HEARTS
don't lie

SUTTON BISHOP

 NliveN, LLC

NliveN, LLC
880 Lennox Drive
Zionsville, IN 46077

 NliveN, LLC

Early Praise for *Hearts Don't Lie*

"This is a beautiful second-chance romance with so many feels! You will cheer and swoon for Mac and Hardin as they fight to find their way back to each other. Filled with heart, sizzling chemistry, and compelling characters who walk off the pages, *Hearts Don't Lie* is a true romantic gem that proves love really does conquer all."

Nina Lane
New York Times and *USA Today* best-selling author

"I had the privilege of beta reading *Hearts Don't Lie*. Sutton has written a totally believable, heart-wrenching tale of young love that never died. Some people do find their soul mates in their youth. Brilliant book and brilliant, believable love story."

Karen, Literati Literature Lovers

Dedication

For those who believe in ever after.

FOR YOU

Marjie Giffin

The weeks, the months, the years
have passed, and for too long
I have longed for you—yearned
for you, so this is my song for you.

I can't give you back what is lost
to you, what is past for you;
but now I can ask time to stand still
for you, so what is true can be.

And what is true is my love for you—
It's always been alive in me. Through
all the years apart we've been,
my heart could never see another.

Refrain
Yes, I have longed for you—yearned
for you, so this is my song for you.
Too long I have longed for you—
yearned for you—so this is my song.

Chapter One

M AC CHECKED HER smart watch after entering the Piñon Grind. She nodded to Kai behind the counter and held up two fingers to let her friend know "the usual" while simultaneously pushing back the long wavy strands from her ear and tapping on the earpiece.

"Hey. I know. I'm running later than I expected. Had to drop Stowe off at camp. Homer got loose again. We finally found him in the dirty laundry. I'm convinced that damned rabbit does this on purpose, knows when my son has to be somewhere. Do you want something else? I just ordered."

Cori laughed on the other end of the call. "The usual is good, thanks. Just letting you know I booked a three-day, leaving tomorrow morning."

"I thought we were booked solid." She inhaled deeply, savoring the aromas of coffee and cinnamon, observing the whir of grinding beans and frothing milks, taking in the conversations and laughter. As usual, Kai's massive coffee loft—a combination of whitewashed brick walls, honeyed wood, and glass, filled with natural light that made the space feel airy yet welcoming—was humming with activity.

"We are, but I called Jess in to cover. She jumped at the chance. Said she could use the extra hours."

"Okay. She's taking it?"

"Um… no. You are, with Chase."

What the hell? It wasn't like Cori to screw up. "No, I'm not. My schedule is full until Stowe goes back to school. Have someone else take it." Mac handed Kai cash and offered an apologetic smile.

"You *were*." Cori took an audible breath before launching into the explanation. "The guy asked for you. Called in as soon as I opened up. I told him you weren't available." She spoke faster. "He insisted. Kenna Eliot. No one else. 'Nonnegotiable,' a private trip, to include Elks Pass and Chasm Incline. I explained we don't send our women guides out on private tours and tried to send him elsewhere, but he said no. He said he was willing to reconsider and compromise. Seriously. He said that. Can you believe it?"

"Cor—"

Cori kept talking. "He said it was fine to send someone else with you. He hadn't thought of that, agreed it was smart policy. He also said it didn't matter because once you realized who he was, you'd insist the trip be a one-on-one."

"Oh, he did, did he? Pretty arrogant," Mac said with a hard edge to her tone.

"Then he asked again what it would take to book the trip. I said $10,000. It was the first amount that popped into my head. Uh… He freaking paid it! He didn't even hesitate other than to ask me if I was ready to take his

2

credit card info." There was a pause, and then she mumbled, "I should've asked for more."

"What the hell, Cor?" Mac asked, dropping her change in the tip jar and moving to the pickup area, now seething, trying to keep her voice down in the sea of customers. It alarmed her that some guy was asking for her specifically, assuming her time could be bought by paying ten times their normal rate for a three-day trip. She hated nothing more than being expected to yield to another person's demands. "No can do. Not even for a million. And even if I agreed… Stowe…"

"Got him covered."

"Thanks, but he has camp and practice."

"Beckett and I will stay at your place because of Homer. Besides, Beck has practice with Stowe. It's just easier. Mike and the girls won't mind for a few nights."

"This is a huge inconvenience."

"Seriously? You're saying this to your bestie? Tsk-tsk. Weak argument. It's not like I haven't pitched in before or you haven't done the same. Running Stowe back and forth to camp is no issue either." Cori got back to what clearly excited her. "Ten thousand dollars! Who pays that? We provide the best experiences, but ten thousand?"

Some rich, high-and-mighty jerk. Dammit. They rarely had people who were a pain in the ass, but sometimes…

"Emory isn't on call for the next three days, so she offered to fill in as we need her, which frees up Van, who'll take your bookings until you return. He's happy to do so. Your client said he'd have his credit card company cancel the transaction if you weren't up for the trip."

"He actually said if I wasn't up for it?"

"Uh-huh. Kind of an in-your-face comment, right? I

sent him down to Elevation for clothing and the other personal items he needs since he basically has nada. I made some suggestions and strong recommendations."

This is becoming fishier by the minute. "Who demands a multiday trip and arrives wholly unprepared?"

"I know, right? Chase is available to go with you, and if you do decide to do the one-on-one, he'll just take you out and then pick you up at the Flag Creek trailhead. If he ends up not going with you, he'll give us the breathing room we need while you're gone. He's packing all the gear as we talk. It's late July in Colorado, friend," Cori said. "In case you can't hear it, I'm drumming my fingers with impatience. Your decision?"

Ten thousand dollars. Intrepid Adventures—their wilderness guided-tours and -trips business in Piñon Ridge, which they had launched soon after Stowe was born, could really use the extra money or Mac wouldn't even be considering it. Besides being her partner, Cori was her best friend, Stowe's honorary aunt, and all-around godsend.

"Did you explain to this guy that the hike is really challenging in parts, as in damned difficult? The majority of the terrain is Class 2, but Class 3 is mixed in. Loose rocks, narrow climbs, big drops. The chasm alone takes three to four hours to scale," Mac argued. "Five to seven miles each day. Piñon Ridge is at 9,600 feet, and we're going to hike unmaintained trails, sometimes no trails, and gain between one thousand and two thousand feet in elevation each day."

"I did."

"Then there's the altitude sickness."

"I explained that to him too. He assured me it won't be a problem. He will 'abide by the guidance given.' His words."

"Seriously? He sounds overly confident. Medical form?"

"Complete, dated and signed, and received. No flags."

"You're not going to let me out of this, are you?"

Cori's laugh was musical. "Nope." Her voice softened. "We could use the money with the expansion of our excursions and activities."

"I know." Mac grimaced, then heaved a sigh. "Fine, I'll guide. Pack helmets. Who is this asshat that called and paid a king's ransom to change my plans?" she sniped, taking their coffees and nodding to Kai in thanks, blowing her a kiss.

"Hardin Ambrose. The soccer god," Cori said dreamily.

The burning liquid did not register as it splashed over the front of Mac's sleeveless summer shirt and shorts and exposed legs, seeping uncomfortably hot into her socks and sports sandals. She didn't feel the man next to her grab her arm as she stumbled and began collapsing, nor did she hear the gasps from others in Kai's coffee shop before she fainted.

"Damn, girl. You scared us all. Feeling better?" Kai asked.

Mac noted the soft expression of her friend, who held out a cup of water to her. "Skipped lunch and dinner yesterday. I think I was way overdue for a meal," she fibbed, noticing most of the customers had gone back to what they were doing. The man next to her watched her carefully. Mac wished a hole would appear and swallow her up.

"Sit up and drink this. You were dropping like a

boulder. Jason here broke your fall"—Kai indicated the man bent over Mac—"or you'd have a nasty something on your forehead and be on your way to the clinic."

Mac sipped slowly, her eyes passing over the grizzled older man wearing a baseball hat. She'd seen him around the area for years but had never met him. "Thank you."

The crow's-feet around his eyes deepened as he smiled. "Happy to help a damsel in distress." He glanced over at Kai. "Looks like you've got this handled." He extended his hand to Mac. "I'll get on with my day after I help you up."

Remembering what had happened before she passed out, Mac blinked and swayed slightly again. She would see Hardin tomorrow. The first time in twelve years. *Oh fucking hell.*

"Okay," Kai said, gripping her by the forearm. "You're still unsteady. Sit for a minute, Kenna," she added, calling Mac by the name everyone in Piñon Ridge and the surrounding area knew her by.

"I'm fine. Really."

Kai pushed one of the Grind's popular breakfast burritos toward Mac—she'd motioned for food as soon as Mac had said she hadn't eaten. "You're seriously going to tell me that after you just passed out in my shop? Uh-uh. Have a few bites of this before you go. And some juice," she said, nodding to the container of apple juice placed in front of Mac.

"I'm only going to work."

"Yeah, I know." Kai sipped from her mug, then lifted her chin toward the burrito. "I insist. A minimum of two bites and wash it down. All the juice. Then you can go."

Mac knew her friend wasn't going to budge, so she took two large bites of the burrito and drank some of the juice. "Damn. You do make the best, I swear. Thanks!"

Two fresh cups of coffee appeared on the table to replace her earlier order. Mac rose, steadier and ready to face her past. She started to clean up, but Kai stilled her hand.

"I'll take care of that, missy."

"Thanks so much, Kai. I feel a lot better. What do I owe you?"

"On the house." Kai stood and hugged Mac. "Friends take care of their friends. See you tomorrow."

"Um, no. I have a last-minute, extended trip," she said, faltering slightly and righting herself immediately. "I'm fine." Mac gathered the coffee and grinned at Kai, knowing her smile didn't reach her eyes and her voice wasn't as light as her words.

2 Chapter Two

HARDIN PACED IN his beautiful modern-rustic suite at the Urban, Piñon Ridge's most upscale boutique inn. The details pleased him—a utilitarian mixture of galvanized metals, reclaimed wood, and glass. A gas fireplace took up half the exterior wall; the other half was taken up by doors that opened to a large balcony with a hot tub, a table and chairs, and a panoramic view of the massive Taurus Range, which embraced Piñon Ridge from the west.

Trepidation suppressed the euphoria that had first flooded him. Mac was here. He would see her again in the morning, and she wouldn't be able to ignore him. He'd have her undivided attention for three days and two nights and would find out how she had become Kenna Eliot.

He'd been recruited before his junior year out of North Carolina University, and as soon as the ink dried on his multimillion-dollar contract, he hired Liberty Quinn of Sentry Investigations to look for Mac. While Liberty searched, he moved to Spain to play soccer professionally in the Men's European Fútbol League and

9

finished his undergraduate long distance in between training, games, and appearances. Playing in the MEFL was a dream come true, but his other dream, that of spending his life with Mac, remained out of reach.

Able to blend in anywhere, Liberty Quinn had proven to be a stealthy private investigator, working tirelessly to track down Mac, but to no avail. It was as if she had vanished after boarding a bus for Joliet, Illinois, years earlier—the last information Liberty had been able to dig up. The trail had gone arctic-cold after Joliet. No one recognized the petite teen with long auburn hair, and cameras turned up nothing. There was no social media presence, nor was there any electronic record of a McKenna Rose Vesley.

He was faced with scouring every state and checking local newspapers and schools. Recently, a woman fitting Mac's description had turned up in an outdoors magazine in Denver, a story highlighting companies that provided the best adventure experiences in Peaks County. She was in a photo with a group of people, but there had been no identifying information, like all the previous leads that hadn't panned out. Liberty forwarded the photo to Hardin, expecting another dead end.

This time though, it *was* Mac, but she was going by the name Kenna Eliot. Liberty was powerless to provide more. Vital records in Colorado were not accessible to the public, so she wasn't able to search Mac online or access any information. Hardin had Liberty fly to Colorado immediately and see what else she could dig up. She quickly tracked Mac to Piñon Ridge, where she owned Intrepid Adventures with her partner, Corinne Wainsom.

Liberty drove to the quaint Victorian town nestled in Peaks County and stayed overnight, spending time with residents, even popping into Intrepid Adventures and talking to Mac herself, discovering she had moved to Piñon Ridge over a decade earlier and was an active, well-liked and respected member of the community. Mac was single and had a child who shared her last name. The child's information was protected by the same Colorado laws.

Now he was here to get more answers—about their past and to determine if a future with Mac was possible.

Illinois, August, Twelve Years Earlier...

A clearing near one of the least-traveled country roads, long forgotten after county residents decided against extending the walking and biking trail in that direction, became their spot. It was where Mac and Hardin's friendship grew and evolved into love. Where they could be vulnerable with one another and not be subject to the influences of family and friends. Where they shared their hopes, dreams, and fears.

Heat lightning flashed along the edges of the thick clouds blanketing the moon, darkening the sky.

"No thunder," Mac observed, sitting cross-legged while Hardin lay prone, his head resting on his forearm. She finished a piece of watermelon and licked her fingers with satisfied smacking. "I think we're good."

"One of the many things I love about the Midwest," he mused, watching the play of light above. "I don't know if North Carolina will be able to measure up." Hardin sat up, his kiss lingering on her shoulder. "I want you again," he murmured. When he wasn't burning to play on the pitch, he was on fire for her.

She smiled and reached for him, her eyes full of heat. "Only if we can forget about North Carolina tonight."

Their galloping hearts were chasing mutual orgasms when the distant beam from a flashlight caught the corner of the ground blanket, narrowly missing their writhing, naked bodies. It continued arcing over the ground and trees, moving closer.

Hardin withdrew from Mac suddenly and shoved an extra blanket at her. "Shit. Someone's here," he whispered breathlessly, urgently, hastily pulling on his shorts.

Steeped in a postclimactic haze, Mac struggled to dress quickly under the summer-weight blanket. She was pulling her skirt down over her thighs and in the process of sitting up next to Hardin when they were hailed by the people approaching.

"Hello? I'm Officer Kozak and this is Officer Smiley," the policeman said, continuing toward them and stopping several yards away. His beam took in their disorderly appearance and heavy breathing. "You two okay? We saw the Jeep off the side of the road. We were concerned given the hour."

Hardin scrambled to stand and helped Mac up. "Yes, sir," they chimed soberly.

Officer Kozak's watchful eyes bounced between Mac and Hardin. "There's a strong storm brewing behind this heat lightning. Probably best not to be out in it. First though, how about some ID?"

Hardin pulled his wallet from his rumpled shorts and extracted his license, handing it to Officer Smiley, who came closer and seemed amused after reading it. "Koz, we've got ourselves a celebrity here," he smirked, handing Hardin's ID to his partner.

Officer Kozak's brows rose, and he whistled before pinning Hardin with a steady look. "Hello, Hardin

Ambrose. I've seen you play. Trident is lucky to have you on their team. You're nothing short of remarkable. Maybe the next Messi. My sons want to play like you."

"Hello," Hardin said, not sure where this was going other than he was often compared to Argentine Lionel Messi, one of soccer's greatest players. It was always a humbling honor. "Thank you, sir."

Mac clutched her hands tightly in front of her. "I don't have mine. It's… It's at home."

"What's your name, young lady?" Officer Kozak asked, studying her.

"McKenna Vesley."

"How old are you, McKenna?"

"Sixteen, sir. My birthday was last week."

"We lost track of time, Officer," Hardin said. "Mac's my girlfriend. Eighteen months now."

"Uh-huh." Officer Kozak nodded slightly. "Where do you live, McKenna?"

"Walden's Field."

"You attend Bowen?"

"Yes."

"Our soccer star's girlfriend attends the rival school. Interesting." Officer Smiley cleared his throat. "Hardin, McKenna, we have a few problems." He flashed a look at Kozak, who nodded. "In Illinois, McKenna is underage. She's out past curfew. Over an hour past." His eyes flitted to the blankets, picnic basket, and candles in jelly jars and then drilled into Hardin's. "We also need to know what the two of you have been doing out here. As I just stated, she is underage. Consent means nothing."

Hardin stared at Smiley, then wove his fingers between Mac's and squeezed. "We know about that, Officer. We were only messing around," he said, lying like a rug and trying not to flinch. "No drugs or alcohol," he added.

Smiley tilted his head and appraised Mac. "Is that true, McKenna?"

Her eyes dove for her feet. "Yes," she croaked, then looked up. "We wouldn't do anything to mess up Hardin's scholarship or ruin his future."

Officer Kozak stepped forward. "Okay, then we're only down to one issue. Curfew. My partner and I will overlook that and take your girlfriend home."

"Can I please? I'll take her straight home. It's our last night together. Please. I leave for school tomorrow."

Kozak shook his head. "Nope. As a gift to both of you, we're taking McKenna home and that's the end of it. Agreed?"

"Can I at least help Hardin pick up?"

"Sure," Smiley said. "Make it quick though, Ms. Vesley."

Mac and Hardin packed up everything in silence, then followed the officers out to the road where the police SUV was parked next to the Jeep, its hazards flashing in the ebony night. The wind had picked up, and trees moaned as they swayed, their leaves lashing about.

Tears coated McKenna's face as she kissed Hardin goodbye. "Hardin," she cried into his neck. "I love you."

"It'll be okay, Mac," he cooed, kissing her, then pressing his forehead against hers to gaze deeply into her eyes. He hugged her fiercely to him. "I love you. I'll talk to you tomorrow before I leave."

3 Chapter Three

T HERE ARE SOME things a girl never forgets, and the memory of her last night with Hardin came rocketing back to her as she walked toward Intrepid. She stepped into one of the small parks nestled among Piñon Ridge's shops, businesses, and restaurants. All alone, Mac placed the piping-hot coffees and her purse next to her as she sat on the concrete skirt of a water fountain in the deep shade of the buildings' wood-and-brick facades. Bowing forward and placing her elbows on her knees, she cupped her forehead and closed her eyes. Remembering.

Illinois, Early August, Twelve Years Earlier, Mac's Senior Year...

Sixteen and a year ahead in high school, she eagerly anticipated finishing her senior year early in December and joining her boyfriend at college.

Hardin Ambrose was the love of her life. They had

spent every moment they could together since their first date eighteen months earlier, when he wasn't playing soccer somewhere out of town, training out of the country with premier clubs, or for most of this summer, at college, taking two classes, working out with his team. They made the most of their time together and could not imagine the future without each other.

Her heart was breaking like the widening fissures in the parched Illinois earth. Hardin was leaving for North Carolina the following day, having earned a coveted starting position ahead of the preseason. A well-seasoned traveler, he was flying to school by himself. His parents had already sent his stuff ahead of him.

The pink-and-yellow sky was awash with gauzy clouds as the sun began its slow descent when she set out to meet him at their agreed-upon pickup spot. It was decided that they would meet there after her mother, Alicia, railed on and on about Mac dating a boy two years older than her, warning that things would turn out very badly.

She knew her mom's story, had heard it her entire life. Pregnant with Mac at fifteen by the son of a wealthy real estate tycoon. He had spurned her, alleging he wasn't the father, and fed the high school rumor mill that it could have been anyone on his football team. He and Alicia knew it was him, but before she could pursue it, he and his family were in a small-plane crash while vacationing during spring break in the Caribbean. There were no survivors. Alicia was the only parent listed on Mac's birth certificate.

Alicia had had no backup plan. When she began to show at four months, she ran away from home, working odd jobs as a waitress and maid, struggling as a teen and then as a single mom to keep a roof over their heads and food on their table. She was a yo-yo of emotions, swinging back and forth between indifference for her daughter and animosity that she had to provide for her. Rarely did Alicia express her love for her only child. To add insult to injury, she insisted that Mac call her Alicia. "Mom" simply didn't fit.

Mac's relationship with Hardin was a stark reminder of what had happened to Alicia, how she had lost her head and a future of possibilities by allowing her hormones to rule her decision to be with Mac's father. Hardin's family enjoyed a stratosphere of wealth similar to what Alicia had tasted close to Mac's age. Been seduced by. The result was pregnancy.

Even more beautiful than Alicia had been at fifteen, Mac's exquisiteness was dangerous, a beacon to lusty boys who used sweet words to get what they wanted. And on occasion, after a few glasses of vodka, Alicia lashed out at Mac with fists and vile words; then they kept their distance while her wary daughter healed from the physical bruises. The emotional ones would stay with her forever under the psychological keloids that thickened each time Alicia lost it.

Somehow Mac retained her sunny disposition, optimistic outlook, and perfect GPA, along with a modicum of respect, born of fear, for her mother. Alicia had big plans for her beautiful, smart, and talented daughter who had her choice of full rides to college. Hardin Ambrose was not part of them.

Passionately in love, Mac ignored her mother's warnings, celebrating her sixteenth birthday and Hardin's return from three weeks of training in Spain by giving him her virginity. It was the most breathtakingly beautiful experience of her young life.

Alicia was at work grooming dogs when Mac eased out of their mobile home a week later, her cute bought-on-layaway sandals snapping and slipping over the rutted ground as soon as she stepped out of their tiny square of yard. Dust from the narrow dirt path clung to her damp feet before she made it to the tired gravel road. Scents of the park wafted around her—Mr. Rasmussen grilling burgers, the Wilsons' open garbage, and the permanent odor of mildew.

Her heart was skittering before she even made it to the county road, before she saw his red Jeep idling close to the mobile home park's entrance, partially hidden by one of the great oaks. Before she saw him and the joy in his aqua-blue eyes.

Hardin jogged around to meet Mac and engulfed her in a huge bear hug, practically squeezing her in half. Two weeks of missing her during mandatory college training and conditioning resonated in his passionate kiss, before he released her and opened the passenger door. He raced back to his, shutting it and then pulling her as close as the bucket seats and stick shift would allow. "I missed you, Mac," he murmured into her wild auburn hair before inhaling audibly. "Damn. You smell so good."

He peppered kisses along her temple and over her cheek before capturing her full lips. She returned his kiss, hungrily. Someone laid on a horn behind them and Hardin separated from her, his eyes dancing mischievously. The corner of his mouth quirked up, wet from kissing, his dark hair still spiky and damp from a shower. He waved his hand over his head at the car behind them; then his gaze swept over her exposed, sleek legs. "Time's a-wastin'. Let's go."

Mac wrinkled her nose and smirked. "You smell like bug spray," she said, buckling up and clasping her hands

18

in her lap because Hardin needed both of his for driving. "Where to?"

"Somewhere we can watch the sunset and enjoy the fireflies."

"That's it for our last night?" she asked playfully.

He shook his head and smiled. "Give me more credit. Check the back seat."

She twisted to look behind her. Several blankets, a picnic basket, tote bag, and a large thermos covered the Jeep's bench seat, along with the ever-present assortment of soccer balls and a bag that she knew held a pair of cleats, socks, and guards. "A picnic dinner! Perfect!"

"Full moon tonight," he said softly, his fingers trailing over her smooth thigh—deeply tanned like the rest of her from hours spent lifeguarding—before downshifting and turning left onto another county road.

Understanding his intent, Mac's heart ricocheted in her chest.

"Repellent and wipes are in the bag by your feet. Get covering. I'd hate for the mosquitoes and other bitey things to feast on your beautiful skin. That's reserved for me." He flashed her a disarming smile that zinged to her core.

The young lovers lay on their backs in the clearing, naked and panting heavily, fingers laced, clothing strewn around, observing the thickening clouds over the full moon. Citronella candles inside mason jars flickered around them, adding ambience to the harp strings of moonlight and doing an admirable job of attracting Illinois mosquitoes to their flames instead of Mac and Hardin. The raucous chirping of the crickets diminished as night set in, and the unholy heat dissipated ever so slightly, helped by an occasional gentle breeze.

The night was close, the air pregnant with moisture. Mac sat up and pulled a mass of curls away from her neck and secured it with one of the hair bands that were always present on her wrist.

Hardin caressed her exposed neck with his lips, then asked, "You okay?"

"Yes and no. I don't want tonight to end." Mac brushed an errant tear from her eye. The last thing she wanted was to dissolve into an emotional mess tonight of all nights. "I already miss you," she whispered, turning to him, full of emotion.

"Me too," he said, reaching for his shorts and digging in the front pocket. He handed her a small, emerald-green velvet bag.

"What's this? I have nothing for you. I... I..."

"Shh," he said, shaking his head, placing his forefinger gently on her lips. "My father sent me into town for a new battery for his watch. I saw this in the jewelry store. It made me think of us. Our love." His voice cracked. "You're all I want, Mac. There is nothing more beautiful you can give me than yourself. I love you."

She loosened the cord and shook the contents into her palm. It was a sterling silver necklace with a square pendant. Mac shifted it in the tendrils of light emanating from the candles and moon, seeking to see it better, then questioned Hardin with her eyes.

"It's a thistle. Its meaning, that's what got me."

"It's beautiful."

"It's made from an old wax seal." He lifted the necklace from her palm and secured it around her neck with the lobster-claw clasp. "The card in the bag explains the symbolism better than I can, but basically it represents protection and remembrance. Also strength, which both of us are going to need during our separation," Hardin said, kissing the back of her neck where the necklace rested. "And sweetness after challenges." He cupped Mac's chin and gently turned her to face him. His eyes pinned hers, then drifted to her lips before searching hers intensely and leaning forward. "Don't forget about me. Or us and our love," he said huskily, his voice dropping into a whisper. "It's only four months. Our love will carry us through."

The pendant nestled halfway between the hollow of her throat and her heart. She covered it with her hand and curved her other behind Hardin's neck, sliding her fingers into his recently cut hair and pulling him to her.

"Thank you," she breathed over his parted lips before kissing him deeply, her tongue sweeping the inside of his mouth. She broke the kiss to whisper, "I could never forget you. I will love you forever."

"I love you, Mac." Hardin lowered Mac down to the blanket and covered her with his body. "Forever," he whispered into her ear.

4 Chapter four

Present Day, Piñon Ridge...

"HERE." MAC SET the coffees down on Cori's desk, then plopped into a soft chair and huffed loudly. "What a sucky morning," she grumbled, glaring at her coffee-stained socks and blinking rapidly.

Cori closed her laptop, pushed it to the side, and took a sip of her coffee. "Thanks, and good morning to you."

"Why is the door open?" Kenna asked grumpily.

"It's beautiful out, too nice to be cooped up inside. What's with the bug up your butt?"

"I don't want to take him out," Mac protested, easing out of her sports sandals and slipping off her coffee-soaked socks. She deposited them in a wad on the weatherproof planked floor, her eyes studying the array of poster-size photos on the walls, then panning across the exposed-brick wall to the enormous monitor that highlighted an array of moments and videos from Intrepid's tours, trips, and other offerings. "Can you do it, or have Chase take him by himself? Say I suddenly came down with the flu. Or my foot is broken. Something." Her brown eyes met the bright blue eyes of her friend, pleading. "Pretty please, with sugar on top?"

Cori came around and perched her hip on the corner of the desk. "No. Remember, your participation was part of the deal. A private tour. Granted, having Chase with you makes it not private unless you opt for private, like Hardin Ambrose believes you will. That's wholly your decision."

Mac stared at the floor, ruminating for a minute before meeting her friend's eyes.

Cori scrutinized Mac and her tone changed to one of concern. "What's going on? You're not acting like you. I realize the guy's a soccer player. Okay, he's a fucking huge international deal. Have you seen him play? Oh my God. He moves like Messi. Beckett can't get enough of him. Neither can Stowe. Like I said earlier, the guy is a soccer god and a drop-dead gorgeous one at that. But hell, Kenna, that shouldn't bother you at all, taking him for a hike. You've gone out with gorgeous guys before, even if it wasn't by yourself. Christ, you seem to date all the guys around here who keep women in wet panties." She leaned forward and tapped Mac's shoulder. "What gives? Is it his money? He's supposed to be richer than Midas."

Mac studied her best friend, weighing how much to disclose, how much to let out of Pandora's box. She opted to keep it shut and slouched into the chair, lifting her long hair before it cascaded over the back and caught on the rivets. It also helped to cool her neck, which banked her ire a bit. She counted the exposed beams overhead even though she knew exactly how many there were. Fifteen.

"I could give a rat's ass about his money. It's just... well... we... We have a history."

Cori rocketed to her feet. "What?"

"I know Hardin. Well, that's not accurate. I knew him, way back when, before he achieved 'soccer god'"—she used air quotes—"status. I haven't seen him since then, and I'd rather not see him now. Let's just leave it at that."

"You want to leave it at what, Mac?" a deep voice asked behind her.

Cori's mouth opened so wide that it could catch birds. Her round eyes mirrored her mouth.

No, no, no! Fuck no! Mac's pulse jackhammered as if she had sprinted to the summit. It was his voice, but deeper and richer than twelve years ago, and it released the memories she had locked away, like the nuances of his breath and body. *Not now. I can't face him. I'll splinter to pieces.* Disbelief, fear, joy, and anger rioted through her system. For the second time this morning, she fought to stay lucid, to inhale. She controlled her breathing and steeled herself before answering.

"You're a day early," she returned icily without facing him, remaining slouched in the chair, wishing she could disappear completely.

"No. I'm twelve years late," he said softly.

"Um... I'm going to go see where Chase is with the gear and supplies," Cori said, pivoting toward the hall behind them, her cell in hand and walking slowly, obviously dying to hear more.

Hardin called back to Cori's retreating back, "Thanks for setting this up, Cori."

Mac kept her back to him. "Please come back tomorrow, Hardin. When we're scheduled to leave. Call

Cori if you have questions." She heard Hardin shuffle behind her and envisioned him as he moved—easy, athletic grace, confident, but now unsure, watching her, weighing what to say.

Finally he spoke. "Okay. I'll go along with what you want. See you in the morning unless you reconsider, as in grabbing a drink or dinner tonight. Or conversation. Catch up."

"No."

"I'm staying at the Urban," he said neutrally before she heard his steps retreat.

Mac didn't move until she felt his presence was gone, then she let out a breath she hadn't realized she had been holding in. *How in fucking hell am I going to do this?* She pushed up and shot out of her chair and ran to the small break room, shutting the door and leaning against it, needing its support as she slid down into a slump. She hugged herself and closed her eyes. Tears raced down her face, and the past surged forth with painful clarity.

Illinois, Early August, Twelve Years Earlier, Mac's Senior Year of High School...

"Thank you, Officers," Alicia said, sounding groggy but glaring at her daughter. "I must have fallen asleep." She waited until their car pulled away, and then she released her fury.

Unprepared, Mac bounced off the thin wall of the trailer. Tears stung her eyes as her hip came into contact with the sharp edge of the counter jutting out into their small space. She swallowed a yelp of pain, knowing from experience that it would only fire her mother up more.

There was nowhere to retreat. Alicia came at her, strident, like her unchecked anger.

"You whore! What in the fuck were you doing out until almost two in the morning? It's past curfew. You're underage. Were you fucking him?" Her hand met Mac's cheek. "What have I told you? You're going to pay for this! So is he!"

Mac rolled away and dodged some of her mother's blows, but there was nothing she could do about her venomous words. Finally she got a hand on the doorknob and ripped the door open. Mac lurched out of the trailer, sobbing, numb and hurting, the taste of salt filling her mouth. Alicia's slurred, abusive words and wicked laughter followed her, meshing with the cracking thunder overhead. Lightning split the black night, and Mac ran unsteadily, not stopping until sheets of rain drowned out the vitriol ringing in her ears.

Mac spent the night huddled under a rotting wooden picnic table on the edge of their small mobile home park, and when she woke—stiff, sore, and wet—a clear day was breaking. She waited, shivering, and watched as Alicia threw a full white trash bag in her trunk before driving off. Only then did Mac feel safe to return to their trailer.

Her breath stuttered when she stepped inside. Light filtering into the dark space through the thin curtains illuminated how Alicia had taken the rest of her wrath out on their meager home. Disbelief washed over Mac as she surveyed the mess. She inhaled and braced herself before gingerly skirting the wreckage to retrieve a small broom and dustpan and begin cleaning, immediately discovering her destroyed cell phone among the shattered glass, broken dishes and ripped books, its SIM card gone.

Determined, she considered her options. By bike, she could probably reach his house, roughly seven miles away, in forty minutes if she pushed it. There was time to see Hardin if she left the mess. Now. She grabbed her bike helmet from the compartment under the couch.

The door banged shut behind her as she ran, then jumped from the stairs, buckling her chinstrap. Mac unchained her bike, then stopped midstraddle. Both her tires had been slashed. She let her bike drop against the trailer. Panicked, she went from neighbor to neighbor. Either no one was home or those who were couldn't assist her.

She flew back into their trailer. She'd run to her friend Hannah's house in town. It was much closer. Mac could explain what had happened, and maybe her friend's older sister or parents could take her to Hardin's house. Her course of action decided, she went to the closet.

The oxygen whooshed out of Mac and she clenched her hands in anger, fingernails slicing into her palms. Now she understood why Alicia had thrown the trash bag in her trunk. All her shoes were gone. Every last one of them, even her cleats and flip-flops. She would run the three miles into town anyway, in her flimsy sandals.

The strap on her right sandal broke after a half mile. Her beautiful new sandals ruined. Mac limped to the side of the road and collapsed behind some dense shrubbery, hiccuping sobs robbing her of breath, her heart and soul in bloody ribbons. The pity she had long held for her mother blossomed into full-blown hate when she realized what Alicia had done. Mac's chance to speak to or see Hardin before he left had been stripped away.

5 Chapter Five

Present Day, Piñon Ridge...

E XASPERATED, HARDIN LACED his fingers over the crown of his head and groaned before heading to the outfitters Cori had recommended. He needed a few things Intrepid Adventures didn't supply their clients, expecting they would show up somewhat prepared for conditions. The mountains to his right beckoned, covered in lush, variegated green and occasional outcroppings of gray rock, the unmoving, empty chairlifts difficult to pick out against the colorful backdrop.

Ten minutes later he was closing in on the base of Granite Peak. The terrain was rocky and grassy and sloped gently until it flattened out near the closed-for-the-season lodges. He sat on one of the empty benches and stretched his legs out in front of him, still jet-lagged from the long flight in from Spain, and remembered.

Illinois, Fall Semester, Hardin's Junior Year of High School...

The curvy, petite cheerleader from the neighboring county's rival high school drew his attention during the homecoming varsity match. She watched him with open curiosity, not the common and effusive over-the-top fawning he loathed. So much so that his penalty shot almost failed. He scanned the sidelines of the opposing team after the kick rocketed in ugly and locked eyes with her. Something primitive sparked between them.

After the soccer game, he walked purposefully, hoping to cross paths with the auburn beauty, but she was gone. Hardin, his teammates, cheerleaders, and friends went to the Scoop to celebrate their win. He entered the crowded open patio to the side of the building, and there she was with her friends. She had changed into fashionably torn, faded skinny jeans, a long shirt over her tight T-shirt, which failed to detract from her curves. She sat at an empty round table, seeming to have claimed it for herself and a few friends.

Entranced, he approached her. "Hi. I'm Hardin," he said, offering his hand, towering over her.

The spark from the game amplified tenfold, making the air feel as if it sizzled between them. The charge flashed through his body, causing him to inhale shakily. Caught off guard, Hardin speared his fingers through his dark hair in an attempt to collect himself.

She cocked her head and glanced up at him. "McKenna." She didn't offer more, nor did she take his hand.

"I saw you cheering on the sideline."

A wide smile broke over her beautiful, freckled, heart-shaped face and carried into chestnut-brown eyes, making her even more breathtaking. "Before or after you almost shanked your kick?" McKenna asked teasingly, her eyes twinkling.

He laughed. "Touché. You play?"

"Varsity girls. Forward. But nothing like you," she said, accepting her ice cream in a cup from one of her friends, who watched with interest but said nothing. "Thanks." She turned her attention back to Hardin.

Something somersaulted in him as her tongue darted out and caught the melted ice cream that had dripped onto her hand. She followed it up with a small helping of mint chocolate chip. "I'd come watch you," he said as her mouth closed around the plastic spoon.

She licked her lips before answering. "Why?"

"Because I'd like to. I'm a junior. What year are you?"

"Sophomore. Shouldn't you be getting back to your friends? After all, you're talking to the enemy."

"Somehow I think that doesn't matter. You're in our territory."

She inclined her head toward her friends, who were deep in conversation. "We wanted ice cream. Why drive back to our town when we can get some here?"

"I have my Jeep," he said, watching her for a response.

Her nod was barely perceptible, but her eyes said it all. Interest. The sizzle between them intensified again.

"Tell your friends I'll bring you home."

"I don't take orders, Hardin," she countered evenly, her eyes dancing with humor.

He speared his fingers through his hair again. "Please? Now I asked." He grinned.

She grinned back. "Since you asked nicely, I accept."

Just like that. They spent the entire evening together talking, laughing, and grabbing a quick burger and fries at the nearby diner.

He asked Mac out before dropping her off at a friend's house where she was joining a slumber party.

"It was fun, Hardin. But no."

She continued turning him down over the next four months, giving him the excuse of studying or practice, and when soccer was over, extracurricular commitments. But eventually she agreed to go out with him.

Hardin's parents' complaints about Mac began as soon as they got wind that he was dating her. She was too young. She was "not the kind of girl he should associate with" but a social climber, a girl who could destroy his esteemed career before it even became a reality. They told him to drop the relationship before it got out of hand, confident their son would listen to them.

He didn't.

The youngest of four boys, Hardin had been the easiest to raise, or so his parents said, the one who never bucked their wishes. Hardin had watched his parents slowly restructure their lives in preparation for being empty nesters since he was in grade school. They failed to see Mac tucked in among the mass of fans at the games. Neither did they notice that he often used the excuse of practices and studying to see her, so certain were they that their son always did as they instructed. They had long ago given him his independence, and for the first time in his life, he ignored his parents' wishes because he knew who Mac was—the love of his life. His heart didn't lie.

What he shared with Mac was raw, hungry, and pure. Their last night before he left for college was everything he had hoped for. Giving her the necklace. Pledging to love each other. Making love. And then it had gotten fucked up sideways.

Piñon Ridge...

That things hadn't gone well with Mac this morning was the understatement of the century. Christ, she wouldn't even look at him, and on top of her cool, dismissive tone, that was problematic. He needed to connect with her, see if what they had in high school still existed or could be rekindled. Instead, she had chastised him, and he'd left like some damned dog scurrying off with its tail between its legs.

Hardin ached to bask in those beautiful brown eyes that had unraveled him each and every time since he had first met her in high school, those eyes that haunted his dreams. He wanted to bathe in the smile she had only for him, the one that made him feel so incredibly cherished and loved. He longed to talk to her, hear that raspy voice that sent electricity racing through him. Enjoy that quirky giggle that became an infectious belly laugh when she was really tickled.

Frustration and anger burned in his gut when he thought of all that had transpired. He and Mac had been railroaded. What a fucking mess. He was furious with Mac's mom but even more so with his parents, who had refused to accept that he had found his forever love in high school.

At this point, Hardin's relationship with his parents was practically nonexistent, having grown more strained as the years passed. Living in Spain and playing most of the year outside the US gave him the emotional and physical distance he needed, welcomed. He'd been able to avoid their unceasing questions and pressure about his social life, and eventually they had stopped hounding him to settle down and start a family. Nowadays the Ambroses talked about the inconsequential during the rare occasions they spoke, understanding that the minute they stepped into Hardin's personal sphere, he would end the phone call. He didn't miss them; his parents had been physically absent and emotionally distant for as long as he could recall.

After a year in the MEFL and no success locating Mac, Hardin became petulant. It came off as an edgy cockiness, and combined with his handsome dark looks and sensational skills, women seemed to find him an irresistible aphrodisiac, drawn to him like bees to honey.

Detached, Hardin fell into bouncing from woman to woman, earning the reputation of a "player" and a "bad boy" when in truth he was the exact opposite. No amount of companionship or sex filled his emotional needs. He remained lonely. Hollow. Tormented. Unable to sustain a relationship beyond a few months because none of the women he dated were anything like who he needed. Who he desired.

Hardin had given Mac his whole heart in high school, and since he'd lost her, the only time he felt whole was when he was on the pitch—practicing and playing his ass off or coaching the next generation of up-and-coming premier hopefuls.

HEARTS
don't lie

Mac tripped down the stairs of the Hickory Lodge, her face lighting up as soon as she saw him. "Hardin!" She launched at him before stepping onto the floor.

He caught Mac easily and hugged her close, kissing her soundly, not wanting to put her down, but they were getting looks from some of the passersby. He was thrilled that their plan of being together over break had worked out.

"I'm so glad you're here," he said, helping her slip into the new ski jacket he'd given her for Christmas. The cobalt blue was a stunning combination with her auburn hair and chestnut-colored eyes. "I worried when your plane was delayed."

They had four days. No training. No family or social commitments. To do more or less as they chose since the accompanying chaperones had large groups of students to keep their eyes on.

Both of their high school ski clubs came here every winter break, but it was the first time either of them had participated in their clubs. Their plan was hatched in the early fall, when Mac got wind of the essay contest and coveted awards made possible by the alumni club— airfare, the student's portion of the dorm room they were sharing with nine other students of the same sex, daily breakfast, and multiday lift pass. Lunches, dinners, equipment rentals, and incidentals were the student's expense. Mac won one of the two awards. Hardin enthusiastically offered to cover all her incidentals.

"You're hungry, right?"

"Ravenous," she said, putting on her cream-colored

hat and mittens, also gifts from Hardin, then taking his hand.

Always the gentleman, Hardin held the door open for her. "Let's go eat."

They stepped outside into the center of postcard-perfect Stowe, which boasted a classic early-nineteenth-century New England village. It was almost dark. Hand in hand, they strolled the cozy town, which was festively lit with holiday lights.

Over the ensuing days, Hardin and Mac made their own schedule, being sure to check in with their chaperones. They relished making the most of their time together, which was usually interrupted by his training and frequent trips out of the country. They hadn't consummated their relationship, but it was becoming more difficult to keep it that way as their feelings deepened.

Never having skied or snowboarded, they took lessons before venturing onto the slopes on their own. During the late afternoons, they explored the village, enjoying hot chocolate and conversation, growing even closer. Their time together was magical.

The night before they left, they made one long trek around the town and ended up at the gazebo all by themselves. The snow fell in big fluffy flakes, dusting everything in an airy white blanket, all but silencing any sound but that of their breathing. Hardin cleared snow off part of the benches built into the sides before sitting.

"It's beautiful," Mac said wistfully, lowering herself next to and facing him. "I'll always remember this moment, being here with you in this peaceful wonderland."

Mac smiled at him, as only she could, taking his breath away. His heart took off like a rocket in his chest.

"I'll never forget this moment either."

"Is this enough for you?" she asked, her eyes searching his. "I'm not trying to string you along, Hardin. I'm just not ready. I know there are so many girls who—"

He placed his gloved fingers over her lips to keep her from saying more. "You're more than enough. I don't want to pressure you, but I do want you to know I want you, Mac. I don't want anyone else but you. When you're ready." He kissed her tenderly and inclined his head, looking down as he covered her hands with his, then fixated on her eyes and took a deep breath. "I love you, Mac."

Her smile lit up the intimate space, bathing him in delicious warmth. "And I love you, Hardin."

They held each other until the cold began to seep in through their outerwear and boots, then made their way back to the lodge to say good night. Hardin's club was leaving Stowe early in the morning. Hers was leaving after lunch.

Unfortunately, by the time Hardin arrived home, the parental grapevine had informed his parents about his time with Mac. His parents met him at the front door, their anger buffeting off him.

"We know everything that goes on. We told you before to quit seeing her." His father's tone conveyed he expected Hardin to acquiesce. "You deliberately disobeyed us. You will not see that girl again. You're to focus on academics and your soccer career. Am I clear, Hardin? It's done. Do you hear me?"

Hardin schooled his features into appearing cowed. "Yes."

"You will apologize." His mother stared at him, her expression cool.

Robotically he said, "I'm sorry, Mother, Father." Hardin's eyes passed over each of them as he spoke their names. Internally, he was boiling. Internally, he redoubled his efforts. He and Mac would find a way.

Piñon Ridge...

Had he done the wrong thing by showing up as he had, without notice? No. It was the only way. Intuitively, he felt Mac had purposely made herself difficult to find. She had severed all ties with the past, including her mother and friends. Twelve years. It had taken him twelve years to find her, ten years of which consisted of Liberty searching intensively. Now, a dozen years later, they were finally in the same town. Hardin had paid for a three-day excursion, just the two of them, and he planned to make every minute count.

Liberty had tracked Alicia down almost immediately after he hired her. Alicia did not have any idea where her daughter was, nor had she seemed the least bit concerned about her welfare. Alicia was enjoying an easier life on the Florida coast, courtesy of her calculated strike at the heart of what mattered to Hardin's parents—money and status. The Ambroses' generosity was another revelation during his search for Mac.

His parents had played into Alicia's plan perfectly and then followed it up by having a protection order filed against Alicia and Mac, effectively ending all contact between Mac and Hardin. Alicia and the Ambroses had shared the same end goal—keeping him and Mac apart. The whole thing made him sick.

She had a son. He was coming to terms with that. At

first it stunned him because they had talked about their future plans, which included marriage and a passel of kids—their own soccer team, they had said and laughed.

Hardin wanted the answers to his growing list of questions. Mac's change of surname indicated she had married. Whom had she married and when? When had she become single? Was she aware of her mother's treachery and the payoff provided by his parents? Why else would she have disappeared without a trace? It just didn't fit her.

He tried to withhold judgment. Mac had always been unfailingly open with him. It was the primary reason he had been able to be vulnerable with her and share every part of himself. *Jesus.* Lies upon lies, neglected, festering and haunting him for twelve years. He had to get to the truth, regardless of the outcome. He needed closure. He'd been in an emotional rut since the day he left for college. His mind replayed the scene before the car arrived at his parents' home to take him to O'Hare.

Illinois, August, Twelve Years Earlier...

He stepped out of the shower of his en suite bathroom the following morning, still groggy from a lack of sleep and feeling deflated and frustrated by how the night abruptly ended with Mac. The policemen's appearance had ruined his romantic evening with her. A car was picking him up for the airport in thirty minutes.

Shouting from the foyer carried up the wide, double staircase and through the massive paneled bedroom door—his parents and a woman. He strained to listen, but after the distinct sound of the pocket doors to his father's office closing, the conversation was muffled. Although he wanted to go downstairs, he didn't. Hardin had been admonished time and again as a young boy to stay out of adult conversations and negotiations.

A nagging sense of worry grew as he checked his cell again and again while he dressed. He'd been trying to reach Mac since he got home from their date. Repeated efforts to reach her went unanswered, the first to text and voice mail, and later to an automated message from the carrier stating the phone number was out of service. There were no calls, voice mails or texts from her. What the hell was going on?

Raised voices drew his attention again, and then it was just as quiet. The pocket doors slid open and light steps clacked over the black-and-white tiles of the grand hall. The heavy front door opened and shut.

Hardin rushed to his parents' bedroom and stepped onto the balcony over the front veranda, seeking to catch a glimpse of the visitor. The rusted driver's door of the dented, familiar clunker complained loudly as it opened. He swallowed convulsively, and sweat dampened his clean, dry polo shirt and pants despite the air-conditioning as he observed Alicia Vesley with a smug expression glance back at their house before seating herself daintily behind the wheel.

6 Chapter Six

Piñon Ridge...

AFTER CRYING IT out, Mac returned to the front office, numb but determined to move forward. She could do this. She had dealt with other challenges that demanded far more from her than Hardin's sudden appearance. Mac put on her professional hat and threw herself into checking the details of tomorrow's trip.

Her first order of business was to find Chase and tell him he wasn't accompanying her on the trip. She found him in the pantry, a large room that served as their equipment room, readying supplies for trips going out that day and the next, including hers and Hardin's. In front of him was an electronic tablet for logging the items for each trip. Mac and Cori were responsible for final inventory checks, comprising gear, navigational tools, first aid kits, and itinerary. Since this was Mac's trip, Cori would take care of it.

"Hey. I only need you for the trailhead drop-off tomorrow. I'm taking Hardin Ambrose out on my own."

Although Chase was only a half head taller than Mac, he was husky, all muscle, and the self-appointed watchdog over his lady bosses. He stopped what he was doing and faced her, squinting his eyes. "That's against policy."

"It would be if our client was an unknown entity," she said, squeezing his arm and smiling, her eyes not wavering from his.

Chase searched her eyes and nodded, seeming satisfied Mac was fully comfortable with her decision. He leaned his hips back against the metal table, crossed his arms, and studied her. "Cori said you know him. He picked a tough trip. Has he hiked?"

"When we were teens, no. Since then? I have no idea."

"How are you going to handle him?"

"He insisted on this excursion, so I'll treat him like he's a seasoned hiker but guide him like he's a novice." She laughed and passed two bear canisters to him, which he noted on the tablet in front of him.

"You'll be careful," he said, studying her, his expression serious.

"Always," she said convincingly. *But what about my heart?*

He shook his head slowly. "Go pull yourself together. I've got this. Cori will do the recheck."

"I *am* together."

"Bullshit you are. Right now you're the least *together* you've ever been since I've known you."

Mac snapped her hands to her hips and pulled herself up to her full height. Her jaw jutted forward. "Listen—"

Chase shook his head again and grimaced, but his eyes danced. "Don't go getting all huffy on me, *boss*." He waved his hand toward the front of Intrepid. "Go do what you need to do. Everything is set for the day."

42

Mac walked back heavily to her desk and dropped into her chair, wondering how Chase seemed to know about the turmoil she was experiencing. Had he and Cori talked while she wept in the break room, or worse, had one or both of them heard her lose it? *Oh God…* She passed the rest of her morning battling the near panic that surfaced between answering the phone, scheduling trips, and talking to walk-ins. A massive, nauseating headache was building between her temples, expanding and filling her entire skull. She tried breathing through her nose, but it didn't help.

Gentle pressure on her shoulder snapped Mac out of a long-compartmentalized memory in the recesses of her brain that had materialized, so vivid it was as if it had happened yesterday.

"Hey!" Cori said. "You're absolutely no good here."

Mac rubbed her temples and glanced up at her partner and friend. "I have a massive headache coming on."

"I'll get you something," Cori said before rifling around in her purse. "Hold out your hand." She tapped some gel caps out into Mac's palm.

Mac tossed the gel caps into her mouth and gulped down most of the water from the bottle on her desk.

"Good. Now go take a walk, and if you're feeling up to it when you return, take my one o'clock. It's Blue Lake. You love that one. A hike will do you good. Get whatever is in your head out."

Mac rose and grabbed her jacket from the back of her chair, then pulled Cori into her arms. "Thanks, sweetie."

"You've got this," Cori said and pushed her toward the open door. "Go. Lunch will be waiting when you get back."

Mac walked the same direction Hardin had earlier, past Hazy Rebel Brewing, past the art district, toward

Limestone Peak, looking for a flatter spot in the uneven, gentle terrain. She was surrounded by acres of green when she eased herself onto the earth and lay back, her head and upper torso cushioned by her Intrepid Adventures jacket. She glanced up at the sky and placed her feet on the ground, then crossed one ankle over her knee, watching the clouds move joyously overhead. The memory from earlier resurfaced, and Mac let it overtake her, wondering if the event was why Hardin's parents had disliked her so much.

Illinois, August, Thirteen Years Earlier, Mac's Junior Year in High School...

Hardin had obviously been in a hurry when he picked her up. Sure, he had taken his time kissing her, but as soon as her seat belt was secured, they were off. "We need to make a detour. I forgot my wallet at home."

"Your parents?"

"Gone, as usual. Off with the Barlows somewhere."

He drove ten miles per hour over the speed limit, barely slowing down when moving from the passing lane back to the right. Hardin drove his Jeep like he captained the team—calmly and confidently. She stayed quiet, feeling safe. Playing finger games with him when he wasn't shifting. What she wanted was to run her hands over the lean muscles of his thighs, feel the coiled power in them. But that action had taken them abruptly off the road last week, so she kept her hands to herself and tugged her jean skirt a little farther down over her bare thighs.

He noticed. "Let it ride, Mac. I've seen more than your beautiful thighs."

Hardin hadn't only seen. He had touched, and she'd willingly urged him to explore more. So much more. She ached to be his, in every way a woman could be a man's, but they had decided they would wait a little longer.

Delicious fluttering flooded her body, causing her to squirm in the seat. "Are you sure?"

"You have to ask? You *know* I am. I'm focused," he said, merging onto the toll road.

Hardin lived twenty minutes from her. They always traveled the back roads. Rarely did they go to friends' homes, and never to hers or his. They preferred to spend their time in remote places, away from everyone else, where they could just be together and talk and kiss and explore. This was new. Her hands grew damp as soon as he exited the toll road and entered Thurston—Illinois's wealthiest town and where Hardin lived. She sensed they were close and discreetly ran her palms down her skirt to dry them and to hide her nervous reaction from him.

Hardin's hand trailed over her thigh. "We're here," he said, downshifting before swinging into the drive, which was all but hidden from the street by a thick hedge. He picked up his speed and continued down a long winding driveway, slowing slightly when a wrought iron gate wedged into the brick perimeter wall came into view.

Mac swallowed audibly as the gate opened like magic, and again as she turned and watched it close behind them.

He wove his fingers through hers and lifted her hand, kissing her knuckles. "Don't let my parents' place intimidate you. It's just a house."

"It's *huge*, Hardin," she whispered hoarsely, pulling her hand back into her lap, gripping her hands together so tightly they hurt. She'd never seen money like this.

He shrugged his shoulders, then downshifted as the

driveway morphed to paved stones. "Yeah." He drove to the side of the French-revival-style mansion and parked by the six-car garage, then turned to her. "I'm not my parents. This house doesn't represent me. Okay?" he asked, searching her eyes.

"Okay." She returned his look, smiling as soon as he did, feeling lighter and surer of herself.

Hardin helped Mac out of the Jeep and held her hand as they strolled up the stone walk before stepping onto the expansive limestone porch and entering through the massive front door under an equally impressive second-floor veranda. Ornate runners covered the double staircase leading upstairs from the black-and-white marble entry and joining halls into beautifully appointed rooms. A large round entry table of glass and wood topped with a large crystal vase of blood-red roses was the centerpiece of the foyer. The cavernous entry felt austere and chilly.

An uncomfortable sickness filled Mac. Shame. For the first time, it hit home just how very different and far apart her and Hardin's worlds were.

She had a single mother for a parent and had no siblings. He had a mother and father and three brothers. Her home was a listing, rusting trailer that jiggled during a light rain. His family home was a mansion. No, scratch that. It was an estate, which probably employed people who earned more money than her mother.

"I shouldn't be here, Hardin. Can you take me home? Please? I... I don't belong here."

He slid his arm around her shoulders. "You do belong here, Mac. With me. I want you here." He glanced around the entry as if seeing it with fresh eyes and nodded. "It *is* fucking intimidating. Ugly. Cold. No wonder my friends never want to come here. Even I prefer to come through the back when I have to be here." Hardin winked at Mac and grinned cockily as his hand slid down her arm and he interlaced their fingers, then kissed her deeply. "It's just us. The staff is retired for the evening. Come on."

She left her gym shoes by the front door, noticing Hardin continued to wear his, then placed her purse on the center table before walking next to him on the wide staircase, her feet sinking into the dense floral design of maroon, navy, gray, and ivory. The upstairs was carpeted in more of the same luxurious pattern that covered the stairs, hushing their footsteps.

"I'll show you around." Hardin led her past the master bedroom in the front of the house to his room.

She peeked in. Unlike the downstairs, the bedroom was dated—a bland room of beige, browns, and creams that struck Mac as tired and surrendered to time. Somehow, that made her feel better.

Striped wallpaper in blues and browns covered the walls of the next two bedrooms. Navy curtains hugged the windows.

"Sam's and Bryson's. Mine is this way." He walked through a connecting hall. "The guest rooms are down the other wing. With Noah's. My parents keep my brothers' rooms exactly as they were the day they moved out. The housekeeper keeps them clean since my parents hope they'll show up with their families, but they seem to prefer spending time with their in-laws," he said with sarcasm.

"Do you miss them?"

He shook his head. "No. I don't know them that well. Maybe that'll change in the future. There were so many years between us. I was the oops baby."

Mac smiled sardonically. "Yeah, I totally get that."

"I know." He pulled her into his arms and kissed her forehead. "What an incredibly wonderful oops you are. I really like you, Mac Oops."

She smacked him playfully, laughed, then grew serious. Her hands reached up and framed his face, and she gazed adoringly into his amazing blue eyes. "And I really like you, Hardin Oops," she whispered, following it up with a kiss, which he returned with even more heat. Mac pulled back and glanced around. "Not here."

"Right." He led her into his room and grabbed his wallet, which was on the corner of the desk, easing it into his back hip pocket.

Hardin's bedroom was more recently decorated, but in a similar unappetizing palette. He had a large bed, bigger than hers and her mother's combined. He also had his very own bathroom. Again, Mac reflected on the differences in how they lived. Her bed was a thin, lumpy cushion on a built-in bench that tripled as storage and a place to sit and eat. She had to curl up to sleep on it and had never allowed herself to think of the things that infested and might grow inside the cushion. She slept on more layers than she wrapped up in.

Mac surveyed the bathroom—a closet, shower, toilet, large vanity, pristine fixtures, and light—bright compared to the flickering dim wattage in the trailer's tiny bathroom. He even had a window.

Mac's showers were restricted to two minutes in a space where, no matter how little she moved, water leaked all over the floor. Water service had been intermittent for years, getting worse as she grew up. Alicia kept several gallon jugs on hand for when the service was turned off, often without notice, or when they received a boil notice.

Sleepovers at Mac's friends' homes had become a priority as soon as she understood the sounds coming through the paper-thin door of Alicia's small room and why their trailer rocked when the boyfriends visited. Some of the *boyfriends* eyeballed Mac leeringly when her body began changing. Despite Alicia's lack of maternal instincts and usual state of drunkenness, she had noticed and protected Mac. She also grew threatened by her daughter's burgeoning beauty.

As soon as Mac began earning money, she started saving for a used bike to provide her freedom and a mode to get away should she need it. And she had, leaving in the deep black of numerous nights, riding her bike into town, the bike's light a beacon guiding her.

Awards and trophies cluttered Hardin's shelves. Mac hadn't been able to keep any of hers except the medals. There was no extra space.

"You're so lucky to have all this room," she said, admiring his All-Academic, All-State plaques. And then she heard the unmistakable sound of a car door, then three more in quick succession. *What the hell?* "Hardin?"

He sprinted to the window and pulled the curtain to the side. "Dammit! My parents are here! With the Barlows!" He ushered her toward the bathroom and opened the window. "Stand in the shower but keep an eye on the windows."

"What?"

He opened the glass door and shoved her in. "Can you see the windows?"

She nodded, speechless and confused. They hadn't done anything. Why were they sneaking around? Mac watched Hardin open a window in his bedroom too.

"I'm going downstairs. I'll put a ladder up to one of the windows. You climb down."

And then he was gone.

The lights in the hallway extinguished. Somehow his greeting to his parents and their friends carried into the bathroom. Maybe he was talking loudly or maybe it was a trick of the house. Mac heard Hardin explain that he had brought a friend over to show her the house, but she had felt sick and forgotten her purse. He didn't mention her shoes that she had slipped off as a sign of respect by the front door, which he closed loudly behind him.

The hall lit up brightly. McKenna backed farther into the shower, trying to regulate her breathing, trying to somehow hide herself behind the frosted glass, but instead she nudged the lever. Cold water trickled down her back. She turned it off soundlessly, tiptoeing out, lodging herself between the toilet and the shower, hoping she was invisible.

Through the doorway, she watched Mrs. Ambrose pad in cautiously after flipping the light switch and stop in the middle of the bedroom, listening. Mac didn't breathe or move. Hardin's mother scanned the room slowly but kept her back to the bathroom. She opened the closet door and peered inside, running her hands through what few shirts hung within. She exited and stood in the hallway.

Mac's heart pounded in her chest as Mrs. Ambrose entered again, halted in the center of Hardin's room, and then got down on all fours and tucked her skirt behind her knees before crouching farther to look under his bed. She got to her feet and became motionless once again, appearing to be thinking and listening as she focused on the open window before approaching and closing it. Pausing again, she listened before going to his closet. Mac fought to breathe slowly and quietly as Mrs. Ambrose moved things carefully around like she thought something might jump out at her. Satisfied, she stepped back and cocked her head, then zeroed in on the bathroom before walking straight to the open window, turning around after shutting it.

Icy blue eyes mirrored the terror in Mac's, who stood paralyzed against the wall, water and sweat sluicing between her back and the thin, striped shirt she wore.

Both of them screamed at the same time. Then, piercing stillness.

In a shaky voice, Mac confessed, "I don't feel so good." And she didn't. Nausea and fear roiled in her gut. Peripherally, she saw the top of a silver ladder wavering outside the window in Hardin's adjoining bedroom. The ladder banged around and then rested on the sill. He had to be kidding.

Mrs. Ambrose whipped around 180 degrees, strode to the bedroom window and threw it open. She extended herself out, hanging precariously over the driveway two stories below. Her white-haired head turned way left and her posture morphed into stillness.

"HARDIN! YOU GET UP HERE RIGHT NOW!"

Heavy steps bounded up the carpeted treads and into Hardin's bedroom. Mr. Ambrose blew into the room, huffing from exertion.

"What's going on here?" he asked loudly. The expression on his lined face changed from alarm to irritation as his eyes shifted between his wife and Mac, who stared at the blue and white tiles and searched for courage.

More steps pounded up the stairs. Thick dark hair entered the room before the rest of Hardin's lean frame. Guilt etched his amazing blue eyes. Hardin skidded to a halt.

"What were you thinking?" The question was

rhetorical because his mother immediately followed with "Take her home. Now."

Her. Did Hardin's parents even know her name? Fear and shame manifested as acidic bile and silence. Mac swallowed convulsively and wished herself into oblivion. She scrambled down the stairs behind her brilliant boyfriend, halting to acknowledge the Barlows on the couch in the living room, holding fresh cocktails.

The husband elbowed and winked slyly at his wife, causing heat to flush up Mac's neck and into her face. Laughter erupted from the Barlows as she grabbed her purse and shoes and raced out with Hardin.

Mac was in tears when she got into the Jeep.

"Dammit. I'm so sorry," he said, gathering her to him. "I'm so, so sorry."

She gulped down the tears until there were no more. "Let's go."

Lost in their own thoughts, they didn't speak as Hardin drove to their special place. He got a blanket from the back and spread it out, helping her sit, then lowered himself next to her. He slid his legs between Mac's and pulled her close. The full moon illuminated her face, showing just how upset she was.

After a few moments, she untangled herself and began crying again. "I felt like an idiot. Your parents think the worst of me. The way your mom glared at me. Oh my god, Hardin. She hates me. And your dad's face. I felt so dirty. I didn't even do anything. *We* didn't do anything."

"My parents are difficult. And my decisions tonight"—he cupped her face tenderly, thumbs wiping gently over the tears on her cheeks—"well, I wasn't thinking straight. I was stupid. I'm sorry for my role in making you feel bad, for making you look bad."

"Dammit! God dammit! Making me look bad? You couldn't have made me look any worse!" She smeared the tears away from her eyes as she seethed, angry and hurt to her very soul. "As far as how I feel? You made me feel... God, you made me feel so... dirty, Hardin. I'm not your dirty little secret!"

"Babe—"

"I'm not done. You don't get it, do you? What you did? You went and got a ladder to have me climb out of a goddamned second-story window. Are you insane?" Mac shook her head and peered at him through her blurred vision, then untangled her limbs from his in jerky movements and stood. Shaking her head, she quietly said, "No. You're ashamed of me."

"Mac—"

"I don't want to be with anyone who's ashamed of me. Who doesn't value me. Ever. I've been raised by a parent who doesn't see my worth. I'm better than that. This would have happened sometime in the future. It's better that it happened now. We're all wrong for each other." She took a deep breath and steeled herself. "I think it's best that we end it. Please take me home."

"Mac—"

"Now."

Hardin scrambled to his feet and stared beseechingly into her eyes. "Please, no. I'm so sorry, babe. Please..." He cried, his shoulders shuddering. "Forgive me," he whispered, taking her hands in his. "Please, baby."

His tears broke through her anger and the humiliation she felt. "I do." She whipped her arms around him and cried with him.

"I'm never ashamed of you. I'm ashamed of my parents. They're... God... They're miserable people, all about controlling me. Every move. Every fucking decision, including being with you. We are so right together," Hardin murmured into her hair.

Mac felt him swallowing his tears. She swallowed hers too, trying to bring her emotions under control. All she was capable of was nodding.

"I'm sorry. This is on me. They found out you were on the ski trip with me after they had told me not to see you. I refuse to bow to their wishes of not seeing you, no matter what shit they try to rain down on me." Hardin separated them gently and took her face in his hands, his wet eyes searching hers. "Go the distance with me. I see you, Mac. I'm crazy in love with you."

"I see you too, Hardin. And I love you so much it hurts, but you're going to have to do better than a fucking ladder."

"Yeah." His lips broke into a broad smile and he chuckled, wiping his eyes with the back of one hand while holding on to her with his other. "What a great story this will make for our kids."

"Kids, huh?"

"Yeah. Mark my words, McKenna Rose Vesley. Someday. We're going to have a whole team."

7 Chapter Seven

Piñon Ridge...

IT WAS EVIDENT from the moment Hardin stepped inside Elevation Outfitters that the owners had a passion for the outdoors. He knew his way around a sports store, but one focused almost solely on outdoor gear and equipment? Not so much.

An attractive, athletically lean brunette came up to him. She was very much the epitome of an accomplished outdoorswoman. "Hi. Can I help you?"

As he removed his sunglasses, Hardin offered her the paper on which Cori had scribbled the list of items he would need.

"Oh my God! You look like Hardin Ambrose," she said, taking a step back, then wagging her head back and forth as if disbelieving who she was seeing, her brown ponytail swishing about like a horse's tail. "You can't be though." She stepped closer and ogled him. "Right?"

He vacillated only for a moment. How to play this? Large bills filled his wallet. Surely he could pay for whatever he needed without using a credit card. He had one focus. Time with Mac. Hardin squinted at her. "Who?"

"I'm sorry. Of course you can't be him." She continued talking nervously. "You could be his twin though. It's unbelievable how much you look like him. He's an American soccer player, as in among the best. I watch him play all the time. Plays for Spain. You might say I'm a soccer geek. Played through college. Do you play soccer?" She smiled brightly and barked a laugh. "Sorry. That was rude. Never thought I could be starstruck. We get everyone in here. Hollywood peeps. Tech millionaires." She inhaled deeply and then extended her hand. "I'm Veronica Chastain. Ronni. My family owns Elevation."

"Nice place," he said, looking around the large store. Brick walls and rough plank floors anchored the space while an exposed high ceiling and rustic industrial fixtures gave the store an inviting, hip vibe. Oversized windows and suspended metal lamps provided ample light in what would have been a dark space. He didn't offer his name but nodded at the paper in Ronni's hand. "Cori sent me down to buy those items."

"Intrepid's the best." Ronni scanned the paper. "Let's get you taken care of. Follow me. I'll help you pick out a backpack first. Where're you headed?"

"A three-day excursion. Elks Pass and Chasm Incline."

"That's an incredibly demanding hike. I hope you're as fit as you look."

Hardin couldn't help himself. A cocky grin broke over his face, but he said nothing.

"When?"

"Tomorrow."

"You're a seasoned hiker," she stated.

"Nope."

She stopped and turned. Her hazel eyes raked over him, then dropped, sweeping over his well-worn hiking boots. "You haven't hiked in those?"

"Nope," he said, smirking. "I wear them because I like how they look and feel."

"Okay. You picked out one of the best pair of boots, and they're decently broken-in, so you had me fooled. They'll serve you well on your trip." Ronni spun around and moved toward a corner of the store at a brisk pace. "Do you have a budget in mind?"

"I have no idea what it takes to outfit me. I want the most functional, best performing."

"I'll show you a number of options. Who's guiding?"

"Mac." *Shit*. "Uh, no. Kenna."

If Ronni had noticed his slipup, she made no mention of it. "Kenna's a beast. She'll put you through your paces."

"What's that mean?"

"It means be prepared. She's one of the best guides in Peaks County, but she'll also compete with you if you're as fit as you seem to think. If you challenge her."

"Perfect," he said. "I live for a challenge."

A broad smile broke out over Hardin's face, rendering Ronni speechless. She handed the first pack to him to try on.

Properly outfitted for his adventure with Mac, Hardin went back to the Urban and dropped off his purchases, then went out in search of lunch. Much of downtown Piñon Ridge was designated a National Historic District and was reminiscent of the small quaint villages in Europe he escaped to when there were breaks in his schedule. The feel of the picturesque town was laid-back yet vibrant.

He strolled past buildings that had stood for over one hundred years and others that were newer, designed to reflect Piñon Ridge's historic character. Occasionally, Hardin stopped at a restaurant and checked out the lunch menu posted outside. Not satisfied, his search continued, taking him past the art district. The doors to the Hazy Rebel Brewing Company were wide open, inviting him to look clear through the dark rustic interior to the back where a large deck overlooked the water. After reading the menu, he noted a few items that interested him along with the handcrafted beer. He was on the early side for lunch, so the host showed him immediately to a small table in the dappled shade under the pergola.

He ordered the special—a brisket sandwich, fries and coleslaw, along with the restaurant's flagship beer, a lager made exclusively with German malt and noble hops that the host assured him finished clean and crisp. It came immediately and Hardin took a deep sip. It was delicious, light, and refreshing. He nursed it while waiting on his food, knowing full well that drinking too much would enhance the effects of the time difference between Spain and Colorado. He certainly didn't want that on top of the altitude change. He also planned to pack this afternoon for the trip and be in bed early.

In short order, the waiter was back with Hardin's lunch. He hadn't eaten since his light breakfast hours ago at the inn; the smell of the tender beef made his mouth water. The first bite proved it was as delicious as the waiter had claimed.

Hardin glanced at the people slowly filling the tables, wondering what it was like to live in Piñon Ridge and if Mac frequented the restaurant. He envisioned them having dinner. A date. Comfortable with one another like they used to be. Talking and smiling over beers. Their eyes meeting, conveying private thoughts under the surface of their discussion. Was his plan going to work?

After lunch he walked Main Street south, noting the mix of commercial and retail businesses that continued up to where the street merged into the highway. Hardin reversed course and headed north. Once back in the thick of Piñon Ridge, he explored the side streets east of the charming village, wandering into an older neighborhood with refurbished Victorian homes and remodeled extended miners' cabins that reflected a similar feel and age. The homes were significantly smaller than those that dotted the sloped bases of some of the peaks. Resort lodging—condo and town house developments—filled in large swaths of land between the village and the ski slopes.

Booming music in the distance caught his attention. He slowed his pace, mesmerized. Just up ahead, where the street T'd into another, was a small Victorian, painted pale green. Dancing and singing and wearing cutoff shorts that showcased her beautiful legs, Mac disappeared behind the red vehicle she was cleaning out, oblivious to him or anyone else. An older Jeep. Hell, it might even be the same year as the one he'd driven in high school.

The recently mowed front yard was bordered by a riot of colorful flowers, bird feeders, birdhouses, and a birdbath on one side and large pines mixed in with smaller purple-leafed trees on the other. He smiled, thinking it all felt so like the Mac he had known. Warm. Welcoming. Full of life. Happy.

From where he stood, he could tell that a privacy fence extended behind the house, gated where the asphalt driveway ended. In front of it was a basketball goal with a collection of sports balls scattered underneath, including several soccer balls. A skateboard lay on its side on top of an inexpensive soccer goal in pieces in the grass. She tossed out an equipment bag, adding it to the pile, then stretched. Her shirt tightened and rode up. He noted her breasts were fuller than in high school and her abs were more toned. Her auburn hair, which had spilled over the back of the chair in Intrepid's office, was clipped into a large, loose wavy knot at the back of her head and shone like burnished copper.

There was no additional movement other than birds visiting the suspended feeders. He ventured closer as he took in the scene, his mind replaying the feel and scent of her warm skin. Two boys rode toward her from the opposite direction. Hardin stepped into the shade and hid behind a large tree.

"Mom!" called the boy balancing on the seat and holding two backpacks while the other boy pedaled them both.

Mac dropped what she was doing, like literally dropped everything. Before she even turned toward the boy, an enormous smile spread over her face and she glowed.

Hardin's heart beat so hard it felt like it would explode out of his chest. He watched, blown away by seeing her as a mother. Mac was the embodiment of grace and love, and it only made her more beautiful.

From his position, he couldn't hear anything else after the boys came to a stop in front of her, dismounted, and chucked their helmets into the grass next to the pile of sports gear. She wrapped her son in a tight one-armed hug and ruffled his mop of dark hair before kissing it. The boy, only slightly shorter than Mac, seemed familiar. He leaned in and wrapped his mom in a two-armed hug around her waist. After releasing her son, she gave the towheaded boy a side hug, and the three of them disappeared companionably into the house.

Taurus Range, Colorado Rockies…

Hardin's admiration for Mac's fitness and agility was the last thought he had before stepping into a deep patch of scree and sliding. His arms flailed as he fought for control and to stay upright and not sail over the knife-edge of the narrow path. The drop-off was sheer; the unforgiving ground appeared to be at least half the distance of a soccer field before it leveled off among more boulders and spindly trees and pines. Sweat broke out over him as he battled, legs and core straining, unaccustomed to the extra weight and bulk of the backpack. He finally won and chastised himself. *Pay fucking attention.*

Above him on the steep incline, Mac had stopped and turned. It was impossible to read her since she wore sunglasses and the dark shadow from the bill of her ball cap obscured any facial expression. Her hands were on her hips, and the impersonal "You good?" didn't make him feel any more confident. He was definitely out of his league up here. This called for a different kind of athleticism.

"Yeah. What would have happened if I'd gone over?"

She cocked her head, seeming to consider before she answered. "As Cori explained when you reserved your trip, all guides carry a specialized first aid kit. All of us are wilderness first responders, trained to triage. We also hold

CPR/AED certification. And I have a SPOT device, so we're being tracked via GPS. Our location is known. Should anything happen, the PCRG, Peaks County Rescue Group, will be activated and escort you to a clinic or hospital. You're covered, Hardin. Feel better?"

He didn't. She was emotionally closed off, fully professional, focusing on guiding him safely. She stayed ahead of him, enough so that talking was nearly impossible as they traversed the demanding terrain among the tufts of long grasses and clumps of wildflowers. He wanted her to talk to him, not sound like some damned infomercial.

"I'm good," he said, then sipped from his dromedary bag, a purchase recommended by Cori. He had refilled it three hours ago with water filtered through the compact microfilter Mac carried.

"We have about another mile before we stop for the day and set up camp. The terrain settles out in another half mile or so. Then it's easy-peasy, especially for an athlete of your caliber," she said, not trying to hide her sarcasm. "Let's go."

Relieved at having dodged possible injury or death, Hardin picked up his pace and followed her more closely. He was impressed with how Mac had become a human mountain goat, appearing to easily maneuver over the steep scree-covered earth. The sun had dropped in the sky ahead of them, and the air was noticeably cooler as they continued upward. He looked forward to stopping, stretching, and cracking through the veneer she had erected, hoping they could have a long-overdue, albeit painful, conversation.

Chapter Eight

M AC LAY IN her sleeping bag, wide awake, her mind churning. Hardin was still up. The glow of his solar lantern was evident through the wall of her tent.

He had acquiesced to her minimal talk all day, giving her a wide berth when she sought time by herself. Tonight he had pitched in—setting up camp, cooking dinner, cleaning up and then making sure the food supplies were secured in the bear canisters over a hundred yards from where they slept.

Hardin had been nothing but accommodating. She also noticed that he hadn't seemed to be aware of the few women gawking at him as they had passed during their hike—either because they recognized him or were appreciative of the trail candy. Mac had spoken little to him all day other than to point things out or to give him instructions. She had successfully avoided looking at him, really looking at him, until they were finishing their early dinner, after retiring their sunglasses due to the rapidly deepening mountain shadows.

He was a beautiful man. She was fascinated by seeing his tattoos up close instead of on TV. All new since she had last seen him, and not for the first time she wondered about their significance.

Hardin had taken her breath away the first moment they met, when he gave her that impish grin and gazed into her eyes. His were the color of the sky after a good hard rain had washed it clean and the sun was radiant, and they were framed by thick dark lashes that only made them stand out more. He was the most beautiful boy she had ever seen. And, it turned out, the sweetest and most considerate.

Nowadays, when she allowed herself to watch him play during the recorded games only after Stowe was asleep, Hardin's eyes had less light in them, and the playful cockiness he had in high school seemed to be replaced by an edgier form, a toughness that wasn't there before. Mac suspected that the level of fame that accompanied being one of the best soccer players to ever play the game could have made Hardin jaded and wary. Aside from that, time had been kind to him. If anything, he was more beautiful, manly, and confident. From the little gossip she read, he was a womanizer, a player.

As they finished cleaning up after dinner, Hardin's eyes seared into hers for the first time in twelve years, searching her soul. Mac stumbled, mumbling an excuse about the uneven footing when the gut punch of desire hit her with a gale force. His hand had grabbed hers, and a current of electricity sparked between them. The knowing look she remembered filled his face, and she found herself exposed and vulnerable. She gulped and pulled her hand away and hurried to her tent to avoid him, hoping to hide from the thick, heady desire setting her blood on fire.

"Good night, Mac," he said before entering his tent. He sounded amused.

Darkness descended quickly, and now both of them were parked in their tents when they should have been exploring the millions of stars sparkling in the sky above them. She had pushed him on the hike, choosing the more difficult options of the trail, yet not taking him as high as she initially planned, watching for any indication of altitude sickness, showing him over and over her prowess in high-altitude backpacking, establishing that she was in control. He had done great. Yeah, he slid and stumbled on occasion, but he did remarkably well for a newbie. In turn, Mac felt like a bitch when she thought about how she had treated him. Tested him. But so much had happened and not happened. There were so many unknowns. So many unanswered questions. She felt adrift.

The last half mile of the day was downhill. They set up camp five hundred feet lower than the highest elevation they had hiked. They were below the tree line in a mostly level depression, which would protect them from the night wind, any pop-up storms, and the coldest temperatures. It would also give Hardin's body recovery time, help with his acclimatization while they slept, when their automatic breathing was at its lowest. A robust stream hurtled over rocks and boulders and emptied into a large crystalline lake some two hundred yards from where they set up camp.

His lantern continued to glow. What was he thinking? Reading? Like her, he loved to read. She corrected herself. He *had*. What other boys would have admitted a love for the classics? Would they have read poetry with her, to her?

The more Mac thought about Hardin, the more her mind churned, and the ember of desire, long banked, flamed. She tried to think of other things, but her brain refused to cooperate. Until she thought of Stowe. She was rarely away from her son. A night here or there; however, this was the first two-night separation. Cori would take excellent care of him. She always did, and Cori's husband Mike was like a father to Stowe.

Mac, overwhelmed by the fierce love she had for her boy, blinked her eyes furiously as tears threatened to erupt from nowhere. She had no idea how love for another human being could be all consuming. As much as she had thought she loved Hardin, that depth of love paled in comparison to what she felt for Stowe. She would give her life for him.

Illinois, August, Twelve Years Earlier...

The day after Hardin left for college, the shit hit the fan.

"If I get wind of you talking to that boy again, I'll have him charged with statutory rape. Do you understand me?"

Mac had lied to her mother. "Nothing happened, Alicia. Leave him alone!"

"Don't tell me nothing happened. Do you think I'm stupid, McKenna? You had his stink all over you, just like other nights."

If Alicia had slapped her, Mac wouldn't have been more astonished. She grabbed some socks and put on her gym shoes, which had miraculously reappeared the morning after Hardin left, and stormed out of the trailer. Mac ran the direction of town, toward Hannah's, hoping her friend was home and that she could drive her to the Ambroses' to get Hardin's number and other contact information.

Mac glanced back at Hannah, who waited behind the wheel of her car, windows down and engine off. She gave Mac a thumbs-up and an encouraging smile.

Sheltered from the hot August rays, Mac stood in the recessed entryway, trembling. She kept her head down, struggling to hold on to her nerves, having noticed the camera in the corner as she approached and remembering when she was last face-to-face with Hardin's parents and their cool demeanor. Her mortification. Hardin's apology and pleas to keep seeing her. She swallowed and reached for the doorbell.

She was about to ring the bell again when she heard the tumblers in the lock move. The massive wood door opened, and a stern woman in uniform stood there.

"May I help you, miss?"

"Hi. I'm McKenna Vesley. I—"

"I have it, Bridgett." Mrs. Ambrose materialized next to her. "Thank you," she said with authority, dismissing the maid.

Hardin's mother's eyes were just as icy as Mac remembered. They passed over the damage Alicia had inflicted on her face.

"Hello, Mrs. Ambrose. I'm McKenna Vesley. I—"

"Leave. Now, young lady. I've filed for a restraining order. You and your mother and her threats have done enough damage. My son could end up behind bars because of you." Mrs. Ambrose's lips drew back and she bared her teeth, looking as if she would attack. "You will never see him again. Disappear, you little bitch," she growled, wrinkling her nose like she'd caught a whiff of rotten eggs, her arctic eyes washing over Mac with contempt before she lifted her chin and firmly closed the door.

Illinois, November, Twelve Years Earlier...

Mac curled over the white porcelain bowl in the private bathroom of the pregnancy clinic and sobbed uncontrollably, her suspicion confirmed. She had traveled to a town forty minutes west of Pleasantdale where no one would know her, taking the commuter rail line operating between Chicago and its western suburbs. The contents of her stomach had emptied of their own volition until all that was left was violent cramping. She lay on cool, icy-white tiles, arms crossed over her stomach, shuddering waves moving through her body, fear gripping her like iron clamps.

Could this level of vomiting harm the baby? And with that question, Mac knew she had made the decision to parent the child she carried. After all, it was an innocent conceived in love, albeit how was perplexing.

An insistent tapping on the door pulled Mac out of her thoughts. She wiped at her mouth with a shaky hand. Physically drained. Emotionally depleted.

"Yes?" she uttered in a croaky voice.

"Are you all right in there, dear?"

Mac stood on unsteady legs and unlocked the door.

A tall woman with graying brown hair, who appeared to be in her early forties, regarded her with soulful brown eyes. She pursed her lips before asking quietly, "Not the news you were expecting?"

Mac shook her head vehemently, and a fresh torrent of tears washed down her face.

The woman pulled Mac into her ample bosom and rubbed her back until the tears subsided. "I'm Carol

McGiver. Here to listen, to talk, or just be. No judgment."

"Thank you," Mac whispered, breaking the hug and looking up. "I'm... I'm Kenna."

"Well, Kenna. Everything is confidential here."

"Can I stay?"

"Of course. As long as you wish. It just so happens today is a slow day. Let's get some food and fluids in you. Come on."

Mac followed the nurturing woman into the small office farther down the hall. As soon as she sat, it was as if someone had fully opened the spigot; she talked at length about her homelife and predicament, leaving out nothing except her real name and where she lived. Carol gave Mac her full attention.

After finishing half of Carol's lunch and keeping it down, Mac fell asleep.

"You're going to be okay," Carol said when Mac woke from a brief nap. She pressed a bottle of prenatal vitamins and a piece of paper into her hand. "I made a phone call while you slept. A friend of mine. We have a network of women throughout the US who provide emotional support for teen moms. She's a distance, Kenna. Colorado. If you can find a way to get there, she'll find a way to help."

"How can I thank you?"

Carol smiled. "By taking care of yourself and the miracle you carry, dear."

Mac gave Carol a heartfelt hug and left. She felt stronger, buoyed by the contact information of Carol's trusted friend and the seeds of a plan that continued to germinate during the train and bike ride home. She would start researching in the community library across the street from the high school tomorrow—things like prenatal care, transportation to Colorado, medical and other expenses—details necessary to keep from Alicia, made easier since she began giving Mac the cold shoulder after the officers had brought her home that early and stormy August morning.

After making herself dinner and doing the dishes, Mac cleaned the trailer, showered, and was in her bed—the built-in bench—before Alicia came home from work. She feigned sleep until she heard her mother snoring, then opened her eyes and sat up, wrapping herself in a thin blanket like a burrito, wondering at the chance that a kind stranger would offer her help. Her thoughts soon became consumed with protecting the life growing inside her as well as Hardin, for the baby was proof that they had indeed had sex.

Resourceful, Mac had squirreled away money from her jobs and hidden it in a compartment under the trailer, out of sight and unknown to Alicia. As luck would have it, Mac discovered a stash of money when she cleaned the trailer. It was in several cosmetics bags, tucked behind the cleaning supplies in their tiny kitchen. Her jaw dropped open as she counted it. Two hundred and fifty thousand dollars in crisp new hundred-dollar bills, strapped in ten-thousand-dollar bundles. How Alicia had put away this much was a mystery.

Her gut said something was amiss, so asking the universe for forgiveness and promising to repay it when she could, Mac borrowed a small amount, and if Alicia failed to question her, she would continue to borrow and add it to her cache before she left Illinois at the end of the semester. All she needed to do now was finish high school and remain under her mother's radar.

Mac was on her own, and she vowed right then and there that she would protect her baby from Alicia, Hardin's parents, and anything else that might be a threat.

Chapter Nine

Taurus Range, Colorado Rockies...

PERIODIC SHARP WINDS buffeted the tent, whistling along the slopes above them. When the wind died down, the gushing and splashing of the water over the rocks resurfaced. The power of the water thrummed through the ground, having the effect of a soft massage under her sleeping bag.

Mac pulled her small tablet from her pack and turned it on. After staring at the words for some ten minutes without absorbing them, she finally admitted that reading wasn't in the cards. Hardin's appearance had cracked the layers of emotional armor around her heart, which she'd long believed impenetrable. She scrubbed at her wet cheeks, then covered her mouth to silence a choking sob. That didn't work so well. Rather than alert him, she grabbed her light fleece and flipped over, burying her face in it and letting the sobs wrack her body as emotions and memories assaulted her.

Illinois, December, Twelve Years Earlier...

"McKenna, wake up." Alicia shook her shoulder roughly.

She blinked slowly and rolled over, sitting up carefully, making sure her growing bump was concealed under the roomy flannel pajamas she'd worn every winter since sixth grade. "What? I was sound asleep." She had told Alicia she didn't feel good last night, when in fact she felt great physically since the nausea had passed, other than being tired. The baby exhausted her. Alicia had left her undisturbed when she went to work. "What time is it?"

"It's after lunch. So you've slept all morning?"

Mac let that go. "What're you doing home?" she asked instead, sitting up straighter.

"I thought you should know I'm celebrating getting you through high school. I packed while you slept like a princess. I'm leaving, McKenna."

"Where are you going?"

"On a long-overdue, well-deserved vacation. Somewhere warm. By myself. I'll contact you."

"You're just up and leaving? Christmas is in a few days." She took in their meager, dark space, noting again that there weren't any Christmas decorations. The responsibility had always fallen to her, but she had been so busy with finals that the few ornaments and trimmings they had remained in one of the bottom drawers of the kitchen. Because they had no room, and no money, Mac recycled the decorations she had made throughout grade school, having fewer to put up over the years as they fell apart or got damaged beyond hope and weren't replaced.

HEARTS
don't lie

"We've never really celebrated anyway. It won't be much different for you. I'd be at work if I were here."

"How? How are you going to contact me, *Mother?*" Mac seethed. "You destroyed my phone in August."

Alicia's eyes flashed at her. "Do not call me that. I did. I expect you've learned your lesson by now."

"What would that be?"

"Never to see that boy again."

A tsunami of powerful longing came over Mac. She started crying. The phone. Then the restraining orders. A double whammy she had been unable to crawl out from under.

"Knock it off," Alicia said impatiently. "He only wanted in your pants. I did you a favor, McKenna. So did his parents."

"Your concern warms the cockles of my heart," Mac said scornfully through her sniffles.

Alicia's face contorted into an ugly mask before she grabbed Mac's cheek and pinched hard. "I've given you everything, you ungrateful girl."

"Ow!" Mac held her cheek, another wave of tears coming in from a different kind of pain. She was going to have a bruise.

"Shut up!"

Enraged, Mac jumped from the bench that had served as her bed for her entire life. "What do you mean, you did me a favor? And Hardin's parents did too?" she shouted, backing up as her mother came toward her.

"I kept you from being in a position to get into trouble, like I did. His parents made doubly sure both of you didn't make any stupid mistakes by serving you with restraining orders here and in North Carolina and making

73

sure your admission was rescinded by the school. I'm sure that cost them some money, but shit, they have plenty of that." Alicia laughed meanly. She glanced at the new watch on her wrist. "Lucky you. You get to go to college, all expenses paid. Only in Illinois. Your second choice is just as good."

Mac couldn't speak. She was too stunned. Until this very moment, she'd had no idea why her offer to North Carolina University had been rescinded. She had been devastated, and yet when she realized she was pregnant, it was a moot point. She had never accepted the offer in Illinois. *You have no idea, Alicia. Too late.*

"The Illinois restraining order named both of us. I saw it. What did you do?" Mac asked, shouting again, not caring that their fight was probably being heard in other trailers. "My full ride is my doing." Mac jabbed her finger in the air at her mother, hating like hell that she had stooped to Alicia's low, that she was sobbing uncontrollably. Shame for revealing her weakness to Alicia coursed through her. "I earned that. You c-could be… pr-proud of me."

"I am proud. I'm proud you don't need me. I'm relieved my job is done, that I'm no longer saddled with you. I have to go, but before I do"—she had handed Mac a crisp, new hundred-dollar bill—"here's your combined graduation and Christmas present. Treat yourself to something special for Christmas. I'll send a postcard."

"Wow. A hundred dollars," she said neutrally. "Alicia, I need more. Please. I need to pack for school, get some things."

"You'll figure it out. You've always been a smart, resourceful girl," Alicia said, nodding at the money in Mac's hand. She pivoted and opened the door, pausing, half in and half out. Her green eyes, shaped the same as

Mac's chestnut-colored ones, washed over her daughter. Quietly she said, "The rent is paid through the end of the month. Then stay with someone until you go to college. I did my best, McKenna. I hope you recognize that down the road. Maybe you'll forgive me for being imperfect and for not loving you as a mother should. I'm still young. I still want the chance to do the things I want to do, things for myself. Things that make me happy. Take care of yourself." Gusting wind slammed the thin door behind Alicia, rattling the trailer.

Even though Mac had been meticulous with her planning, she was gobsmacked. She fell back onto the bench and mulled over the situation. In her anger and astonishment, she hadn't heard her mother drive off. Had Alicia actually just said goodbye forever? Without so much as a hug?

Actually, Mac couldn't remember a time Alicia had hugged her, nor could she recall her ever saying "I love you." She peered out the tiny window that faced the patch of dirt where her mother parked. The space, as well as the county road in front of the trailer park, was empty. Alicia was gone.

Mac locked the door before going to the cabinet where her mother had hidden the stash of money, the same stash she had carefully borrowed from over the past few months. Alicia had never noticed. Luckily, she had taken a little more each week as her trip to Colorado grew closer, because now the money was gone. Every single bill.

Mac spent the Christmas season in emotional hell, dealing with the abandonment, alternately hating her mother and the Ambroses. Hardin failed to show, and she didn't hear from Alicia. There were times she felt she would suffocate under the weight of all of it. All alone, Mac gave in to the fear and grief battering her. Sometimes she screamed. Sometimes she wailed. And when she was spent, Mac sobbed until she was numb and then fell into a dreamless sleep.

Feeling the baby move for the first time pulled Mac out of her prolonged pity party, reminding her she had someone else to think about. Someone who, no matter what, she wouldn't abandon.

"I've got you, little one," she said, then silently vowed to be a better mother to her child than Alicia had been to her. She patted her stomach tenderly, again experiencing awe and a fierce need to protect her child. The first glimmerings of fortitude asserted themselves. She would find a way.

Alicia had left her stranded. No transportation since her bike was useless in the ravaging winter and no phone. But she had a paid roof over her head, and staying until the end of the month would be the financially prudent thing to do. Before heading over to her neighbors to ask for a ride into town, she showered and made herself presentable. Mrs. Rasmussen took her into town for supplies. Mac used some of her borrowed money to buy healthy food, extra water, and a prepaid cell phone in addition to a new winter coat, hat, scarf, gloves, and boots. Mrs. Rasmussen didn't blink when Mac explained that the rugged duffel bag she bought was a more malleable storage option in the trailer.

Mac bided her time until she left—she ate when hungry, showered when the unreliable water in the trailer park was working, and slept when tired. When awake, Mac went over the plan for her and the baby's future, refining it until she believed she had all scenarios covered as much as she could, given the unknowns.

The contact in Colorado—Issa Fleming, who was a good friend of Carol, the compassionate woman at the pregnancy clinic who had given her safe harbor—offered her a place to stay temporarily until they were able to figure something else out. Mac gratefully took Issa up on her offer.

A few days before leaving, Mac again asked Mrs. Rasmussen to take her into town. This time she bought for her trip—healthy snacks, a water bottle, a filter straw, and more prenatal vitamins. After hemming and hawing over it for days, she decided to buy a tablet. The justifications for the expense were many. Now that she had graduated high school, access to the internet was no longer possible since she had to return her rented device to her school. Without transportation or others to depend on, it would be far easier if she could access information directly. Mac also added a large gift card to her purchase and applied it to the account she opened while in the store. She could draw off it for additional e-books during her bus trip and for future necessary items once she got to Colorado. All she had downloaded was a maternity book and two thrillers.

That night Mac counted her money, checked the bus schedule once more, packed carefully, and set the alarm on her cell. When she rose the next morning, she was able to take a quick shower because the water was working, then called a cab to take her to the train station. She had just finished getting ready when it pulled into the trailer park. Mac stepped outside and waved it closer. As the driver loaded her duffel and backpack into the trunk, she said a silent goodbye to the only home she had ever known. Tears pricked her eyes even though images of her mother's physical and emotional abuse flashed through her mind. Her tears came harder when the cab pulled out of the trailer park, passing the spot Hardin used to wait for her with his red Jeep. Mac took a deep breath and reminded herself it was just her and her baby now.

Taurus Range, Colorado Rockies...

An eerie sense of calm pervaded her soul. Mac had long stopped crying, but she gently palpated around her eyes to reduce any telltale swelling. Not too bad, just gritty feeling. She grabbed the saline out of the first aid kit and put a few drops in each eye. That certainly felt better.

Now it was time for some answers.

Mac slipped on her fleece, picked up the lantern and exited the tent. Outside, she righted her boots and slipped into them, then quietly walked the short distance to the neighboring shelter. "Hardin?"

10 Chapter Ten

"COME IN, MAC," he said, unzipping the flap. His forward movement did nothing to quell his raging erection, a recurring condition he had dealt with since they had struck camp, made only worse after he connected with those brown eyes that had haunted him. Her high, tight ass and shapely legs—quads, hams, and calves—had kept him in some state of attention throughout most of the day. When not focusing on his footing, he enjoyed watching her toned muscles gliding over each other while they covered the challenging terrain. Even her arms and back were sculpted. She was obviously fit—a vision of lean, honed strength.

"Um, hi." She scuttled into the tent in her fleece and sat facing him, her eyes skipping around his tent before flitting to his, then away, before finally landing on his lantern and staying put. Mac turned hers off and placed it next to her knee as she sat back on her heels. She rubbed her hands and began awkwardly. "I realize I haven't talked all that much today. Of course, it was a tough climb. And I was dismissive yesterday. Uh, okay, maybe rude. It's just, well, you, showing up after all this time. I—"

"Hey." He waved his hand between their faces, then dropped it into his lap.

Her eyes flew to his and rounded.

"I'm right here," he said quietly. "Not where the lantern is. But I get your reaction."

She squeezed her eyes shut, bowed her head and raised one hand, palm facing him. "Give me a minute."

Hardin watched Mac struggle for control, mesmerized by the long wavy hair cascading over her face and shoulders, blocking his ability to gauge what she was feeling—this girl, now a woman, who had always been an open book with him. He had spent a lot of time caressing those silky tresses, and his fingers moved from the memory of gently loosening the curls when they'd become tangled.

She inhaled deeply and exhaled slowly, then sat in silence.

While he waited, Hardin concentrated on breathing normally and slowing his tattletale heart, which was beating furiously with rioting emotions. Fear mixed with anger at her not speaking to him the majority of the day. A kick-in-the-gut desire so powerful that it was all he could do not to act on it. To touch her. But he wouldn't. He was the one who had shown up without notice, turning her seemingly bucolic life topsy-turvy. Was there anything left to salvage between them? *God, I hope so. Coming to Colorado was my only option. Patience,* he told himself.

Finally, she spoke. "Why are you here? What do you want?" She kept her head down, her words snapping and snarling, buffeting the inside of his small tent. "I'm beyond pissed at you! I'm so fucking pissed off, I can't even look at you! Goddammit, Hardin! Why did you show up after all these years?" Mac's eyes locked on him and her voice was harsh. "I feel... I feel..." The first tears plopped onto the hand gripping her thigh. "...unmoored," she cried. Her shoulders slumped forward and began shaking, and she sniffled as she wept.

"Mac," he said quietly. He felt a tear break free, and then more followed in an unbroken stream. Hardin clenched his jaw as he rubbed at his eyes with the heels of his hands. "I'm here because I want you. Period. It's always been you."

"Too much time has passed," she said tonelessly, avoiding looking at him. "Too much has happened."

"I'm praying that isn't the case. I've never stopped loving you." He reached toward her cautiously with one hand, touching her.

At first she resisted but then softened, allowing him to pull her into the circle of his arm. Hardin dropped his face into the crook of her shoulder, inhaling the scent that was forged in his soul, welcoming the comforting feel of her body up against his.

"I've missed you so fucking bad," he whispered into her ear, his tears mixing with hers, his other arm reaching around to encircle Mac and hold her close. "Give us a second chance."

Mac's arms slid around his waist and she burrowed deeper. Eventually her weeping stopped, as did his. She'd cried herself out and fallen asleep. Hardin laid her down carefully and stretched out next to her, covering them with his camping blankets. Her warmth and his tears had made him drowsy. He smoothed back the hair that had tumbled over her face, kissed her forehead, and was asleep in minutes.

Hardin's cold backside stirred him awake hours later. He had shifted onto his side while he slept, spooning her from behind. Mac slept like the dead. She was toasty warm, nestled within his body heat, his sleeping bag, and the blankets she had stolen while sleeping. He moved carefully so as not to wake her, positioning part of his sleeping bag behind him and adjusting the blankets over himself while keeping her covered. Hardin propped his chin in his hand and watched her, illuminated by the softly glowing lantern.

If possible, she was more alluring at twenty-eight than she'd been at sixteen. The round youthfulness she had carried in her face was gone. Not surprisingly, Mac wore no makeup. She hadn't been a fan of it in high school. Neither had Hardin.

Her lips were still full, and the few times she smiled during the day—at other hikers, not him—they had spread generously over her straight white teeth. God. How they used to kiss. The hunger. The tenderness. Hours and weeks and months of kissing, which eventually led to exploring each other's bodies and learning what they liked. He had loved nothing more than to please her, and when they had given each other their virginity, well hell… He had no words for the first moments of moving inside her. Of being fully, completely hers. And her belonging fully to him.

Her thick auburn lashes had been replaced by much darker ones. Faint circles under her eyes indicated she wasn't getting the sleep she needed. A faint scar was evident under her left eye. The faintest crow's-feet extended from the corners of her eyes, and she sported a frown line between her eyes, yet her dimples were deeper than ever and laugh lines were evident outside them. The character lines only enhanced her natural beauty. *I hope you've had a happy life, Mac.*

As if she'd heard his thought, Mac's eyes blinked open and met his. "Hey," she said, smiling slowly, cautiously. "Why are you staring at me?"

"I've been watching you sleep, blanket hog." He smiled back. "You're even more beautiful than you were in high school."

Her smile vanished and the tenuous intimacy broke. "I didn't mean to fall asleep in here. I... I came to talk. To get something off my chest." She reached for her lantern, then started to rise.

"Wait."

She stopped and adjusted her fleece top. "What?"

"There's too much left unsaid. I have more to say. And I have questions. I wasn't trying to find you because I enjoy a grand treasure hunt. I didn't spend years and hundreds of thousands of dollars without intent. Losing you, losing us, broke my fucking heart, Mac." *Goddammit.* He swatted at the tears that leaked from his eyes, then sat up, crossed his legs, and reached for his fleece. "Please stay," he said huskily. "Please." He pinned her with what he hoped was an earnest look. "Can we talk? Please?"

Hardin recognized Mac's subtle shifting to giving him her full attention, to fully listening to him, the way no one had in a very long time. In high school she had recognized *him*—the insecure teenage boy who feared buckling under the weight of his parents', coaches', and the community's expectations. She had easily seen beneath his mask of bravado and cockiness, encouraging him to trust her in a way that defied his parents' and others' understanding. She had saved him. Loved him fiercely for who he was, and he'd loved her back just as fiercely, without reservation.

"Okay. You first, then me. Agreed?" she asked, tilting her head.

"Even if it takes until the sun comes up."

One corner of her mouth drew up in a quirk, accompanied by a dimple. "Yes. Lucky for you that I make kick-ass camp coffee. It'll light you up."

Hope burst forth. He smiled and nodded, beyond grateful for the chance. His voice broke. "Thank you." He inhaled deeply and wrapped his blanket around himself. "What I say may be disjointed, but these are the things I know with certainty, and they didn't necessarily come to me in chronological order or early in our separation. I want to be totally candid, Mac. I've never been anything but honest with you."

"I know," she said solemnly.

"I've felt some level of hollowness since the police escorted you home that night. I'll start there, okay?"

Her answer of yes was more like a sigh, but he heard it. She took one of his blankets and wrapped it around herself, mirroring his position.

"Are you warm enough?"

"I am, thanks."

"Good." Hardin sighed and held her eyes as he began. "I left when you did that night, as you know. Not happy how things had gone at all. I wanted to take you home. Kiss you, damn… kiss you so much more." His fingers touched his lips. "I never could get enough of the feel of our lips and tongues moving over each other. I still have

84

dreams where I feel the electricity that sparks over my lips and remember how sweet you taste."

Mac cleared her throat and lowered her eyes to her lap.

He peered at her and pursed his lips. "Sorry. It's just that no one else has made me feel like that." He had to know. His heart pounded as he asked, "Was it like that for you?"

Her eyes snapped to his, hardened, but she answered. "I reserve comment. You're doing the talking right now."

"Fair enough." He nodded before looking down and blinking several times. *Quit being a pussy. She hates pussies.*

"I texted you when I got home, to say good night again. To make sure you were okay. I knew how upset Alicia got with you from time to time. You didn't respond. Actually, I don't think I slept at all. Too worried. I started calling and texting as soon as I got up. No answer. No response. I only stopped when an automated message said your number was no longer in service. What the fuck…" He shook his head. "I didn't even know how to react."

He noticed how sad Mac appeared, how her eyes were full of unshed tears.

"Want me to keep going?"

She nodded slowly, her eyes never leaving his.

He inhaled loudly and continued. "Before the car that was taking me to the airport arrived, I heard loud voices coming from downstairs. Not shouting, but close. Heated. Angry. Then the doors to Father's study closed and it was quiet. The next thing I heard were footsteps I didn't recognize in the hall. The front door opened. I rushed to my parents' room and stepped out onto their veranda. Mac, it was Alicia."

"Alicia?"

"Yeah. I didn't even know she knew where I lived. But anyway... She glanced back at the house before she drove off, looking smug as fuck. I had a really bad feeling. I ran downstairs. Confronted my parents. They said their conversation with Alicia was private. It was none of my concern. I didn't believe them. I knew it had to be something to do with you, with us. Arguing got me nowhere. My mom told me not to upset them when I was leaving, that saying goodbye was hard enough. Right," he said sarcastically. "What a fucking excuse, like my being away was ever an issue for them. I left it because the tension in our house was so thick you could cut it with a knife. I was fucking miserable when I left."

"You can't blame yourself for your parents' actions. Just as I can't blame myself for Alicia's."

"You're right. It's so fucked up, Mac. There's more." His brows rose, asking her silently if he should continue.

She wiped at a tear that ran down her cheek and held her hand up when he leaned over to comfort her. "I'm okay. Keep going."

"We loaded my luggage in the car and left. I continued to call and text your number all the way to O'Hare, in the concourse, and on the plane until we departed, but the message was always the same. Your number remained out of service until it was reassigned to someone else at the beginning of October. Then I stopped. I wrote you too. But all my letters came back unopened, with 'no such person at this address.' I was flying home at the end of the semester. I was going to come see you. Celebrate your graduation. Beg for forgiveness even though I didn't know what I had done to make you turn your back on me. Get us back on track." His voice cracked with emotion.

"Tell me."

"My parents decided that a last-minute vacation in the Bahamas was just what we needed. They sprang it on me the day before my last final by overnighting my passport and flight info. I called and told them I wasn't going. It got really ugly. That's when my father told me I was not allowed to see you under any circumstances because Alicia had threatened to press charges of statutory rape against me. That was why she had shown up at our house that morning."

"She what? Oh my God! Oh, Hardin." Mac sounded stunned, blinked furiously.

"It gets worse, Mac." He sat up taller and drew in a shaky breath. "I ended up going with my parents, and while we were in the Bahamas, I was privy to the finer details about what else happened. I eavesdropped. Father was celebrating having played great golf that day. He and a few of his investment and attorney cronies were pounding down drinks, laughing over their *win,* how easy it had been to protect the golden boy. Me." He sneered, then rubbed at his eyes, which burned with unshed tears, before saying hoarsely, "A quarter mil to your mom to make her threat disappear and keep you away. They had her sign the nondisclosure agreement. Then my honorable father had you both served with a restraining order in Illinois, and there was one ready to be served in North Carolina too. Just in case. He fucking crowed about having your acceptance to NCU rescinded."

He ground his knuckles in his eyes, but the tears flowed over them as he wept. "When I came by your place in May, at the end of the semester, you were gone. Someone else was living there. They hadn't heard of you. I asked your neighbors. No one knew where you had gone." He bowed his head and his body shuddered. "They fucking destroyed your dreams and mine."

11 Chapter Eleven

MAC AND HARDIN had been each other's rocks in high school. He had spoken of the pressures of being a soccer phenom and the baggage that accompanied it; the worst was the prevalent feeling of being regarded as chattel rather than a beloved son. She had shared what it was like to be raised with indifference, to not feel loved, to be emotionally and physically abused. They were each other's best friend, a safe haven, and they discussed whether what they sought from each other was what they were missing from their parents. After many months of examining their growing feelings for each other, they accepted that what they felt for one another was real. And it had been so real. For her, she had never been as close and intimate with someone as she was with Hardin.

She scooted closer to him, and he leaned into her. Mac's arms slid around him as he wept, her hands rubbing his broad, corded back, her cheek at home on his chest. He was more muscular than in high school but still felt like Hardin. He melted around her. Warm. Welcome. His unique scent enveloped her. It was soothing and stirring at the same time. More of her emotional armor came apart. Having Stowe only magnified what she had felt for Hardin but had locked away—a deep, abiding love. *What am I going to do?*

Everything had shifted within Mac as Hardin told his side of the story. His anger and grief were palpable. She had always admired how he showed her that a man could feel and express emotion, that it emanated from a place of strength.

She found herself affected by his obvious distress and drawn to his vulnerability, unable to hold the boundary of emotional distance, more than willing to be there for him. Realizing it had been misplaced, any rancor she had for him dissolved, but her resentment toward his parents escalated into red-hot rage. What the Ambroses had done to keep them apart was unconscionable. The deceit and injustice were mind-boggling, seemingly driven by a belief that she was completely wrong for their precious son, that she was beneath him. But she was cried out for now, numb.

"Alicia was a guilty party in destroying us too."

He gazed at her somberly. "Yeah."

"Well, now I know where her cache of money came from." Mac pulled her knees up and wrapped her arms around them. "Her actions don't surprise me. I shared her story with you back in high school. Alicia was always about Alicia. Only out for herself. Damn the consequences."

"She was."

Feelings attributed to being abandoned by Alicia resurfaced. Raw. Stinging. But instead of loathing her mother, Mac felt pity—born of compassion and understanding, from walking in shoes similar to those of

Alicia's. "I get that Alicia came from a place of survival, but I can't overlook her need to hurt others in the process of getting what she wanted. I can't forgive what I suffered being raised by her, if a person can call it that. It was no way to treat and react to a child. Ever.

"I can give her grace. She put me in soccer when I was five, more to have time for herself. Unintentionally, she also gave me a gift, provided me with role models who exhibited kindness and fair discipline, who challenged me. Those coaches and other parents provided me life examples and lessons, and those became my foundation, impacting my academics and friendships. My relationship with you. Motherhood." Fuck. It just tumbled out. Mac stumbled over her next words. "I'm glad you came and shared what you knew. Thank you."

"Don't cut me off, Mac. I know you have a kid. I know you were married because of your name change, but you're single now."

"Your PI dug that up?"

"She did."

"I see. What else?" The edge in Mac's voice masked her fear.

"I'm hoping you'll fill in the rest. I'd rather hear it from you."

"There's a lot you don't know, and please, don't presume to know. You don't know me."

"I knew you. The foundation of what is you, that person I gave my heart to. I'm confident she's still there. I want to learn these new aspects of you."

Interesting. Mac adjusted the blanket around her and searched his eyes. "We were teenagers, Hardin. Young and naive."

"We were also wise beyond our years."

"In some ways, yes." She took a deep breath. "I don't want to talk about my name or my history since I saw you last. I don't want to discuss my child with you other than to say he's what I hold most dear in this world, and if there's one thing I'm most proud of, it's the parent I am. Please respect my wishes and don't ask me again."

"Fine. I'll wait until you're ready to tell me."

"What does that mean? Don't you have to be back in Spain for training soon?"

Hardin narrowed his eyes at her and shook his head, an impish grin on his face. "Wow. You've been keeping track of me."

"Hardly." She scoffed. "My son is an enthusiastic fan. He leaks like a sieve."

"Sounds like a cool kid."

"He's the coolest ever, and you're skating on thin ice. Dangerous for a renowned soccer player." She rose, bent over because of the tent's low pitch. "It's terribly late. I'm tired and I need to have my wits about me so that you're safe tomorrow. Like it or not, I'm responsible for you while we hike. My reputation is on the line."

"I'm a thoroughbred, Mac," he said teasing.

She turned on her lantern and grasped the flap, ready to step out into her boots and make her way back to her tent. "On the pitch you are, but not out here. The wilderness can sneak up on the best of us at any time. Later, Hardin."

Back in her tent, Mac slid into her sleeping bag. Intrepid Adventures used only the best products for their activities and trips. Questions had been answered, but Mac had so many more. Two things were clear—they were going to talk more, and the topic of Stowe was safe for now. Hardin had always been honorable, and he'd behaved so tonight.

In her mind, she kissed her son good night and ruffled his floppy dark waves before tucking him in. *I love you more than you'll ever know.* Peace filled Mac, and she relaxed in her toasty sleeping bag, falling into a dreamless sleep.

Mac woke to the raucous chattering of birds. She sat up, disoriented, not remembering having fallen asleep. Something thumped to the ground.

"Shit!"

Apparently Hardin was having a challenge. Mac unzipped the tent flaps and stuck her head out. The air was crisp and the sun sparkled in a cloudless sky, a promise they were going to see some spectacular views on their hike. Already shadows and light accentuated the soaring, craggy peaks in the distance. The highest of them—Devil's Brow—speared through a halo of snow, its twin hornlike formations drenched in brilliant light.

"What's going on?" she called, slipping into her boots, noticing he was holding his hand and a pot was on its side at his feet. "How bad is it?"

"Ugh. You made this look easy. I grabbed it wrong. It slipped. I let go or it would have been worse."

"I told you I make kick-ass camp coffee. That means me, not you. Let me see."

He flashed her a look of thanks and came toward her.

"It doesn't look bad at all. Get your water. I'll get a clean bandanna."

Mac went into her tent for the first aid kit and her

toothbrush. She applied the cool, wet cloth after instructing him to sit on one of the large boulders around the stove, then started the coffee. "I'll be back soon," she said and turned toward the water, intent on addressing her morning routine.

"I'm good," he said behind her.

She kept walking, calling out, "Yes, you are. Wait until I return to play with the stove again, okay?"

"Yes, ma'am."

Hardin held his coffee with both hands. "You weren't kidding about making kick-ass coffee. Hits the spot." He took another long sip. "You were sleeping so soundly I didn't want to wake you. Last night you listened to me. Really listened. No one listens like you, Mac. You didn't share your side of things before you fell asleep. I was trying to be considerate."

"I appreciate the effort, but I'm your guide, so I do everything unless I ask or direct you to do otherwise. Got it?" She stared at him, then drained her first cup and started making breakfast. "Hungry?"

"Like a bear." He stood and looked over her shoulder. "What're you making?"

"Pancakes and eggs with vegetables."

"Damn. Sounds good."

"It's prepared ahead of time mostly."

"Can I help?"

"You can. Just sit there."

"I feel funny, Mac, just sitting here, having you wait on me."

She whipped around and gave him a hard stare. "You helped last night, more than I should have let you. Did you or did you not hire Intrepid Adventures, specifically me, to guide you on the trip?"

"Uh, yes." He tried to look sheepish but failed miserably and ended up with a stubborn expression. "But come on. It's you and me."

"I'm in my element. You are not."

"Fine. I'll empty my tent and pack it. How's that?"

"Think you can?"

"I'm not an imbecile. I paid attention to Chase's demonstration."

"Go for it." She waved her hand at him, then poured herself more coffee, watching as his confident, easy stride ate up the distance to his tent. Electricity zinged though her. Hardin still had his charm and that swagger. She blew into her coffee and took another sip, raising her eyes to peer through its steam. He gazed back at her and winked before disappearing into the tent.

Mac changed clothes and repacked her gear and the first aid kit. While she cleaned up after breakfast, Hardin packed the tents. Despite sleeping in, they were ready to resume their hike earlier than she had expected. They'd be able to take a break and snack in one of her favorite spots.

"Well done. You get a gold star," she said, impressed with his effort.

A beaming smile lit those damned eyes of his. "I'll pass on the gold star, hoping maybe I can barter for something else later."

She broke eye contact before she succumbed to swooning and ignored his comment, surveying where they had camped. It was as if no one had been there, as it should be. Leave no trace. "Let's go. We'll fill our water when we pass the lake."

He had done really well yesterday, a testament to his fitness. Even though she had challenged him, she kept them at a lower altitude than originally planned. He might drive himself too hard during the hike, thinking he could push through it.

"Hardin," she said, filling her water. "I want to reiterate what Chase told you about altitude sickness."

"I did great. I feel like myself."

"Yeah, you did. But today is tougher, more vertical. Because you're fit, you might believe you won't be affected. There's no way of knowing. I need you to tell me if you experience any symptoms, okay? I'm responsible for you." Along with the set expression of his jaw, which told her he was listening and taking her seriously, she saw her reflection in his sunglasses. She appeared as earnest as she had sounded.

A slow smile spread over his face, one that unleashed the butterflies in her gut. "I like that, you being responsible for me."

She stood and attached her bottle to her pack. "Ready?"

During the three-hour-long hike, Mac and Hardin were surrounded by tall pines so dense they were in deep shade. The trail was at times thickly carpeted in twigs and other organic detritus, enveloping them in a pungent fragrance as they crushed the pine needles beneath their feet. The first time the sun peeked through, they stopped to take in the beauty in the dappled light. In front of them, variegated gray-and-brown peaks grizzled with pines and other trees soared above them, contrasting against boundless paradise blue threaded with tufts of cloud. The peaks' silvery edges seemed to shimmer in the light.

He whistled softly. "Damn. This is something else."

"Wait until we get where I'm taking you."

"Better, huh?"

"So much better."

"Do you take photos with your clients?" he asked, turning to her.

"Sure."

"Take a few selfies with me." He slipped off his sunglasses and let them rest against his broad chest, suspended by a colorful cord. She watched as he pulled his cell from his front pocket. He grinned at her, his blue eyes beckoning. "Please."

Her feet moved forward of their own accord.

Hardin draped his arm over her shoulders, pulled her next to him. "Sunglasses off."

She perched her sunglasses on top of her mass of dark auburn hair.

"Smile," he said, extending his arm.

Her entire left side connected with his right. She was all too aware of his lean, hard body. How he towered over her. His smell. She wanted to bury her face in his skin. Mac felt heady and wasn't sure she had smiled until he said, "Good." Then she just stood there, mute and still.

"Mac? You all right?" He had a barely there smirk on his face.

"I'm just taking it all in."

"Uh-huh."

"Let's go. Keep going the same direction." She kicked

herself for dropping her guard and stepped in front of him.

The landscape changed as they moved through the subalpine terrain. The dense pines thinned to wind-twisted, dwarf versions of themselves. When the path vanished or was impassable, they scrambled across steep slopes, sometimes needing hands to maneuver over the loose rock. To their right was tundra and an expansive, sheer, rocky incline bordering the other side of a glassy blue lake created from snowmelt.

"We're here." Mac stopped and put her hands on her hips, spinning slowly, taking in her surroundings, a dreamy smile on her face. "Follow me and then we'll take a break."

They approached a massive boulder overlooking an enormous waterfall, some distance from other hikers who had stopped to enjoy the view. Sparkling water thundered over the boulders and rocks, the spray hitting Mac and Hardin when the light breeze shifted. The sun was blinding and the sky cloudless, the earlier gauzy clouds having evaporated.

Her eyes raked over Hardin's washboard abs, which were briefly displayed when his shirt rode up while he was taking off the light quarter-zip, then her gaze darted away, becoming engrossed in the play of the water just as his head appeared. *Jesus. He didn't have those in high school. I can't unsee those, nor do I want to.* The sound of the cascading water muffled her shaky breath.

He followed where she focused, glancing at the tumbling water and then taking in the tranquil lake farther out. "You do not disappoint. Spectacular."

"It really is," she said deliberately, not looking at him.

"One of my favorite places just to *be*." She nibbled at her trail mix and found herself entranced by the rapids.

He sat next to her and inhaled his snack, chasing it down with water. "Do you have more?"

"Maybe taste this one?" Mac handed him another packet.

"Ha ha ha," he said good-naturedly. "Midwest girl, transplanted to the Colorado mountains, owning a wilderness guide business that includes backpacking, hiking and peak ascents, and rock climbing. It begs the question of why, especially since I know you didn't do any of this as a kid or teen."

Mac considered how to best answer without revealing too much. She sipped her water, studying him, then shared her story in the briefest, most truthful way possible. "A friend of a friend suggested I move here, and even though it was winter, I knew immediately I wanted to stay. I met Cori almost right away and we became fast friends. She's about five years older than me, a native Coloradan."

"This is the same Cori I met?"

"Yes." Mac nodded and smiled. "I went out hiking and on a few primitive camping trips with her after summer arrived, and I was hooked. She enthusiastically shared her dream of having a wilderness guide business. I had a little bit of money saved, as did she. We started small, working out of our homes and sharing storage with another business in Piñon Ridge. Going after our certifications, like wilderness first aid and CPR, and permits for commercially guided activities. Cori's grandfather passed away and left her some money, which allowed us to rent our storefront with a storage area and hire some key staff. After our first six months in business, we branched out from backpacking and hiking trips, adding team building and survival training and outdoor skills. Those programs were geared toward specific age groups, like middle schoolers, teens and adults. We were able to get our information out to schools, way ahead of the summer season. Our middle school and teen camps have been full every summer. Of course, we're members of Piñon Ridge's Chamber of Commerce, which helps to further promote Intrepid Adventures. It's been challenging and lean, but so much fun. Every day is different. I love living here."

Hardin slid his sunglasses onto the top of his dark head, then reached over and squeezed her shoulder, his fingers seeming to linger, the act sending wonderful sparks through her body. "You're amazing, Mac," he said earnestly, smiling wide, spectacular eyes beaming with pride.

She was speechless. His touch. That blinding smile. Those aqua eyes. All she could do was swallow and nod, then smile weakly.

He stood and slid his sunglasses back into place. Hardin's smirk had a naughty edge to it as he extended his hand to Mac. "Shall we? You told me this morning we have a long, rigorous day."

12 Chapter Twelve

AFTER LUNCH THEY had scaled the chasm, donning helmets and gloves because they needed hands to climb over the steep scree- and boulder-covered slope. It was the most vertical ascent of any hike she guided, and not often at that. Her arms, legs, and core had burned while she fought for purchase. Hardin admitted that he'd been challenged too. Her body was pleasantly tired, clean after a dip in the frigid water before a satisfying taco dinner.

Mac figured she'd conk out soon after crawling into her sleeping bag since she had wanted to nod off during dinner. It was not to be. Instead, her mind returned to the man in the other tent. Her body hummed in response, her pulse skittering wildly. Too warm despite the drop in temperature, she unzipped her sleeping bag and flipped the top away from her body. The churning circle continued, her emotions and desire amping up with each cycle. Her mind and body were on fire.

The hell with it. She crawled forward and unzipped the flaps, finding her cold boots right where she had left them. Mac glanced at Hardin's tent glowing softly from his lantern and then the starry heavens. The brisk air and the concentration needed to slip her boots on in the dark slowed her pulse. But as she walked toward his tent, her heartbeat ratcheted up. She had questions after listening to his side of their history, and her body begged for answers to others.

She inhaled deeply and was just raising her hand to tap on the tent when he said, "Come in, Mac."

"How did you know I was there?" she asked sheepishly, stepping in after dropping her boots outside.

Hardin sat up, a tablet in his hands, its screen glowing softly.

"What're you doing?"

"Reading. You told me the bears are bashful, and I was pretty sure it wasn't one of those mountain goats we saw today. They'd prefer to stay clear of humans, you said. I watched the lantern move from your tent to mine." Hardin smiled, but it didn't reach his eyes.

"What're you reading?"

"Seriously? You want to know what I'm reading?" He squinted at her. "Weak segue, Mac. What's this about?"

She raised her brows and shrugged.

He sighed impatiently and closed the cover of the tablet. "Your nocturnal visit. As in why are you here? You've been abundantly clear there are things you don't wish to talk about."

"That's not so. I didn't have the opportunity to tell you my side of things."

Hardin exhaled harshly. "Bullshit. Do not bullshit me, you of all people. We can talk about this but not about that. Your marriage. Your child. Why you moved here."

"Your language is coarser."

"Yeah. It's the world I live in. Arrogant, false gods who think people are at their beck and call."

"Is that what you've become, Hardin?"

"That you'd even ask me that pisses me off," he said bitterly, a harsh expression passing over his face.

"Sorry. That was low."

"Apology accepted. And for the record, your language isn't as sweet either. Cut to the chase. You're skirting things, Mac. I know you. I know your soul."

"You used to," she said, hedging. "I have my reasons and you agreed to my terms."

"I did and I shouldn't have. But I did and now I'm pissed off. I told you everything I know. You told me nothing. There's your whole side of our story, like why you were gone when I came to see you in May. Where were you?"

She folded herself onto the end of his sleeping bag. "I left because Alicia left me. She fucking left me. With a hundred dollars." Mac's voice became more impassioned as she recounted what had occurred, in snippets that barely touched on the devastating events that had brought her to her knees time and time again. "I left because my boyfriend's parents slapped me with a restraining order. I left because my scholarship was rescinded, and I hadn't had the foresight to accept another because I planned to attend the same school as my boyfriend and had no idea his parents were going to fuck me over some more." Her throat burned with unshed tears. She let them flow. When she felt more in control, she said, her voice cracking, "I left because I had nowhere else to go." Mac sniffled and wiped her face on her sleeve. "End of story."

"No. Not end of story," he snarled, his fists clenched.

"I've been trying to find you for twelve years. Since our last night before I left for college. I've never stopped."

She sat back on her heels and regarded him through her tears, wiping again at her eyes and running nose. "I don't understand," she said with disbelief.

"I hired a private investigator ten years ago to find you. Immediately after signing my first contract. Liberty Quinn. She—"

"I met her last week. She popped into Intrepid. I talked to her about our tours and adventures." Mac gazed at him with rounded eyes. "She was smooth. I never would have guessed she was a PI. She works for you?"

"Yeah. Lots of starts and stops. Dead ends. I sent her out to Colorado after she showed me a photo she came across in a magazine. After discovering you were one of the owners of Intrepid Adventures, Liberty was able to track you to Piñon Ridge. I sent her there to find out anything else she could. From your name change, she assumed you had married, but she couldn't access the public records. She asked around once she got to Piñon Ridge. Discovered you're not married and you have a kid."

"As I said last night, I don't want to talk about any of that. Quit bringing it up."

"When will you? I have limited time here."

"Then leave as soon as we return. I'm not on your schedule, nor am I beholden to you."

"No. I'm not leaving until I get the answers I came for and to give you some."

"I don't need any or anything from you. I've moved on, as you can tell. I have a wonderful life in Piñon Ridge."

"You're single, right?"

"That's been established," she said, feeling defensive.

"Let me clarify. Are you involved with anyone?"

"That's none of your business," she hissed at him.

"You aren't."

"I am."

He shook his head and chuckled. "You never were a good liar, Mac. You haven't improved."

"Fine. I'm not seeing anyone right now, and my love life is none of your business. You need to call me Kenna."

"Fuck that. I'm not calling you Kenna. To me, you're Mac. You always were and always will be. Why'd you change your name?"

"I was ready for a change. Decided I like Kenna better."

"I'm not buying it. You know what I think? I think you're hiding something. I think you covered your tracks purposely, that you didn't want to be found. Hell, Alicia had no idea of your whereabouts. Look how long it took me to find you."

"You found her?"

"Liberty did. Within a few days of me asking her to look."

"And?"

"She was living the life in Florida. Married an octogenarian who was in the last stage of terminal cancer. She stood to inherit a nice sum of money. Had a much younger guy on the side. Want to know more?"

"I'd rather not," she said disgustedly. "I'm over her."

"Are you over me?"

"What's your end game here, Hardin?"

His eyes flashed and he grabbed her hands and held them, pulling her closer. "You. Us. I haven't been able to move past us, no matter how hard I've tried."

She attempted to pull free, but he held firmly, somehow not hurting her. "Really?" she spat out. "You live a charmed life that's astronomically wealthier than what even you were raised in. Why in hell would you want to be with me, a poor girl who never will travel and doesn't want to travel in your circle? From my view, it seems you've moved past me just fine. You have your pick of powerful, influential friends. Fast, expensive cars. Beautiful women who probably can't drop their panties fast enough. I mean, how many women, Hardin?"

He let go of her hands, leaned back, and smirked. "So you keep track of the women?"

"I've heard things," she said with contempt.

"Interesting. I've been with women—"

She couldn't help herself and gave him a scathing look.

"Okay, more than a few women. You don't know the situations or context, so park your judgment."

"I'm not judging. I'm simply mentioning it. The boy I knew, who was singularly committed to me, appears to have evolved into a major player. And I'm not speaking of soccer."

"Tabloid fodder, Mac. This is tabled for now, just like any discussion of your relationships and child. Fair?" He stared at her with a grim expression. "I want to get back to the crux of my being here."

"Fine," she uttered warily.

"Look, I don't want to fight. I came to ask you to just be real with me, to find the courage to bare your soul to me. Can you? Be real with me? It's just us. Everything else... I want it to fall away. I want this time with you. It's why I insisted on you as my guide. You and I owe each other the details."

"I told you before. I don't owe you shit," she said angrily, feeling her hackles rise as Stowe flashed through her mind.

"Yes, you do. You know you do. And I owe you. I wasn't some teen boy with a perpetual hard-on. When I said forever, I meant it. Let's start there. No matter what Alicia and my parents threw at us, we had something incredible, a love that most people can only dream about. Please, Mac." His eyes drilled into her.

She swallowed and nodded, unable to find the breath to talk. Tonight it was just him and her. He wasn't the international soccer god, the athlete who made tens of millions every year and more with endorsements, the pro that young kids and teens dreamed of playing like. Neither was he the gorgeous bad boy women wanted in their beds. Tonight he was just Hardin, the grown-up version of the beautiful teen she'd fallen in love with.

She sighed loudly. "I meant it too, Hardin. I fell so hard for you that losing you took my breath away. I had no one. I was so scared. So empty. I had to keep going. I had to." Tears erupted again. "I—"

Hardin leaned in and pressed his forehead to Mac's, his lips brushing over hers, then captured her mouth and kissed her like a drowning man.

13 Chapter Thirteen

"I CAN'T," SHE said, shutting her eyes and scooting away from him, her breathing matching his. "You don't want me to, trust me. I'd be listening to only my body, and I need to listen to my brain. I want to talk. I need to get through what I wanted to say last night and today."

He reached out. His hand traveled through the air, then dropped heavily into his lap. "You're right, of course. It's just that, well, it just feels so right to kiss you. To hold you again."

"There's more than just the physical, Hardin."

"You don't need to remind me of that," he said with an edge. "If there wasn't, I wouldn't have been looking for you all this time."

Her eyes searched his, then dropped to her lap before she looked him straight in the eyes. "I'll recap what's occurred since I left Illinois, some of which you know. Do you promise not to interrupt me?"

He pinned her with his eyes, then held up his hand and said solemnly, "I promise."

Mac changed her position so that she mirrored Hardin—sitting on her butt, legs crossed in front of her, elbows resting on her thighs, hands clasped in her lap. "That last night, after the police brought me home, she went off on me full throttle." Her fingers touched the pale scar under her left eye. "Alicia cut me with her nail or some cheap ring she was wearing. I didn't realize she had opened up my face until the next morning. Probably because my system was overwhelmed by the pain from multiple slaps and punches and being slammed into the walls and counters. I was numb and hurting all at the same time, like it would move through my body in waves. I couldn't distinguish between my tears and the blood. All of it tasted salty. Alicia split my lip too. She banged me around so much I could barely stand. Called me a whore," Mac said, looking away from him, her voice breaking. "Who calls their daughter that?" she asked softly, brushing more tears from her cheeks.

He assumed Mac's question was rhetorical, so he didn't answer, but God how he wanted to. Her mother was a fucking bitch. Some people shouldn't be parents, and in his opinion, Alicia Vesley topped the list.

"When I was able, I opened the door. Stumbled down those rickety stairs and ran. It was raining cats and dogs by then. I spent the night under the picnic table on that rise on the edge of the court. You know the one. Thank God it was a warm night. It kept the worst of the rain off me, but I still woke cold and stiff."

Hardin ached to take Mac into his arms but settled for holding her hands in his and stroking them periodically to signal he was listening and to encourage her to keep going.

"When I got back in, as I said, I'd been bleeding. The bruising was already there, and it got worse in the coming days. The trailer was a mess. It looked like someone tossed it, but it was Alicia having one of her famous tantrums." She shook her head and looked past him as if she was envisioning what she'd returned to. "So much had been broken. Destroyed. Including my phone. The SIM card was missing. I panicked, trying to figure out how I was going to see you, contact you. I decided I'd ride my bike even though I didn't look so great." A sob escaped her.

Fuck it. Hardin pulled her forward into his arms. "Baby—"

"I'm okay." She took a few deep breaths as if to brace herself and pulled back from him.

"Mac—"

"You promised me. Please. I need to get through this. I've never told anyone what Alicia did." She looked at him with a questioning expression while searching his eyes.

"Okay," he said, combing her hair back. "It's just so hard to watch you struggle through this. I wish I could make it go away. Make it not hurt."

"You can't. The only way to make it go away is to go through it, shatter its hold on me."

"You're right. I'm sorry. I'll try my hardest to not interrupt again or to hold you."

"Thank you." Her chin quivered, and she rubbed at her eyes before speaking again. "She had slashed my tires. Alicia fucking slashed my tires," she said bitterly. "I decided I'd run, right? I was fit. I needed my gym shoes, but they were gone. Every single last pair of my shoes were gone. I'd seen her throw a trash bag in the trunk before she took off, which was odd, but then I understood why. She had effectively kept me from getting to you. I have to give Alicia credit." Mac gave him a wry smile. "She thought of everything. I wore the sandals I

111

had on from the previous night, the new ones I had just gotten out of layaway. I had slept in them and they didn't last long because they really were all for looks. Lesson learned," she murmured.

The silence stretched out, reminding him of how comfortable they had been in the silence with each other, never feeling the need to fill it but embracing it for what it offered, space to be together without attached strings. The ability to absorb and navigate their worlds. Room to heal from the onslaught of expectations and lack of appreciation and validation. Time to garner perseverance. He sensed Mac was gathering more courage to go on and covered her slim hands with his.

She smiled slowly at him. "Thank you for that. For the silence. For giving me the space, Hardin. These were layers of the saving grace we offered one another."

He returned her smile and nodded, prepared to wait patiently until she was ready to share more.

"Alicia didn't return until the evening of the next day. She didn't apologize of course but asked if I'd learned anything from *my* behavior, if dinner was ready. I didn't answer her. I couldn't. I couldn't even look at her. I think that's the first time I understood how someone could hate another. I left and took a walk down the road, barefoot. My feet bled again. I had scraped and cut them after my sandals broke. I didn't go back in until I knew she was asleep, and that's how I got through the semester. Leaving before she woke. Not coming home until after she was asleep. Alicia did give me my cleats back for the season and one pair of gym shoes. How kind of her," she said snidely.

He grunted in support and slid closer until their knees touched.

112

"None of my friends had your number. Hell, I didn't even know your number. Hardin, why did we only plug our numbers into each other's phones? Why didn't I *know* your number? I would have been able to call you from someone else's phone. Maybe our story would have been different. At least we would have been in control of it."

He lifted one of her hands and kissed it gently, savoring the scent of her skin.

"We were served the restraining orders. And then my offer to North Carolina University was rescinded. It was the final straw. I had no other way to contact you. Oh my God…" She cried softly for a while, then pulled herself together.

If only. He could kick himself. It killed him watching her, knowing that Alicia and his parents were at the root of their separation and their pain. What hadn't they done? Their devious cooperation sickened him.

"I left after Alicia gave me my graduation gift. A hundred-dollar bill. There was nothing to look forward to. No you. No us. A friend of mine had a contact in Piñon Ridge, so I got on a bus and came out with money I *borrowed* from Alicia. I found her hidden cache when cleaning. I had no idea how she had accumulated such a large amount. I didn't begin borrowing from it until one thing after another happened. A little bit at a time, hoping Alicia wouldn't notice or would wonder if she'd spent some of it when she was drunk. As luck would have it, she never discovered what I'd been doing. I always intended to pay her back, but things have been lean and now that I know your parents bought her compliance and silence, that's not going to happen."

So engrossed was he in Mac's story that he didn't realize he had opened his mouth to speak.

She held up her hand again and shook her head. "I'm not done. I moved out here and got on my feet and made a life. And here we are," Mac said with a meaningful look and a flashing smile, indicating she was finished.

He narrowed his eyes at her, fascinated how she'd quickly wrapped up twelve years, especially the period after her arrival in Colorado. "That's all of it?"

She contemplated him warily. "I told you what was off the table, so yes." Mac unfolded to stand bent over, her shoulders brushing the tent ceiling. "All this talking has drained me. I'm going to turn in. Thanks—you always were a great listener. I feel better getting all that off my chest. Night."

He didn't feel better at all. So many questions. Hunger to know more. But he acquiesced, remembering how she dug her heels in, praying she would, as she had in the past, come forward with the other details if he gave her the time and space. The problem was there was little of either. "Night, Mac. I'm here if you want to unload the rest."

"I'm good," she said, giving him a dismissive smile, then exiting.

He watched the light from her lantern travel, fading after she entered her tent and then to nothing as she extinguished it. Bullshit if she really believed he was going to leave the off-the-table stuff alone. Hardin hadn't come out to Colorado in search of evasion, half-truths, or more lies. He wanted the unvarnished facts no matter how uncomfortable or how painful. He'd seen her son—granted, from a distance. Mac was going to be pissed when she realized he knew more than she wanted him to and when it became clear just how determined he was to get her back.

HEARTS
don't lie

The third day of hiking ended too quickly for Hardin. Most of the day he and Mac talked and laughed like they had in high school. But occasionally, during the breaks in conversation and more and more toward the end of the trip, he felt her erecting her guard again or disappearing deep within herself. They'd made some great headway, but he wasn't anywhere close to being satisfied. Hardin had no intention of giving up.

These three days gave him hope. There was more than a spark between them. There had been moments that reinforced his belief. When Mac forgot to keep her emotional distance and beamed a smile at him before shuttering it. When her fingers brushed his as they passed his binoculars back and forth. When they had kissed.

Hardin had to be back for mandatory training in a few days. However, he had no desire to leave and planned on calling Arlo as soon as he got back to the inn. He'd direct his bulldog of an agent to negotiate more time with the team's owners. He was staying longer in Piñon Ridge, and if he had to pay fines, so be it.

Hardin got some great photos of the shaggy white mountain goats, the pearl necklace of snow circling the majestic Wolves Peak, and of Mac when she wasn't looking—refilling water and smiling beatifically while she explored the vibrant wildflowers, inhaled the fresh scent of pine, or absorbed the unsurpassed beauty around them. It was obvious she was in her element in the mountains. A few times they asked passing hikers to take photos of them in front of breathtaking backdrops, and he had relished the feel of her leaning against him, wholly relaxed, thankful no one had recognized him.

Chase was waiting for them at the Flag Creek trailhead—an area where a number of trails began—wearing a ball cap, his sunglasses hanging from a strap. He was with his SUV, its rear cargo door open, waiting on them to show.

Mac greeted him with a shoulder bump and a kiss on his cheek, placing her backpack in his outstretched hand. "Hey there," she said, smiling, opening the passenger door and using the running board to get into the front seat.

"Welcome back. So, what'd you think?" he asked, directing the question to Hardin while taking his pack and putting it in the cargo area with Mac's. "Back seat's open."

"Beautiful. Invigorating. I might have to make hiking a regular thing."

Chase closed the cargo door and got into his seat, appearing to consider before asking, "They allow professional soccer players of your caliber to do stuff like the kind of hiking Kenna took you on?" He put the SUV in drive and entered a narrow road.

"Well, hiking isn't specifically banned in my contract," Hardin said, buckling his seat belt.

Mac pivoted in her seat and scowled at him. "Goddammit, Hardin. What if you'd torn something or suffered a career-ending accident?"

"Knock it off, Mac," he said hotly. "I didn't. My risk, not yours. I filled out all the forms and signed your waiver. You were protected."

Her heated response matched his. "Was I? Chase brought up a good point. It makes me feel exposed. What about Intrepid? Shit. Your owners have more money and power than I can even comprehend."

Discreetly, Chase shot Mac a sideways glance before returning his eyes to the road.

Hardin lowered his voice, hoping to deescalate Mac's anger even though he was enjoying her eyes shooting daggers at him. "Nothing happened, and if it had, I would have taken responsibility. My decision. Leave it."

"It could have," she said before whipping back around in her seat.

"I signed the waiver. You did have an attorney draw it up for Intrepid Adventures, right?"

"Do you mistake me for being stupid?"

Hardin couldn't help himself and snickered. "Stupid? Never. Stubborn? Yes. As hell. I've missed your fire."

"Goddammit—"

"You two fight like an old married couple," Chase interjected, sounding like he was stifling laughter. He signaled and turned onto the highway in the direction toward Piñon Ridge.

Mac gave Chase a scorching look.

"Ouch. That burned, boss." He chuckled, shaking his head.

Hardin decided it was best to not say anything else and watched the scenery through his window, thinking about how he was going to move things forward with Mac.

⌒∼

Chase pulled up to the entry of the Urban and pulled Hardin's gear from the cargo hold while he climbed out of the SUV. Mac's farewell was a perfunctory "thank you for your business" and a handshake. Hardin fought to keep his expression neutral while his stomach churned with acid at being so dismissed. No. That wasn't how they were going to part.

"Mac." He lowered his sunglasses, smiled, and winked at her.

Her mouth dropped open and her brows rose in surprise, giving him the hope he needed, the confirmation that there was a chance. All he had to do was find a way in, a way to anchor himself in her life again before he left.

Hardin walked into the inn with a big grin, a plan beginning to take shape.

14 Chapter Fourteen

MAC SHOOK HER head and smiled in wonderment as she inspected Stowe's room. It was down the hall from hers, separated by their bathrooms and a linen closet, giving each of them a modicum of privacy despite being a small house. The room was as neat as a pin, unusual for his age but typical of him. He liked his space organized and tidy. She let Homer out of his pen to roam the house, noting her son had given his rabbit fresh bedding, hay, and water, and the litter change was recent as well.

"Hey, buddy. How about some exercise?"

True to form, Cori had stripped all the beds and remade Mac's bed after sleeping in it. She had also hung fresh towels in the hall bathroom—which doubled as Stowe's—and hers, then started the laundry with the linens from his twin beds and run the dishwasher.

Homer followed her around as she unpacked and tidied up. She did a quick clean of the bathrooms, emptied the dishwasher, and then pulled a carrot from the fridge.

Even though her son hadn't seen his mom for a few days, he would not appreciate an unexpected appearance from her at camp. The plan was that he and Beck would ride home. Sometimes they rode their own bikes. Other times they shared a bike with one pedaling while the other sat on the seat. She couldn't wait to see him, to ruffle his silky dark hair that was weeks overdue for a cut—something he was fighting her on—and inhale his gamey boy smell he'd have after running drills all day.

No one had been able to convey how a person could love so hard, so completely. Eleven years after his birth, it still amazed her. She blinked her moist eyes, grateful she savored all time with him, even the tough times, which had been infrequent so far. Mac knocked on the lower wood cabinet as she folded to the floor. Some superstitions had a way of sticking around. Knocking on wood for luck, she did that one a lot.

Mac had been so fortunate to have Stowe with her, homeschooling giving her more time with him than if he'd attended their public school. But a big change was on the horizon. A small-town boy, he knew most of the kids. He had begged and then set out to convince her to send him to traditional school. Sixth grade seemed like a reasonable insertion time, and he was registered to begin next month.

Stowe was asserting his independence, exploring how he fit into the bigger picture of the preteens and teens in Piñon Ridge. He now shied away from hugs and any other public displays of affection, and although she understood it was a normal stage of his development, sometimes it stung. When home though, he still snuggled with her, often climbing into her bed during her late mornings, sipping hot chocolate or juice while she drank her coffee. Their conversations were lively, jumping from topic to topic. Her son's mind was sharp, curious, and compassionate. Like her, he loved to read and ask questions and turn everything on its head.

"Homer, look what I have." She waved the carrot. The Holland Lop ran over and licked her hand before nibbling on the carrot. "You sweet boy." Mac patted her thigh. "Come up?"

The affectionate rabbit hopped into her lap. She kissed Homer and then stroked his soft, mottled gray and white fur while reflecting on the only topic Stowe steered clear of—his father.

He didn't want to know.

Mac had tried since he was old enough to understand, but the minute she raised the topic, his face visibly shuttered and he tuned out. With each year that passed, Stowe grew more adamant, especially after one of his friends became a pawn in an ugly custody battle. He had been visibly shaken and then cried, admitting his biggest fear was losing her. She hadn't tried to revisit the topic since then, nor did she dare share that her biggest fear was the same—losing him—and that it would destroy her.

Stowe's paternity was the secret they mutually protected. Their answer to anyone who asked was an evasive "father is out of the picture," and that included their closest, most-trusted friends. While it was factual and worked, it hid the truth—Stowe had no desire to know the identity of his father and had no idea that the man who'd helped create him was clueless that he existed.

She wanted Stowe to have the truth, to know his full story of who he was. His parentage was part of his identity, and she'd read enough parenting books and been a mother long enough to know that the psychosocial stages of development were very real. Her son needed the information about his father so that he'd be able to make his own decision when he was ready, and of course Mac would support it. She feared the freedom of time was running out, and it scared the living shit out of her. How would he take the news? And how would he feel toward her? Regardless, she was going to have to push the topic, and soon.

Mac shook her head and exhaled forcibly to clear the barrage of thoughts and feelings assailing her. She gently lifted the Lop and kissed him on his cute little nose, then set him down on the old hardwoods next to her before rising to her feet. "I've gotta clean up, mister. I'm a little ripe. No way for me to greet the love of our lives, right?"

Satisfied that everything was done, including some peaceful time with Homer, and that her son would slide into clean, crisp-smelling sheets tonight after he showered, Mac entered the laundry and put the washed load in the dryer. She undressed and dropped her clothes into the washer with the towels, then padded into her bedroom at the front of the house, enjoying the freedom of moving naked though their cozy home, unseen by neighbors or her son, and stepped into her shower.

Mac was dousing her head under the spray and reaching for the shampoo when the thought that the small space would be a tight squeeze for Hardin and her came out of nowhere. *What the hell?* She winced from scrubbing her scalp too hard.

Seeing Hardin, being with him for three days, had upended her world and the life she had built for herself and her son. Being told of the lengths to which his parents had gone to keep them apart had made knots form in her stomach. Their power frightened her, and the actions they had taken made her blood boil.

"How dare they," she spat out as the water flowed over her.

She swallowed convulsively to keep the nausea down when thinking about what else they might have done if Stowe's existence had been discovered, thankful that she'd left Illinois and taken the steps she had to protect the identity of herself and Stowe. Because of them, Mac had faced the hardest decisions and choices in her life. She had faced fear and moved through the stages of grieving Hardin.

But there had been unexpected gifts too. Overcoming emotional and financial obstacles had made her fastidious, purposeful, and determined, a planner who liked to oversee her life and that of her son and prepare for things far in advance. What Mac hadn't planned on was Hardin's unrelenting search to find her and his showing up out of the blue. Neither had she planned on her love for him to burst forth again—she'd believed it was dead and buried. What she still felt was all the more stunning because he said he felt the same. What was between them as teens still existed.

How could that be? She had grieved him and was able to watch him play with an emotional distance, although she still resorted to loud armchair coaching from the privacy of her bedroom long after Stowe had fallen asleep.

All those emotions. All that desire. It came racing back at breakneck speed, practically suffocating her with its power. If he had pushed just a little bit more, she would have had sex with him, and she suspected that as incredible as it was in high school, being with him again would take her to new heights, possibly break her forever.

Stop it. Just stop it, she chided herself as she toweled off. *It's done. You got through it. Intrepid has a cushion to expand thanks to Hardin's insistent generosity. Breathe.*

She slid into a clean sleeveless tank and cutoffs and went into the kitchen to prep Stowe's favorite dinner. Homemade mac and cheese with broccoli and red pepper, and a fresh fruit salad. Nowadays her son was ravenous, one of the first indications that hormones were firing. It was likely the boys would graze when they showed up, so Mac preheated the oven and pulled out the ingredients for chocolate chip cookies as well as a can of concentrated lemonade from the freezer while she mixed a batch of Stowe's favorite treat. The cookies would be warm, just out of the oven, when the boys arrived.

The front door banged open. "Mom! Hey, Homer. Come here, dude. Shut the door, Beck."

Mac spun around, her smile huge, trying to figure out how to squeeze her son to pieces while he held his rabbit. She cleared her throat, raised her eyebrows, and opened her arms wide. Wisely, Stowe handed his rabbit to Beckett, his best friend and Cori's oldest, who stood next to him, his blond head even with her son's equally dark one.

He smiled lovingly at his mom while he moved into the circle of her arms, relaxing into her bear hug. His head rested over her shoulder. "I missed you," he said softly. "You smell good, Mom." He lifted his head and winked at her. "Almost as good as those cookies."

Mac pushed him back. Her smile and joy radiated from her heart. "Oh nice. I missed you too, honey." She wrinkled her nose. "You two stink. Here's my offer. You can shower and have some cookies inside, or you can have a plate outside with some iced lemonade."

"Uh, Aunt Kenna. That's a no-brainer. Outside." Beck reached for a warm cookie on the cooling rack. "I'm starving."

She playfully swatted his hand. "Wash your hands, both of you. I'll get everything ready." Mac pulled a plastic plate and glasses from the cabinet.

She opened the door with her hip and stepped onto the back patio, placing a tray laden with a large plate of cookies, three glasses of ice, and a pitcher of lemonade on the table. The boys tumbled out and joined her. While they stuffed their faces, she shared stories about her trip, sans her client's identity. Mouths full, they listened politely but grew more animated after their hunger was appeased, filling her in about camp and their plans for the evening—a tent sleepover at another friend's house.

"Can I, Mom? I know I haven't seen you for a few days, but—"

"It's okay. Summer is almost over." Mac smiled, connecting with her son's bright eyes, masking her disappointment. "Shower first though."

"You got it."

Beck rose with his glass, taking it to the kitchen, the door halfway open. "That was great! Thanks, Aunt Kenna. I'd better shower too. Meet you in thirty, Bro," he said before the door closed behind him.

"Thirty?"

"Um. They're having a cookout too." Seeing her reaction, he followed up with, "Uh, I can go after we have dinner."

"Nope. It's fine. You go have fun with your friends." She stood and ruffled his hair. "We'll do dinner tomorrow night."

"Sure?"

"Yes."

"It's a date." He grabbed the plate, his glass, and the used napkins. His eyes flashed up to hers, gratefulness evident. "I love you, Mom."

Mac searched her son's eyes, so much like his father's.

125

Tears tickled her lashes and her voice cracked as she whispered, "I love you more."

Deciding to make Stowe's favorite dinner anyway, she opened a chilled bottle of red zinfandel and selected a country playlist to listen to while beginning preparations, occasionally singing along. She took a long sip and let the wine mingle on her tongue, thinking back.

Mac and cheese, renamed by her son as cheese pasta pie, had been a staple for as long as she could remember. It had been an inexpensive, one-pot, easy-to-manage meal that filled her up. After having Stowe, she had elevated it, making a healthier version from scratch.

Alicia never cooked, so Mac's meals had consisted of PB&J, cans of concentrated soup, macaroni and cheese, or a grilled cheese sandwich. Fruit and vegetables rounded out her diet, courtesy of the school lunch program. On rare occasions, she'd treated herself to a burger with money squirreled away from working odd jobs.

Gnawing hunger had been part of her youth. Until Hardin. She sipped again from her glass. Hardin took her out to eat whenever their dates occurred over mealtimes, which was more often than not. He also surprised her with incredible picnics. Her world and palate expanded, and the hunger pangs had vanished.

After being abandoned by Alicia and moving to Colorado, money was tight. Mac had intended on returning to the meager diet she had known, determined to support herself and the life growing inside her. But what happened was Issa Fleming. A true force of nature.

Tall and rawboned with beautiful, long dove-gray hair, Issa was Carol's best friend, part of the national network that quietly supported girls and women who found themselves in difficult situations. Issa took her in and oversaw her diet and showered Mac with motherly love and pragmatism. She also helped Mac find work where she could earn enough money to increase her nest egg, some of which was used to legally change her name ahead of the baby's birth. Issa also nurtured her emotionally and spiritually and introduced Mac to her daughter Cori. The young women became fast friends, and their friendship had only deepened over the years, with Cori embracing Mac and Stowe as family.

Mac asked Issa to be in the delivery room and, when she gave the final push on that beautiful May morning—straining, shaking, and yelping from the pain as Stowe slipped from the warm recesses of her body, it was Issa who placed the swaddled infant into her waiting arms.

"You have a beautiful healthy son," she said quietly, her hazel eyes shining with unshed tears and love.

Mac beheld the face of her son. All emotional and physical pain evaporated. In that moment she forgave Alicia and welcomed and wholly embraced her fierce love for Stowe.

The timer went off and Mac blinked her damp eyes. *I could cry over him anytime.* She shook her head and smiled to herself as she lifted the slightly undercooked pasta from the cooktop and emptied it into the colander in the sink to drain. Next, she pulled a bowl of crumbled bacon from the fridge, something she kept on hand because she and Stowe added it to all sorts of dishes. Her eyes roved over the vegetables and other ingredients on the counter. The cheese pasta pie was almost ready to be assembled.

Mac placed a large cast-iron skillet on the counter and added butter to the saucepan on one of the front burners, deciding to start the roux after she finished her glass of wine. She was relishing the delicious jammy blueberry and peppery notes when there was loud knocking.

She had locked up after Stowe left for Clint's house. What a fun night for her son, she thought as she made her way toward the front of the house. A cookout and scavenger hunt in addition to the tent sleepover. He was expanding his circle of friends before starting school next month. God, she was going to miss homeschooling him.

As she drew closer, all Mac could see through the small pane of textured glass at the top of the solid oak door was a dark head. A man. Hm.

"Yes?" she called.

"Mac?"

What the hell?

Chapter Fifteen

MAC FLUNG THE door open, the glass of wine in her hand, her brow furrowed. "Hardin." She took a sip and cast a cool look in his direction, blocking his entry.

"Hey," he said, feeling tongue-tied as his eyes traveled her body. She was barefoot with navy-blue toenails, wearing short cutoffs showcasing shapely lean legs and a red-and-blue-striped sleeveless tank that skimmed her flat stomach and perky, full breasts. There wasn't a woman alive who had anything on the beautiful McKenna Rose Vesley Eliot. His gaze lingered on those chestnut-brown eyes. He blinked in response to her hard stare and the thickness pressing against his fly. "Yes."

"What're you doing here? And how do you know where I live?"

"Um…" His eyes watched the movement of her lips as they covered the glass and sipped, then traveled the delicate column of her neck as she swallowed.

She shook her long wavy ponytail, then cocked her head. "Oh, never mind. I forgot you hired a PI." Mac took another sip and pivoted, saying over her shoulder, "Come in, I guess. Shut the door behind you. Homer's about."

Her kid is named Homer? He shut the door and locked it and slipped off his sandals. Movement in the hall caught his attention. A small gray-and-white bunny with long floppy ears hopped slowly in front of them. "I see a rabbit."

She continued walking. "Well, aren't you astute? Homer has run of the house when we're here. He doesn't bite and, before you ask, he's litter trained."

"Hm. Okay." His brain cells seemed to have short-circuited. Mac had worn more clothes during their trip, and far looser. What she wore now left little to the imagination. He focused on the space around him. She had made the old house a home. Small, the bungalow was a mishmash of color and texture, bohemian style. It felt cozy, warm, and very much like her—well, the Mac he knew when her guard wasn't up like it was now. "I like your home."

"Thank you. It works for us. I was just making dinner. Hungry?"

He was ravenous. For her. "Yes, that'd be great." He winced, hearing himself. Too enthusiastic.

"It's just a simple dinner, Hardin. So if you'd prefer something fancy, you might mosey back into town."

She was as edgy as hell, but he was going to try to win her over. He'd made inroads during their trip between her bouts of closing herself off and reerecting emotional walls. "I'd like to have dinner with you."

Cooked pasta sat in a colander in the sink. Red bell pepper and broccoli lay on the counter along with a large bowl filled with different colors of freshly shredded cheese and two smaller bowls—one with crushed crackers and the other with bacon pieces. Mac pulled milk from the fridge and a large cutting board from a shelf beneath the small center island, then turned on the oven.

"You want a glass of wine?"

"Sure, but I can get it." He began to move around the kitchen and opened an upper cabinet.

"I'll get it." She pulled a glass from the cabinet near the hall, filled it a third full, and handed it to him.

Their fingers touched and an electrical current raced through his body. He was positive Mac had felt it too because she pulled her hand back as if she'd been burned. The air in the kitchen sparked with sexual tension.

"Sit yourself down." She pointed to the other side of the island with a large knife. "I was just getting ready to chop the veggies up when you knocked."

The big knife cooled him right back down. Hardin made himself comfortable on a stool, propping his elbows on the stone surface, observing how relaxed Mac became as she concentrated on her task. When she was finished chopping, Mac filled a measuring cup with milk and turned the gas on under the saucepan.

"What're we having?"

"Cheese pasta pie."

"Never heard of it."

She turned away and focused on making the roux. "It's an Eliot family favorite. My version of mac and cheese."

"Geez. I love mac and cheese. The only time I got it was when I spent the night at friends' houses or after I went to college. My mom refused to make it. Said it held no nutritional value. Had a bunch of crap in it. Drove me crazy. It was so damned good."

"You remember that crap was a staple in my life? It

was the first thing I learned to make because I had to eat something. I think I was five or six," she said softly, adding flour, salt, and pepper to the melted butter.

"I'm sorry. I forgot. I didn't mean to bring up an unpleasant memory."

"Don't worry about it." She looked over her shoulder and flashed him a genuine smile, continuing to stir, then whisked in the milk. "If it was unpleasant, I wouldn't be making this version."

Out of habit, he tilted his glass and viewed the wine. It looked clear, yet was dense near its edges. Swirling to coat the glass, he noted that the deeply saturated liquid clung to the inside of the glass and how the legs ran, promising a robust flavor. Hardin took a sip and was not disappointed. The flavor was ripe and mouth-filling. "This is really good. What is it?" he asked, looking up right into the amused eyes of Mac, who had turned to watch his tasting ritual.

"A red zin. My favorite summer wine. I buy it by the case. Think I wouldn't know anything about wine?"

"Not exactly, but a lot of people don't know much about wine."

"I don't know much either, other than what I like. We have a great wine store in town. The owner, a friend of mine, turned me on to this. And a few others." She continued stirring.

"I see," he said, immediately regretting his words and accusatory tone.

She fidgeted, then whipped around. "No, you don't." Mac pointed at him with the large nonstick spoon she was using. "And our friendship is none of your business." She faced the stove again, shoulders rising with a deep inhale. "You can help me."

"What can I do?" he asked warily.

"Bring me the cheese."

Hardin sidled next to her, delighted to help.

"Add it in slowly. I don't want the roux to burn. It's a perfect brown color now."

He watched the cheese melt in the hot roux.

"Okay, that's enough cheese. We want to save some for the top. Well done." She handed him the spoon without glancing at him. "Keep stirring while I mix the vegetables in with the pasta," she said, placing the large cast-iron skillet on the other front burner and depositing the mixture into it. "Okay, pour the cheese sauce over."

Mac lowered the flame and stirred to combine everything.

"It smells incredible."

"Wait until it comes out of the oven." She turned off the flame and topped the pie with more shredded cheese and crushed crackers and bacon. "Okay, this is ready. Can you open the oven?"

After the oven door was closed, he asked, "What now?"

"We wait." She set the timer on her smart watch, refilled her wine and added to his, lifting her glass in salute, her genuine smile reaching her eyes. "And drink more wine. Cheers."

They ate at the round teak table on the patio, which glowed under the soft party lights and glimmering candles she had lit. The meal was one of the best he'd had in years.

Mac's guard had lowered with each sip of wine, and she now lounged back in her chair, her glass empty. "We can open another bottle if you want."

His posture mirrored hers. "I want." He definitely wanted.

"I thought our trip was closure."

He shook his head and chuckled, staring deeply into those brown eyes of hers. "Not even close, Mac." He watched her swallow, pleased his comment hit its mark. "I'll get the wine."

"No, you won't." She rose and gathered the dishes and utensils. "You're my guest."

He didn't respond but watched Mac disappear into the house, once again admiring her beautiful shape. She appeared steady on her feet. Good. He hoped her head was just as steady. Hardin didn't want to be her *guest*. He wanted more. Much, much more—to reclaim what they once had and build on it. His gut told him their foundation of friendship, trust, and love was still there. Solid beneath all the lies and deceit. The wine and his patience were slowly but surely cracking her open.

Mac came back out with an opened second bottle.

Hardin took it from her and poured the wine and held up his glass, saluting Mac. "To more of this wonderful evening and getting further reacquainted."

"To a nice evening. Thank you. It's been pleasant." She raised her glass and drank, then walked over to the patio seating and sat on the all-weather wicker sofa, drawing her legs up sideways.

He settled into a large Adirondack facing her, stretching his long legs out in front of him, thoroughly enjoying the fact that her shorts had inched higher. "I'm always pleasant."

"When you aren't being a cocky ass."

"You helped me tone that down long ago."

"It seems your cockiness has made a resurgence, Hardin. Not pretty." She motioned her glass at him. "Yellow cards. Red cards. Parties. Women."

He set his glass down on the side table next to him and leaned forward. "Interesting. You said that during our hiking adventure."

"So what?"

"The *so what* is that you mentioned only the women. Said I was a player. Now you're adding parties and the price I pay for"—he looked up at the starlit sky, then back at her and gave her a sexy grin—"playing soccer passionately. Strikers and effective mids draw cards." He pushed off his chair and squatted in front of her. "Do you miss me? You keep tabs on me."

"I don't."

"Liar. You do." His fingers brushed over her calf and he watched the reaction—the trail of goose bumps. "The honest truth?"

She nodded, her eyes big.

"My partying is behind me. The women? The vast majority of them have been window dressing. Vacant heads on nipped-and-tucked bodies or agenda-driven females hell-bent on bagging some fucking famous, rich, professional athlete. None of them were interested in me, the real Hardin Ambrose," he said bitterly. "It's lonely at the top, honey. I'm so fucking tired of it." Hardin closed his eyes. "I want out," he whispered.

Mac's glass clinked as she set it down. He sensed her kneeling in front of him and then was sure of it when her scent wafted over him and delicate, strong fingers moved over his head and into his hair, massaging his scalp like she used to do in high school. "No one serious?"

"No." *Not like you. Like us.* Her touch was soothing,

taking away his stress. Intimate. He bowed his head, leaning into her touch, his body igniting, feeling her everywhere. After a few minutes, her fingers left his head and skimmed over his face to gently bracket his scruffy jaw.

He lifted his chin and opened his eyes when her sweet breath caressed his face. *Can she feel me trembling?*

She was on her knees between his splayed legs. Her eyes had turned dark, their pupils dilated, and were unflinching as she seemed to consider what he had shared.

Hardin recognized that look and his heart galloped in response, feeling as though it would burst from his chest. His hand covered one of hers and lifted it to his lips, leisurely kissing each finger. "I miss you so much it burns a hole in my gut," he said, his voice cracking, eyes searching hers.

Mac blinked and her hand moved to her heart. "I've missed you too," she said, her voice quivering. She stood. "I need to blow the candles out."

"Uh, okay," he said, watching her extinguish the candles, knowing he sounded deeply disappointed that she was calling an end to the night. He could spend forever with her.

A mischievous grin lit her eyes, then she giggled. "Wow, the Hardin Ambrose I knew was never one to give in so easily." She grabbed the wine bottle by its neck. "Get the glasses. Let's get *further* reacquainted."

He passed by her on the way in, then waited while she flipped off the party lights and locked the back door, wholly committed to letting her lead, watching her lock the bunny in its cage and then following her to the front of the house and into her bedroom. It wasn't the largest master by a long shot, but it was cozy, and Mac had stamped it with her artistic flair. Nothing matched and yet it totally worked.

Hardin enjoyed the feeling of his bare feet sinking into the thick shag rug while he admired the large colorful painting of sunflowers—her favorite flower—done with a palette knife. "Yours?"

"Yes," she said, smiling, lighting the candles on her dresser. "Sunflowers have always brought me joy."

"I remember. You gave me a smaller one, similar to this. It hangs in my villa. This is beautiful, Mac. Do you still paint?"

"When there's time. So rarely." She set down the bottle and glasses on her nightstand and faced him, her expression expectant and sure, seeming to pass the lead back to him.

The air crackled in the silence, and he found himself at a loss for words as they held each other's eyes, understanding she had opened herself up to him. All he had to do was accept her offer. He realized he was scared shitless.

Of being turned down.

Of disappointing her.

Of finding out what they had in the past was a dream.

His swallow and shaky breath were audible. *Dammit.*

"Are you scared?" She spoke barely above a whisper, but he heard her clearly.

"Yes." His exhale whooshed out of him. "I am. Christ, I feel like a damned virgin all over again."

"Both of us were virgins, Hardin."

True, and their coming together had been sweet and pure. He stepped closer, his heartbeat slamming in his chest. Energy crackled between them, so much so that he felt every fiber of his being strain toward her. Magnetized. Mesmerized.

Hardin caressed the soft underside of her jaw and throat with the pads of his thumbs and rested his forehead against hers, inhaling her scent, attempting to calm himself. Her pulse jumped crazily under his touch.

"Goddammit, Hardin," she whispered. "Just kiss me. Please."

16 Chapter Sixteen

MAC'S INSIDES SPUN. She looked up into his eyes, which had turned dark and hungry-looking. His mouth looked hungry too. Mac licked her bottom lip and rolled it between her teeth. The ember that had burned in her since opening the front door and seeing him standing there flamed into a raging fire of need.

His hands bracketed her waist and slid over her hips. Hardin pulled her close, sharply sucking in his breath when his hands moved over her ass, pressing her against his rigid length.

She came up on her tiptoes and shamelessly ground against him in an attempt to soothe the sweet ache that was growing more insistent.

He captured her bottom lip and sucked, groaning as she rubbed against him and again when her tongue licked him in return. He broke from her, practically panting. "You're going to make me bust, honey. Is that your intention?"

"I'm there too. Please don't stop," she said, sounding

as breathless as him, falling back onto her bed and bringing him with her. She loved the feel of his size and weight covering her.

It was so good.

So right.

Mac grabbed his ass and encouraged him to ride her roughly through their clothes. There was no time to strip. She was so close. On the edge.

She threw a leg over his hip and yanked him against her more tightly, unleashing more heat and moisture between her legs, needing to relieve the ache. The pace picked up and their mouths slanted over each other's, lips fused, tongues sweeping and tangling while they cradled each other's heads and gazed deeply into each other's eyes, intensifying the connection as they crested together.

He stroked her temples and kissed the tip of her nose before chuckling softly. "Hm. That reminded me of high school," he said quietly, his grin carrying into his remarkable eyes. "You okay?"

She smiled back at him and said, her voice breathy, "Yes." Truth be told, she felt great. But how quickly she had succumbed to her desire for him had her all out of sorts. *It's the wine,* she lied to herself. *And it did feel like high school. A good place to pick up from?*

"Can I stay tonight?"

His question caught her unaware, sharply reminding her that the boundary with him was no more. "Here?" *How about no?* She couldn't manage to say that word. *What the hell?*

"Uh yeah, unless you want to sleep at the Urban with me. I like it much better here. It's private and cozy." He watched her as he pulled gently at a tendril of her hair. A corresponding ache tugged at her sex, and it was obvious from the smug smile Hardin wore that her subtle response registered. "We're not done tonight, honey. Not by a long shot. I need you and you need me."

Mac opened her mouth to speak, but Hardin leaned closer, brushing her lips with his before kissing her slowly and with so much heat it rendered her mute.

"I'm gonna clean up."

All she could do was nod, then ruminate over what she wanted while he was in her bathroom. Thank God it was clean. Thank God she had fresh sheets on her bed. Mac shook her head and snickered, amused by her thoughts. *Well, I guess I've made my decision. Hardin in my bed.* Her heart banged around in her rib cage as she rose to her knees and reached for her wine, not feeling the least bit tipsy. The desire coursing through her had to be working like adrenaline, breaking down the effects of alcohol.

Sipping the claret-colored wine, she considered what it was going to be like to have sex with him after all this time. If his kisses and the dry humping were any indication, epic. Her heart revved even more in anticipation, making her breath short. *Calm down, woman.*

Mac had been intimate with a few of the men she'd dated. The experiences had fallen short, leaving her wanting. Maybe because she'd unknowingly selected men she wasn't compatible with. She hadn't been invested, but then neither had they. The question tonight was, of course, was she invested after twelve years apart? Her racing heart, quivering body, and wet panties were screaming yes. Wisdom said yes too. Of course, she was better prepared now. She knew her body. She knew her mind. She was using birth control. The bathroom door opened. *Oh shit.*

Hardin reappeared just as she was wondering whether he had anything he could pass on to her besides sperm. He was dressed as before—a vintage-inspired short-sleeved button-down and jeans. His belt was unbuckled and the fly was unzipped, and he stood in the doorway of the bathroom, waiting.

Smart on his part, still wanting her to lead their dance.

He seemed to look right into her, missing nothing. "Mac? What's going on? You look like you're thinking things over."

God, he could still read her. No point in being less than candid, especially since they had just gone gangbusters on each other fully clothed. "Do you have a, um… Do you—"

He laughed so hard that it surprised her. "Mac, the first thing I'd let you know would be if I had an STD. Sorry, it struck me as funny. I've always gloved up."

Maybe he did, but she knew for a fact that gloving up wasn't always a sure thing. Feeling brave, she asked, "No little Hardins running around out there?"

His expression turned serious. "No."

"I needed to ask."

"Absolutely. How about you?"

"All good and I'm on the pill."

Hardin studied her thoughtfully. "We can go commando then?"

Her heart kicked up another notch. "Yes."

A shit-eating grin broke out over his face. He stepped forward and his hand engulfed hers. A jolt of electricity shot through her system when he pulled her against him.

His eyes blazed with heat as his fingers stroked her jaw, encouraging her to look at him. "This time I'm going to

142

take you naked." He nibbled the shell of her ear. "Slow and deep. You're going to shatter for me, Mac," he murmured in a husky voice that melted over her like warm honey.

Need unfurled in Mac's core. Her brain short-circuited, jumbling her thoughts. Her body responded to his voice and touch, thrumming and tingling. Her skin was hot. On fire. Unable to speak, she nodded.

"Are you sure? Because I don't think I can stop once I start."

"Yes," she said, sounding as breathless as him.

She didn't want him to stop. She wanted him to hurry.

To take it slow. Make it last.

"Mac… Baby…"

Mac slid her arms around his shoulders and laid her head on his chest, over his pounding heart. "Quit talking."

While Mac's response was what Hardin had hoped for, it was also sobering. He searched her eyes. Her pupils were huge. She spoke the truth—her need rivaled his for her. Mac's gaze never wavered as he gently raked his fingers through her hair and dragged the band from her thick ponytail, gathering some of the silky strands and rubbing them between his fingers, his blood igniting.

He had dreamed of seeing her again. Talking with her. Holding her. Loving her. Recovering what they had. Was it possible? Minutes ago, their coupling had been so frantic that they came together fully clothed. Literally. But now…

Hardin kissed her again. Reverently. Drawing it out, savoring her taste under the layer of wine, like the sweetest nectar. She shivered as his fingers slipped under her top and trailed over her stomach and cupped her breasts, teasing her tight nipples through the lacy bra with a feathery touch.

"You're so beautiful," he whispered. "I want to see you."

She pulled the top over her head and tossed it onto the chair in the corner of her room.

Hardin impatiently unbuttoned his camp shirt, which she helped him out of. It joined her shirt on the chair.

Mac's fingers traced the array of tats covering his chest, abs, shoulders, and arms, honed to lean, ripped perfection from years of playing the most elite soccer in the world. "You have so many. What do they all mean?" She stopped on a small inked area over his left ribs. Her throat constricted with surprise. "Stowe?" she whispered, her voice thick with emotion.

"Yeah. Telling you I loved you, hearing you saying it back to me. It was incredible."

"It was." Her heart flew around in her chest like a caged bird. Mac inhaled deeply and asked teasingly as she touched another tattoo. "This one? What does it signify?"

He glanced down. "It's a rune. Uruz. It represents endurance. Determination and persistence."

Her finger dropped lower, and she gave him a questioning gaze. "This one? It's kind of squiggly."

"Later," he growled sexily and gave her his famous bad-boy smile. "I'm really not interested in discussing my tats right now." He shed his jeans, his want for her fully evident, straining against the material of his boxers. "I didn't think you would be either. Are you?"

She bit down on her bottom lip, seeming to concentrate as she stroked his thick length, then circled

144

him as much as the fabric would allow. Her eyes darted to his. "No."

He stilled her hand because he was too close.

"I'm being blocked here."

"It's temporary. Take off the rest," he murmured.

Mac slowly shimmied out of her cutoffs, bra, and panties and lay back, her auburn hair fanning over the pillow, smoldering eyes locking with his, breathing heavily. She glistened in the flickering candlelight.

Hardin's hand drifted to the space between the swell of her breasts, which were fuller than they'd been in high school. Mac's heart drummed against his palm. His pulse and breathing matched hers.

He licked and sucked, wishing he could drink her essence as she squirmed and moaned under him. He drew back and watched her undulate as he trailed his fingers tortuously down the midline of her body, between her breasts, over her ribs and abs, lingering at the apex between her thighs.

"Jesus, you're fucking beautiful." He was painfully erect and full and enjoying every heartbeat of the sensation. Her eyes were heavy with lust and her breath, like her heartbeat, was fast and shallow. Needy. For him.

"I want to taste every inch of your perfect skin, Mac."

She sighed, her hips arching for his fingers. "Yes. Please."

Hardin encouraged her thighs to open. "Give in to me, baby." His mouth descended, lips and tongue gliding leisurely along the inside of her legs from her knee to her core. Mac writhed and bucked as Hardin lapped at her and sucked, finally crying out before going over the edge.

Hardin could no longer wait and slid his boxers off.

He marveled at her as he sought entry, groaning as he thrust, bracketing her hips as he drove deep again and again.

She met him each time, whimpering and crying.

Mac. Home. Forever.

Chapter Seventeen

NO MATTER HOW tired he was, Hardin had no problem waking up. He was disciplined from years of training and playing. He would sleep later. No, that wasn't accurate. He would crash.

He and Mac had stayed up most of the night. When they weren't rediscovering one another or making love, they were talking. They had padded into her bathroom just as the sun broke the horizon, agreeing a shower was probably a good idea after hours of sex. Shimmying into her small shower was comical, but taking her once more, against the tight confines and slick walls with her legs wrapped around his hips, was a human engineering feat, one that had him straining and shaking as he emptied himself into her slick heat.

They had toweled off and literally fallen into bed. She snuggled next to him in the cooled room and began purring immediately. He pulled the sheet over them and closed his eyes, falling into a deep sleep until the need to fill his belly became unrelenting.

Hardin slipped from the bed, careful not to disturb her, watching Mac as he dressed. She lay on her belly, the lovely curves of her back and shoulders exposed, head turned toward him, a soft smile gracing her features. She looked so content. He hoped he was the reason for that expression. Thick lashes caressed her pink cheeks and those long locks of hers were all over the pillow—hair he had woven his hands into and played in while he moved in her. While they gazed into each other's eyes.

He surveyed her room, seeing it more clearly in the morning light. She kept it neat. The chair, bed frame, and dresser appeared old, possibly refurbished. Had she done that? Photos topped her dresser. Curious, he moved closer to inspect them. They were all candids—her son hiking, fly-fishing, snowboarding, and more. The kid was obviously active. It was hard to make out the finer details of his features in the dim light and also because he wore sunglasses and a ball cap in all the photos.

His eyes teared up when looking at Mac holding him as an infant, the largest photo. The pride and love shining in her face made him ache and swallow hard. It should have been their infant. That had been their plan—their own soccer team. Whoever captured the moment was someone with the best timing. God, she glowed.

Something hung from the side of the photo, draped over the corner of the handmade wrought iron frame. His pulse quickened as his fingers touched and then held the thistle—the sterling necklace he had given her their last night. Hardin's heart squeezed and thumped against his ribs; after all this time, Mac had kept it. He wondered if she ever wore it and glanced back at her. She'd noticed his Stowe tat, but not the thistles designed to appear as if they were woven throughout it.

Mac didn't appear as if she'd be getting up anytime

soon. Hardin smirked and nodded to himself. He'd worn her out good, and she had done the same to him in return.

Exploration of the kitchen turned up a coffee maker and filters, but so far, no coffee. *What the hell?* He went into another cabinet. Loose paperwork fell out and scattered over the counter and floor. *Dammit. Nothing like disturbing her stuff.*

Of their own accord, his eyes scanned the papers as he tried to organize them. Forms for enrollment. A medical form. Past education. She had homeschooled her son. Hardin's pride in Mac only magnified. He placed the next paper on top. A birth certificate.

Stowe Ambrose Eliot.

Ambrose.

Hardin looked at the date and dropped the birth certificate on the counter, bracing himself, sucking in air as if he'd sprinted for his life. He rapidly blinked his eyes, not believing what he was seeing. The line for the father's name was blank and the date of birth easily coincided with the timing of the failed condom the night before he left for college. He was dizzy from the shock, fear, anger, and elation assaulting his senses. He felt like he was going to fucking pass out.

"Hardin?"

His eyes met hers, not sure how he appeared. Distraught? Pissed off? Confused? She was beautiful and wild in her half-awake state, wearing an oversized shirt that barely covered her ass. The thought that she was probably naked underneath stirred him to attention despite what he was feeling.

Mac's eyes flitted from him to the open cabinet, then to the papers under his hand. She sounded unsure when she spoke. "Hardin?"

He took a deep breath to fortify himself, to find his voice. "I was looking for coffee. Paperwork fell out." He motioned to the open cabinet, then walked over to Mac, taking her hand and rotating it palm up and open, placing Stowe's birth certificate in it.

He struggled to keep his voice even. "Is he ours?"

She looked at him, wide-eyed, appearing so frightened his heart ached for her. Mac's voice trembled. "Yes."

"Why, Mac?" He scrubbed at his face, then pushed the heels of his hands into his eye sockets to stanch the flow of tears, trying to absorb the news.

"You know why," she said quietly. "We talked about all the whys when we were on our trip. Your parents. Their actions. Alicia." She inhaled and exhaled loudly. "I was s-so… af-afraid," she stuttered through her tears. "They might… they might have… taken him." If anything, she cried harder. "He's all I have," she whispered, the tears running off her chin and splashing onto her feet and the hardwoods. She placed Stowe's birth certificate on the counter, then wrapped her arms around herself and rocked. "He's everything."

"Come here, baby." He gathered her into his arms. "No one is taking him from you."

She began shaking so hard he thought she was going to come apart.

"Mac. Hey. Are you listening?"

"Y-yes."

Christ, her teeth were chattering. "Babe, I'm not going to take him from you. Is that what has you scared out of your mind? Why you've been so secretive?"

She nodded and keened. His shirt was soaked. It was if a dam had busted loose.

Hardin kissed the top of Mac's head and rubbed her back, trying to soothe her. As much as he was struggling, he couldn't even imagine what it had taken to keep their son's paternity a secret, to keep Stowe safe from his barracuda parents. After she quieted to sniffling, he said, "We've got to talk about him."

She stared back at him with eyes that reminded him of a frightened animal.

"Please, Mac."

She seemed to have herself under better control, but her eyes were red and her face was puffy from crying so hard. "Okay. I have to get dressed," she said in a monotone.

"You do that. I'll make coffee. Where do you keep it?"

"I'm out. I was going to grab some at the Grind before I went into work." She swallowed nervously. "That's my normal routine, plus I support my friend Kai. She owns the Grind." Her voice trailed off, and she inhaled a shaky breath. "Oh shit. Work. I'm a mess."

She was a gorgeous mess. "When do you need to be at work?"

"Before ten."

He noted the clock on the microwave. "You've a couple of hours."

"I'll call Issa."

"Issa?"

"Stowe's grandma, one of them. Um—" She corrected herself when noticing the confused expression on his face. "Fictive grandma."

"Fictive—she is like a grandmother to him? Accepted as his grandmother?"

"Yes."

"Part of Stowe's story?"

"Very much so," she said, smiling softly. "She's Cori's mom. A godsend to me."

"Your business partner?"

"Yes."

"Does she know about me?"

"Issa? No."

"Does Cori?"

"No one does. My phone's in my room. I'll be back." Before leaving the kitchen, she turned back. "I promise I'll tell you all of it."

He had no words and searched her eyes, then nodded and dropped onto a stool at the island, trying to absorb the fact that he was a father of an eleven-year-old. Hardin felt like he couldn't breathe. The tears continued to well up and leak out. He wiped at them, impatiently trying to think coherently. His life had just been turned upside down. And what now?

He didn't know the first thing about being a father. But what Hardin *was* sure of was that he wanted to know his son, be part of his life. The certainty hit him with a gale force.

He had been cheated. His initial instinct was to lash out at Mac, but he understood her too well to think she'd done what she had out of spite. He surmised her decisions had been made solely from the need to protect their son, herself, and even him. At this moment, he despised his parents and their lies, deceit, and power. They had done everything possible to keep him and Mac apart.

Mac's voice carried into the kitchen. "You're a lifesaver." There were a few beats of silence. "I love you too." She entered the kitchen, cell phone in hand, having slipped on jeans and a gray T-shirt with the Intrepid Adventures logo on it. Her hair was in ponytail. "Issa's dropping off coffee. She'll leave it on the porch in a few minutes since she's late for a meeting."

"That quick?"

"Uh-huh. She lives a few doors down. I—"

"We need to talk."

"I know. But not now. We're slammed. Cori texted me and asked me to come in early."

"Mac? This can't wait," he said, watching her squirm under his direct gaze. "The cat's out of the bag."

"I—"

"Look, I'm not doing anything. Why don't I come in and help? There's got to be something I can do."

She contemplated him, then exhaled loudly. "Okay. Thanks. You can probably help Chase. Can we keep this between us for now?"

"Sure. How are you going to explain me, my appearance and assistance?"

"I'll think up something plausible." She clasped and unclasped her hands and took a deep breath. "Something's been eating at me since I last saw you. I've never understood how... how... We were careful."

Hardin's eyes held hers. He nodded. "We were, but when those cops showed up, um... things didn't quite perform the way they were supposed to. When I was pulling out... Fuck... It crossed my mind, but I thought, *what are the chances?*" He rubbed his face and shook his head. "I never got to tell you. I was going to, but then everything just snowballed."

Her expression was difficult for him to read.

"I'm sorry. I was going to say something, but—"

153

"What were the chances that all this would unfold as it has?" She gave him a sad smile. "At least you've solved the mystery. I couldn't figure that out for the life of me."

"We have a lot to talk about."

"We do."

"When are we going to tell Stowe?"

"Tell me what?" Their son materialized with a confused expression, gripping a thermos of coffee, his eyes—the same shape and shade of aqua as Hardin's—moving between them. Surprise filled his face. "Wow! You look like Hardin Ambrose!"

How the hell to handle this? Stunned speechless by the appearance of his son, of seeing a younger version of himself, Hardin looked to Mac for guidance. How was he supposed to act? He didn't want his son to think he was some pussy.

Mac cleared her throat and encircled their son with her arm, squeezing him and giving him a peck on his cheek. The transformation from anguish to being present for her son was astounding. "Morning to you! Thought I'd see you later this morning, after breakfast."

"Didn't sleep so well. Grady farted all night—our tent smelled like dookie."

Hardin burst out laughing, and that went a long way to easing his tension. He looked up and caught his son's grin and proud expression. Was it because he'd made Hardin Ambrose, the international footballer, laugh?

"I see. And breakfast?" she asked, smirking.

"We kinda inhaled the food. I'm still hungry."

"How 'bout I make some bacon and eggs? You see to Homer. Are you hungry, Hardin?" she asked, looking past their son, whose eyes were as big as his open mouth, her brown eyes dancing with merriment.

"You are him?" Stowe asked, astonished, turning to his mom. "Is he?"

"I am," Hardin said, feeling gobsmacked and smiling warmly while reminding himself to be cautious. Take it slow. Put himself in his son's shoes. A stranger vying for his mom's attention. "I can always eat." He winked at Mac while Stowe was engaged in looking at her. *Two can play this game, babe.* She flushed a pretty shade of red.

"You never said you knew him!"

"'Him' is in the room," she admonished their son, nodding at Hardin. Then, more gently, she explained. "Hardin and I knew each other in high school."

"That is *so cool!* Why didn't you ever say anything?" Stowe's brow furrowed, and he studied Hardin intently. "How well did you know my mom?"

It was all Hardin could do to not squirm in his seat under his son's intense examination, so he stood instead. "Mac, why don't you take this?"

"Mac?"

She narrowed her eyes at Hardin, then answered her son. "Hardin used to call me Mac."

"Come on. I still do."

"Why?" Stowe asked.

"For McKenna. Mac was Hardin's nickname for me."

"McKenna? Aren't you Kenna?"

Hardin crossed his arms and leaned against the island, wanting to see how she handled the disclosure with Stowe. His crash course in parenting was now in session.

"I am. I was ready for a change when I moved to Colorado. Kenna felt fresh."

Hardin kept his face devoid of expression. It was an honest answer, a safe answer. For now.

18 Chapter Eighteen

A FTER BREAKFAST, MAC walked to work with Hardin on one side of her and Stowe on the other, all of them wearing ball caps and sunglasses. She felt as though she were in a surreal dream. During breakfast, they had both offered to help at Intrepid when they heard how slammed she and Cori were with excursions. They mostly walked in silence until Beckett approached on his bike.

"Hey, Bro. A bunch of us are going fishing. Wanna come?" Beckett's eyes strayed to Hardin as he straddled his bike, pushing along with both feet, keeping pace with them as they walked.

Stowe glanced at Mac in question.

Her eyebrows rose at her son, signaling him to make introductions, but he appeared to have either forgotten or didn't want to. "Beckett, this is Hardin," she said nonchalantly even though her heart was pounding.

"There's a soccer player with the same name. Hardin Ambrose. He's American but plays for Spain."

"You don't say," Hardin said wryly, his smile just this side of cocky.

Mac held her breath as Beckett kept talking.

"I told Bro a few times when we were watching Hardin Ambrose play that he kinda looked like him. Where're you going, Aunt Kenna?"

"Intrepid."

"Mom went in early."

"I know," Mac said.

Beckett's attention returned to Hardin. "You kinda look like Stowe too. Are you related?"

Mac noticed how Stowe became overly interested in the houses and trees on the other side of the street.

Beckett didn't seem to pick up his best friend's lack of engagement and eagerly launched back into his original topic. "Ambrose is like the best player ever! Our favorite! Right, Bro? Fast as lightning. Agile. Me and Stowe, we *never* miss his games. Do you watch soccer?"

The amusement in Hardin's voice was evident. "Sometimes."

Stowe looked uncomfortable and grimaced.

"Where at, Beck?" Mac asked.

He blinked at the abrupt change in the direction of conversation. "Huh?"

"Where are you planning on fishing?"

"Oh. The gulch."

She stopped walking and inclined her head at the towhead, a soft smile on her face. "I know that, you silly boy. Where along the gulch?"

"Sorry, Aunt Kenna," he said sheepishly. "Chalk

158

Creek. It's shallow but running good with all the rain we've had. Mom and Dad said it was okay."

"Of course you can go, honey." She squeezed Stowe's shoulder, which he shrugged off. He moved toward Beckett. "Just stay out of the water and be back by"—she glanced at her watch—"three o'clock. Do you have your key?"

He had turned sullen, not like him at all. "Yep."

"You need food and drinks. And sunscreen and bug spray. Figure it out between the two of you." She nodded at the boys. "Oh! I moved your tackle box to the shed since it was smelling up your closet. And take a SPOT."

"I have one packed already," Beckett said.

"Good. Have fun and be careful." She leaned over and kissed her son, whispering in his ear, "We'll talk later, okay?"

Stowe nodded curtly but didn't look at her.

"Stowe?"

His head rotated toward her, the pain on his face evident. "In the Box?"

"Yes." Her heart was heavy. It was their private code for serious things to examine and discuss, just between them.

He cracked a weak smile and then launched himself at her, hugging her tightly, an unusual display of public affection. "I love you, Mom."

"I love you more."

Lost in their own thoughts, Mac and Hardin walked companionably along Main Street, which was already bustling. The green space ahead of them was empty.

"I know you need to be at work, but can we take a few minutes? Discuss what happened back there? Please?" He indicated a bench in the dappled shade.

"I'd like some more coffee."

"We'll get it, even if I have to go for it after dropping you off."

She sighed deeply and removed her sunglasses, facing him. Hardin removed his too and smiled, remembering how Mac demanded he never "talk to her through his shades" during their first of countless discussions and some passionate arguments. It had become ingrained in him when he quickly realized that communication was more authentic when people were looking into each other's eyes unobstructed.

"You remembered," she said, smiling.

"I never forgot. Our son—"

"Stowe was miserable. He's not normally sullen. I think that when Beck said you look like Stowe, well, it got him thinking. He knows." Tears escaped from her shimmering eyes. "I wish… I wish I didn't have to work today. He needs me."

Hardin wiped at her tears gently with the pads of his thumbs. "Maybe it's good he's fishing with friends? As much as I'm stunned, I can't even imagine what he's feeling or thinking." He pulled her onto his lap and kissed her forehead. "I'm fucking reeling."

She relaxed against him and felt their combined tension ease. It felt so good. So right.

After a few minutes, Hardin sat up straighter and lifted her chin, pinning Mac with a deep look, his eyes full of unshed tears. His voice cracked. "This isn't even enough, but… thank you. He's beautiful," he whispered.

Mac's torrent of held-back emotion erupted. What she felt for her son overwhelmed her, as did finally sharing him with his father. All she could manage between crying and sniffling was an enormous smile and to bob her head.

Mac was thirty minutes late for work, puffy-faced and physically drained. What could no longer be contained had cleansed her. Euphoria and renewal filled her.

Hardin's hand was at the small of her back as he opened the door for her, and they entered Intrepid. "I'll be back with your coffee, honey, and to help." He kissed her soundly in front of the Intrepid staff in the front office.

She really could not have cared less. "I—"

He winked at her. "I know what you want." A confident smile covered his face as he left, leaving her head and body zinging like crazy.

"Sorry I'm late. Something came up." Mac glanced around, taking in the surprised expressions.

"I'll say." Cori chuckled from her seat at one of the two desks. "You *will* fill me in later."

She ignored her and addressed Chase, Van, Jess, and Emory, who watched wide-eyed. Mac cocked her head and regarded each of them in turn, then sat at her desk. "What? Let's get to work. Where are we with today's bookings?" she asked, opening her laptop.

"A heads-up, Kenna. Cori. I need to lead first. I'm on the late shift," said Emory, who worked in rescue and recovery with Mike, Cori's husband.

"Can do. Thanks for filling in again, Em," Cori said. "You've been a lifesaver."

Emory cracked a grin and rolled her eyes. "Weak one, Cori."

"You're packed and ready, Em. Your group should be arriving any minute," Chase said as the door opened again, on cue. "I'll drop your group off with Jess's."

"Where're Lee and Shep?"

"I took them out with a larger group earlier. Dropped them off at Salt Creek. They're doing an all-day with lunch and fishing."

Mac nodded. "Perfect."

"Hi, maybe you can help me. Do you by chance know Ma—Kenna Eliot?" Hardin asked the blonde manning the register.

"I most certainly do." She beamed a megawatt smile at him. "I'm Kai, a friend of Kenna's and the owner of the Piñon Grind. How can I help you?"

"Hardin. Nice to meet you." He perused the enormous blackboard behind her and pulled a twenty-dollar bill from his wallet. "She sent me in for her coffee. I'd typically just get her black, but you've got so much to choose from, or maybe she likes something special every once in a while?"

Kai nodded. "Every so often she has a Raspberry Mocha Latte with coconut milk."

"Hm. Hot or iced?"

"Hot."

"Is it supersweet?"

She laughed. "Surprisingly no. Just really good."

Hardin and Mac had only had a cup each from the thermos Issa had left for them. "Can I have two of the sixteen-ounce please?"

"Sure." Kai wrote on the cups with a black marker, then handed Hardin his change.

He deposited it in the tip jar and sensed a presence close to him. Glancing to his right, he spotted two women, roughly his age, appraising him openly. Each of the blondes gave him an encouraging smile. "'Scuse me," he said, moving toward the pickup area as a high school boy replaced Kai at the register.

She quickly made his order and placed the coffees in front of him. "Here you go, Hardin. Tell my friend good morning."

He grinned and nodded at Kai. "Will do."

Mac glanced at the front door as the overhead bells chimed. Hardin held the door open for two twittering blond women who smelled like money and did nothing to hide the fact that they were ogling him. She got it. He was so easy on the eyes.

Hardin set down the large coffee in front of Mac, slipped off his sunglasses, and lowered himself onto the corner of her desk. "Kai says hello."

"Thank you," she said, taking a sip. "Oh man. I haven't had one of these in forever. Yum." Her attention turned to the women. "Hi, ladies! Can I help you?"

Out of the corner of her eye, she caught Hardin touching his lip and looking at her meaningfully. She wiped the foam from the spot he'd indicated.

"We came in to book a hike."

"Unfortunately, all of our guides are out for today"— Cori searched though the computer in front of her— "through the next, um, three weeks, and then we're still pretty full."

"What about you? Are you available?" the statuesque blonde asked Hardin, changing her posture to jut out her ample breasts and display her shapely behind, which was encased in snug, fashionably torn jeans. She looked as if she was going to start drooling. "You don't look like you're occupied."

Hardin narrowed his eyes and grinned wryly. Mac cringed inwardly at the woman's overt pass but kept her face expressionless. *Fucking unbelievable.* How was he going to respond?

"The boss has my dance card filled for the day," he answered sardonically, then rose, giving Mac a sly smile and a thumbs-up, and a wink only she could see before he ambled toward the break room.

"You can leave your name and number with us. If anything comes open, we'll call," Mac said evenly. "Just know the chances are slim. We have a wait list."

The less curvy blonde challenged Mac. "Does that happen?"

"On occasion," Cori said, looking from the blondes to Mac.

"I see. We'd like him. That man who just left. What's his name? He looks familiar."

Cori pushed an open spiral pad toward Miss Statuesque. "Write your contact information down. We'll call if anything opens. It would be very last minute."

"We're only here for a week, so do your best. I made a note that we want *him,*" she said with an edge, writing firmly on the pad, clearly accustomed to getting her way.

Oh, yes ma'am. Mac swallowed her rising anger. *Fuck you and your money.* She heard a chuckle from behind her. Hardin was in the break room, with the door open, listening to the full exchange.

The blonde raised her voice so that it carried into the

hall. "We're staying at that quaint little inn down the street, the Urban."

"Wonderful," Cori said. "Enjoy PR and the scenery." She read the fresh entry in the ledger. "Mina."

"PR?"

"Piñon Ridge."

"We certainly will if it's all as nice as him."

Mac envisioned tossing them out the door, watching them splatter all over the pavement as they landed, but she stayed glued to her seat and sipped her coffee calmly. Jesus. Was Hardin subjected to this kind of shit all the time? The women's flagrant sexist treatment toward him made her blood boil. They only saw him as eye candy, and yes, he was gorgeous, but there was so much more to him. It pissed her off.

She chewed on the inside of her lip as they left, wondering how much worse it might have been if they'd known who Hardin was. How on earth did he deal with bitches like these women and people who objectified him? It was something she'd never given serious consideration until now.

Large, warm hands squeezed her shoulders. "Hey," Hardin said, kissing the top of her head. "You're really tense, babe."

She tilted her head back, finding calm in his aqua-blue eyes, and smiled. "Hey, yourself." She reached to stroke his scruffy face. "Those women treated you like a piece of meat."

"Uh-huh. It was better I left. I guess they followed me. They were in line next to me at the Grind. I don't think man-eaters are going to become extinct anytime soon. No point in making a scene. I didn't want my words or actions to impact you or your business negatively in any way."

"Thanks, but their behavior burns my ass."

Mac saw Cori observing them in her peripheral, but it didn't bother her. Being with him in public, touching him, allowing him to touch her and kiss her… It felt… natural. Right.

"It's my life," he said, quietly searching her eyes. "One of the many reasons I want out." He pulled her out of the chair to face him and gave her a lingering kiss. "Show me what I can do to help you today, boss."

"Uh, Kenna?"

Mac was feeling light-headed from his kiss when her eyes switched to her business partner, who looked confused. "Yeah?"

"You have *so much* to tell me."

Hardin glanced at Cori, squinted and the corner of his mouth hitched up. "Take a number and get in line behind me, okay?"

She returned his crooked grin and gave him a thumbs-up. "You got it. Why don't you get your instructions from *the boss?* And thanks for helping. We're stretched thin today."

Chapter Nineteen

M AC LEFT INTREPID in the capable hands of their employees at two thirty, intent on being home to greet Stowe. When he finally returned from fishing, an hour later than they had agreed, Stowe greeted her coolly before heading to his room. Instead of lighting into her son for his attitude and for being late, she trailed behind him, not saying anything, torn between giving him space and her desire to talk.

"Stowe—"

"Not now, Mom," he said before shutting the door.

Unaccustomed to its use, the lock sounded loud. Mac stood outside her son's door, wringing her hands, heart pounding with uncertainty. Shit. Had she failed him by not forcing the discussion of his father? The thing was, they needed to talk, and before Hardin arrived for dinner. His shower turned on, so she went to take a quick shower herself.

Stowe came into the kitchen and sat at the island while she was putting a pan of brownies into the oven.

"Catch anything?"

His answer was to stare at her.

"Look. A verbal answer is appropriate. I raised you to be courteous and respectful."

"Does that apply to only me?"

"What exactly does that mean?" she asked, facing her son, leaning across the island to touch his hand.

He withdrew it just as her skin brushed his and dropped his head.

Mac's heart broke and she moved around the island, next to him, but didn't attempt to touch her son even though she craved pulling him into her arms to offer comfort. His breathing was jerky and shallow, and he rhythmically clenched and unclenched his hands in his lap, swallowing and blinking rapidly.

Softly she said, "Stowe…"

His eyes snapped to hers. His expression injured, his eyes shimmered with unshed tears until first one fell and then another. He brushed at them angrily and his chin quivered. "Is Hardin Ambrose my father? Beck thinks he is."

"Yes."

"Why?" he whispered hoarsely. He was crying now. "Why didn't you tell me?"

"I'm sorry, Stowe." Her eyes welled up and her chin quivered in response. "I was weak. Every time I tried to tell you, you pushed back. It became easier to give in, and I shouldn't have." She gulped her tears and continued, stroking his face. "I'm so, so sorry."

"Has he known about me all this time?"

"No. Not until this morning."

"Why not?"

"It's a long story, honey. A complicated one. Your father and I are just now putting the pieces together."

He snarled at her. "Don't call him that! And don't expect me to call him that. I don't even know him, and he doesn't know me."

"Hardin wants to know you."

"I don't want to know him! I don't care who he is. Hardin Ambrose and his millions and his fame need to leave PR. Now!"

Mac slid her arms around her son. His trembling eased as she rubbed his damp back. She didn't speak again until she felt he was calmer. "Honey, that's not going to happen."

"Why's he here now?" Panic filled his voice. "Is he going to try to take me from you?"

"Ssh... Ssh... No. No one is going to take you from me. Ever," she said, quietly but with heartfelt conviction. "Hardin's not like that."

"What *is* he like? When's the last time you saw him?"

"This afternoon. He was helping us at Intrepid."

"Before that. He was here this morning. What was he doing here so early, Mom?"

She mentally crossed her fingers before telling her son a little white lie, having no desire to hint at anything intimate between herself and Hardin. "We had dinner and then stayed up most of the night talking, getting reacquainted."

"You had that much to talk about?"

"It's been a long time. There's been a lot to cover and uncover. As I've said a few times, Stowe, it's complicated."

"Did you love him?"

Mac framed Stowe's face in her hands and looked deeply into eyes that marked him as Hardin's. "I loved him so much that when I lost him, I could hardly function. But when you came along, I discovered"—tears splashed down her face—"a different kind of love. Losing you... Losing you would be the death of me."

"I love you, Mom. I'm sorry I was a turd." He squeezed his arms around her waist and buried his head against her galloping heart.

She hugged him tightly. "I'm sorry too. I love you more, my sweet boy."

Ten minutes passed before her heart returned to normal and Stowe had eased his hold on her. He glanced up at her. "So, dinner and sleepover at Beck's tonight?"

"No dinner. The sleepover is a maybe."

"Hardin's coming for dinner?"

"Hm. How'd you get so smart?" She tilted her head and smiled at her son. "Yes, Hardin is coming for dinner and he's nervous."

"Is Hardin smart like you and me?"

The twinkle in Stowe's eyes and the question with its embedded assumption amused Mac. Laughter bubbled up. "He does okay."

"What time?"

"Six thirty."

"I'm going to hang with Homer," he said pushing off the stool. "Unless you need help?"

Mac ruffled her son's hair and shook her head. "I've got it. You can help later. If the rain holds off, we'll eat on the patio." She needed to text Hardin and give him a heads-up that Stowe knew he was his father.

Hardin knocked on the side of the screen door, on time and nervous. He wore khaki shorts and a neatly pressed soft pink button-down, sleeves rolled up, hoping he looked casual but appropriate. He shifted the bottle of wine and a large bunch of sunflowers into his left hand, uncertain of the welcome.

"Hey!" Mac greeted him with a smile, which grew even wider when she saw the flowers, and clapped her hands. "Sunflowers! Oh, thank you!"

"You're welcome." His eyes scanned Mac's sleeveless floral-patterned blouse and the denim skirt that showed off her beautiful legs before connecting with the eyes of his scowling son standing behind her. "Hey, Stowe."

He grumbled something and turned away from Hardin.

Shit. Expecting his son to accept him out of the blue was unrealistic, but he had hoped.

She gave Stowe a look. "Where are your manners?"

His eyes simmered as they roved over Hardin, avoiding looking him in the eye. "Hello, Hardin."

The greeting was chilly. Hardin would have preferred she hadn't forced the issue, had let their relationship develop organically, but it was what it was. He was going to have to find his way through it.

Between the elation of being with Mac all night, little sleep, and the stunning revelation of having an eleven-year-old and not knowing how to bridge those years, Hardin had fought to balance on a tightrope of emotion, feeling as though he was barely holding it together. Back in his suite at the inn after helping Mac and Cori all day at Intrepid, he had researched parenting and how to bond with an adolescent. He certainly couldn't rely on his parents' example.

His brain was a mishmash—overloaded with information, expert advice, and incessant worry. Hardin had gone on a five-mile run, then showered and popped into the wine store and flower shop. His renewed but temporary confidence waned the closer he got to Mac's home, hitting an all-time low when Stowe turned away from him.

She took his hand and held on to it. "Come in. I hope you're hungry."

"Pretty much always."

Stowe trailed his parents into the kitchen, where she released Hardin's hand to get a vase for the flowers and a wine opener. "Will you open the wine, Hardin?" She placed two outdoor wineglasses close by and recut the flowers. As she added the sunflowers and water to the vase, she tried to draw their son out. "I haven't had sunflowers in so long, right, Stowe?"

"Uh-huh."

"Mother's Day. You got them for me."

"They're your favorite."

"Yes, they are." She smiled to herself, then kissed him on the temple. "Would you please set the table, honey? We're eating on the patio."

Hardin sidled next to Mac after Stowe went outside and gently lifted her chin. "Hi again," he said before ghosting her lips, then capturing them and kissing her fully until both of them were panting. He stepped back, his thumb brushing over her swollen, wet lips. "I want more of that later, Mac." He searched her face, and she gave him a subtle nod and smiled with her eyes.

"This isn't going to be easy. We're all reeling."

"I know, babe. Challenges test our mettle."

172

"They bring to light that which is most important."

"Yes. There isn't anything more important than him, you, and me."

"I want that, Hardin," she said, her voice cracking with emotion.

"As do I. With my heart and soul. And sweetness after challenges."

"Yes."

They smiled at each other and kissed again, stepping apart as the lever on the backdoor turned. Stowe's expression was stormy as he looked from Mac to Hardin. He shoved between his parents and stomped to his room and slammed the door.

Mac and Hardin were halfway through dinner when Stowe came outside. He didn't take a seat but a deep breath, shifting his weight from one foot to the other. "I'm sorry, Mom. You raised me to be better than that." He held out his hand to Hardin, his chin quivering, eyes blinking, fighting like mad to maintain his composure. "I acted like a brat. I'm sorry, Hardin."

A huge wave of emotion hit Hardin. Appreciation, respect, awe, and love. He stood and faced Stowe and accepted his handshake—the peace offering, man to man. Touching his son for the first time was surreal. It was as if his heart and soul recognized Stowe for who he was. Hardin contemplated his son and cleared his throat, but his gruff voice betrayed the emotion roiling in him. "I get it, Stowe. Let's just take this at a pace that works for all of us, okay?"

"I'd like that because I don't know how to have a father."

A smile split Hardin's face. "I don't know how to be a father, so bear with me. I expect I'm going to fu—"

Mac cleared her throat and raised her eyebrows at him.

"Uh… Yeah." He scrubbed his hand over his face, a naughty smirk appearing when his hand dropped below his mouth. "Sorry, and point made. I'm going to mess up plenty, Stowe. Not intentionally."

"Grace and patience," Mac said, looking at each of them deliberately. "That includes me. Agreed?"

"Agreed."

"Yes, Mom."

"Your mom made one heck of a dinner. Hungry?" Hardin had had a voracious appetite for as long as he could remember. He eased back into his seat and picked up his fork.

Stowe plopped into his seat. "Starving. Mom's fajitas are kinda famous."

"Really?"

"Yeah. Owen wanted the recipe for his restaurant."

"Owen?"

"He's one of the owners of the Hazy Rebel. He and Mom used—"

She shook her head. "That's enough, Stowe."

Hardin sipped from his glass and considered. There was so much to unpack. How much time did he have? Whatever the amount, he needed more.

20 Chapter Twenty

THEY KEPT THE conversation light throughout dinner, moving indoors just before the storm erupted. Mac shooed Stowe and Hardin out of the kitchen, content to give them some one-on-one time.

When she checked on them, they were playing a game on the console in Stowe's room, so she left and started a load of laundry—there was always laundry—and swept the floors. When she next checked, Hardin had moved to the beanbag chair behind Stowe and had Homer on his lap. Both he and the rabbit appeared to be asleep. Stowe had his headphones on and was playing intently. She tapped her son's shoulder.

Stowe paused the game and took off his headphones. "He's a lightweight, Mom," he whispered, looking over his shoulder at Hardin and back at her. "Said he was going to close his eyes for just a minute, after I trounced him in *Super Mario*. He sucks."

She kept her voice low too. "You trounced him?"

"Yeah."

"Maybe he's never played. Did you ask?"

"He said he's played some. Uncle Mike's played some, but at least he can hold his own with Beck and me."

"*Some* is a relative term."

"So you've told me, Mom."

Mac glanced past her son and saw the smile on Hardin's face. Her eyes flickered between the matching sets of gorgeous aqua eyes. It was almost too much. Her breath caught, but Stowe didn't notice. He was staring at the screen, focused on getting back to his game.

"Did you have fun?"

Hardin inclined his head forward, as if he was straining to hear Stowe's answer.

There were a few beats of silence while Stowe stared at the screen, and then he said, "Yeah. He seems all right. Pretty chill."

Mac's eyes swept over her son and held Hardin's gaze. "Fair warning, honey. There are few who are as competitive as him."

Stowe's voice rose. "Do you think he was playing me?"

In her peripheral, behind their son, Hardin shook his head. "I don't. It's just not part of his DNA. So I'm with you. He sucks."

Stowe burst out laughing.

Hardin scowled at her, put the Lop down carefully, and rolled out of the beanbag chair. "What's so funny?"

"You fell asleep," Stowe said and frowned. "With Homer."

Hardin's eyes locked with Mac's, out of Stowe's line of sight, looking pleased. "I didn't get much sleep last night."

Stowe pulled out his imaginary violin and played it for

Hardin, who looked surprised, but then he smiled.

Mac smiled too. Their son teasing him was a step forward.

"I guess you'd better go then. Get your beauty sleep."

"Stowe!" she said sharply.

"Sorry." He swiveled his chair to face Mac and Hardin and shrugged, a smirk on his face. "I'm tired too. My best behavior keeps getting in the back seat. I don't know how to act around you, Hardin."

"I get that. How about we focus on being kind?"

Stowe nodded and swiveled around in his chair again, considering the frozen screen in front of him. He took a deep breath and turned it off, stood and faced Hardin, all cockiness gone. "Do you fish?"

"I have."

"Better than you game?"

"I'm not sure. I was a boy, around your age."

"What about your father?"

"Nope."

"Sisters? Brothers?"

Hardin shook his head. "Just brothers. Three. All older. They weren't much interested in their little brother."

"How little were you?"

"Nine years under my next youngest brother."

"Like you were an only."

"Kind of, yes."

Stowe nodded, looking considerate. "I like to fish. Flyfish. Do you… do you maybe want to… want to do it sometime?"

"I'd like that. You'll have to guide me."

"I can do that." Stowe flashed Mac a look, then focused on the Lop, who had hopped into his pen. "I really am tired, Mom. So is Homer. We're gonna say good night."

"Good night, Stowe."

"Hardin."

"Night, honey. I love you."

"I love you more, Mom."

Her cup runneth over. "Impossible. Sleep tight," she said softly, closing the door and smiling up at Hardin.

⟡⟡⟡

They walked to the front door holding hands. Hardin pressed her against the wall gently and began kissing her, quickly deepening it. She returned it with equal need, fire sparking through her veins. Soon they were grinding against each other, using the wall to brace themselves.

He separated from her when she whimpered, breathing heavily. "God, how I want you. Not here." He pushed the hair away from her face, his eyes full of heat. "It's been precarious tonight. I don't want to chance making it worse. I'm going to go. You need sleep. I need sleep."

He opened the door. Lightning cracked overhead, so bright that it lit everything, including the sheets of rain.

Mac stilled him, grabbing his forearm. "Hardin?" He should leave, but everything in her was screaming for him to stay.

He spun around. His mouth crashed against hers, his tongue seeking, ravaging.

She returned his passion, coming up for air to beg. "Please."

HEARTS
don't lie

Hand in hand, he tugged her out of the house, down the slippery steps, and around to the shed in the side yard, practically ripping the door from its hinges to get them inside from the pelting rain. Clearing the workbench in one sweep, he lifted her onto it.

Their mouths were still sealed as Hardin laid Mac back and shimmied her rain-soaked skirt over her hips and wet panties from her body, then climbed onto the bench, hovering over her. She impatiently fumbled with his shorts—unbuttoning and unzipping. He was commando, thank God. She lost no time freeing and guiding him into her, out of her mind with lust through the first rough thrusts.

He pushed up on his hands, suspending himself over her, buried deep within her core, and growled. "Look at me, baby."

Through the dirty cracked window, lightning split the night and illuminated his features. Thunder boomed loudly, reverberating in the shed and through the workbench she was spread out on. His aqua eyes had turned almost black as he slammed into her again. Looking into his eyes was her undoing. His expression seared her, and she whimpered and moaned and came apart, struggling to breathe as wave after wave of euphoria rippled through her entire body.

Hardin was right there with her, groaning loudly as she bucked under him, trying to take him even deeper, milking him dry. His arms shook as he lowered himself onto her, spent. "I'm really loving your workbench, honey."

Chuckles intermingled with her pants. "Got it at a garage sale. I'm just glad it held."

21 Chapter Twenty One

TWO DAYS LATER, Hardin was en route to pick up Arlo Cruz in Gambol—the tony resort of the über-rich thirty minutes north of Piñon Ridge. His longtime agent was flying in, having insisted on hashing out Hardin's request face-to-face, probably more like trying to convince him to show up for mandatory training. Every day and every team meeting Hardin had missed resulted in a substantial fine.

Like I give a shit.

There was nothing like in-person pressure, and Arlo was among the very best. Hardin also counted the Spaniard in his small circle of trusted friends. He had faith that once Arlo had the full story, the scope of his and Mac's history, he would do everything in his power to help him.

It was the first time Hardin had been behind the wheel since arriving in Piñon Ridge over a week ago. What a week it had been. Reacquainting with Mac and realizing that the love he had for her was everything he believed and that she had feelings for him. Then discovering he was a father and now navigating a relationship with an amazing young man who ran hot and cold without warning.

Getting on even footing with his son was the challenge of his lifetime. No one had come close to putting him through his emotional paces since Mac, but Stowe did, with a finesse Hardin admired.

Arlo would stay in Hardin's roomy suite while he was visiting. There were no vacancies in Piñon Ridge. Summer rivaled the ski season in popularity, what with all the outdoor options. Hopefully his friend had calmed down during the flight in from Spain. Arlo had gone ballistic when Hardin told him he'd be delayed returning to training and asked him to look for loopholes in his recently renegotiated and signed two-year contract, reverting to speaking his native tongue in a frenetic speed.

Hardin was proficient in Spanish, but when Arlo launched into his tirade, he couldn't keep up. He had tuned out instead and reflected on how upset Arlo had been last month when he wouldn't commit to a longer contract because of the wear and tear on his body, even though he had avoided being seriously injured. What he demanded now was something that would rock international premier soccer.

Most players retired before the age of thirty-five. Yeah, there were a small number of players who were older and held on to their peak play, but that came with costs. At age thirty, Hardin had no desire to be another member of that club. He had seriously given consideration to retiring last year, but dammit, he had allowed the money and pressure to seduce him once again. He had said as much to Mac when they were on their hiking trip, before he knew about Stowe.

Hardin's thoughts turned to his son, simply the most

incredible surprise he'd ever received and one that required heaping amounts of patience, understanding, and tenaciousness as both of them peeled back and explored the layers and layers of soul-stirring wrapping. For the most part, Mac stayed on the sidelines, only stepping in when she felt Stowe needed a knot jerked in his tail for being rude or Hardin required redirection. But those moments, like Stowe's early flashes of anger and surliness, occurred less often as the days passed.

His cell rang over the Bluetooth. It was Mac. "Hello?"

"Hardin?"

No, it was Stowe using Mac's phone. "Hey, Stowe. Morning."

"Good morning. Where are you? It sounds windy."

"Driving to pick up a friend at the Gambol airport. Sunroof's open."

"Oh… Um…"

"Hold a minute." Hardin closed the sunroof. "Some of what you were saying was going out the roof."

His comment was met with Stowe's laughter.

"Okay. That's better. What's going on?" This was the first time Stowe had contacted him, and he enjoyed his son's laughter. Hardin signaled and took the off-ramp from the interstate and headed for a parking lot that was close to the ramp, designated for people who carpooled to Denver and other larger cities. The lot was nearly empty at this early hour on a weekend.

"Um… Uncle Mike is taking Beck and me fly-fishing. Do… Do you want to go?"

Hardin pulled in and put the Range Rover in park, fully focused on his son. *Of course I want to go.* He had planned to spend the afternoon with Arlo, examining the finer points of the contract, looking for a compromise, or better yet, a way out, without being made an example and fined into the poor house. His heart pounded. "What time?"

"Well, we were going to leave as soon as possible, but you'll need waders and boots. Mike has an extra rod and reel you can use. And we need to go into the local Parks and Wildlife office so you can get a license and stamp. It's next to Elevation. Bring ID."

The excitement of Stowe asking him to do something trumped his need to talk with Arlo. They could talk later. Hell, Arlo would probably be hungry and jet-lagged and want to eat and nap. If not, he could explore the town or hike. "Sounds great, Stowe. I'm coming right back."

"Okay. Um… I can call Ronni or Asher and see if you can maybe go in before Elevation opens."

It took Hardin a second, and then he remembered that Ronni was the woman who had helped him at the outfitters. Her family owned the business. Who Asher was, was a mystery. "Sure. Call me back, okay?" He could drop Arlo off at the Urban and walk right over if Elevation would open up for him.

"Okay."

"Your mom with you?"

"She's in the shower."

The engine revved loudly.

"Are you speeding?"

Christ. Hardin pulled his foot from the gas pedal, which he had pushed to the floor when envisioning water cascading over Mac's beautiful form. Their urgent coming together in the shed was still fresh. His body stirred and he smiled slowly. That was something he wasn't ever going to forget. "No. My foot slipped."

"You need to be careful," Stowe said, admonishing him like a parent.

"I have it under control. Let me know, okay? And tell your mom I said good morning." *That I'm thinking of her,* he wanted to add.

"Okay." Stowe disconnected and Hardin banished all thoughts of a naked Mac before putting the luxury vehicle into drive and heading the last five minutes to the airport.

~~~

The Bluetooth signaled he had another call. Mac's number popped up again on the screen. "Hey, Stowe."

"It's me. The boy is addressing his caterpillar-coated teeth."

He grimaced and then laughed. It was an image he was unlikely to part with soon. "Morning, honey. That bad?"

"Uh, not really. I'm exaggerating a bit. That said, he isn't going about his day with dirty teeth."

Hardin made a mental note of the importance of Stowe's hygiene.

"I'm headed into work. Our son asked me to follow up. Asher, Ronni's brother, will be expecting you when you get back to PR. Stowe will be with me. You can take him to Elevation with you. He loves looking around. If you want, that is."

If he wanted. Of course he wanted to have his son with him. The question was their son's expectations. This was a delicate dance. "What do you think he wants? Actually, answer this. Did you have him invite me along?"

"Inviting you was his idea, which is great. But that said, be on your toes."

He wanted to shout from a mountaintop. Stowe inviting him was a major step forward. "Wow," he said quietly.

"Yeah. Progress. Keeping you in the loop. We were at Cori and Mike's for dinner last night. Issa and Doc, Cori's parents, were there too. While the kids were playing outside, the topic of you came up, as did questions, specifically regarding the uncanny resemblance between you and Stowe. Anyway, I told them about you, about us. Very briefly. They know and will act appropriately. I just wanted you to be in the loop because Mike will probably bring it up while you fish if you end up out of the boys' earshot."

"Understood. By the way, does Stowe need anything?"

"No, but that may not keep him from asking or begging. He is a child after all. If, and I say if because this is your decision, you do decide to get him something, please try to be, um, reasonable. Not get something I couldn't afford or wouldn't agree to. Please."

Hardin pulled into the airport and began looking for Arlo. His friend waved at him from the far end of the terminal.

"Thanks for the heads-up," Hardin said calmly even though he felt otherwise. He wished Mac would be with him, that they could field the questions and comments about Stowe together. "As far as Elevation or anything else along those lines, I support that." Finances were something they needed to talk about. Mac's days of supporting Stowe and herself were coming to an end.

Her sigh of relief carried easily through the Bluetooth. "Thank you. Knowing you, I'm thinking you're nervous."

"Nervous as hell."

"You're going to do great, Hardin," she said supportively.

"Thanks. When can I see you?"

"I'm not sure. Stowe's at Issa and Doc's tonight. Grandparent night. I'll be out with the girls."

Disappointed that he wouldn't see her, Hardin decided Arlo and he would address his contract after fly-fishing and maybe do something later if they were still talking to each other by then. "I've got plans too."

"You do?"

"Yeah, a friend has flown in and I'm in Gambol picking him up as we speak. Hold on." He pulled the Range Rover to the curb and motioned Arlo, who wore an unhappy expression, into the vehicle. "Hey, Arlo! I've got to go, honey."

"Call me later?"

"Of course."

Chapter Twenty Two

"YOU CANNOT DO this, Bro," Arlo said while securing his seat belt, clearly frustrated. "It's just not done."

"Hello to you too."

Arlo turned to him; his mouth set in a firm line. "Hello. You're crazy."

"Find a way," he said, demanding.

"What the fuck? You do realize that you're being fined out the ass?"

"Yeah."

"That doesn't bother you?"

"Not even close to how leaving here would."

"What the fuck does that mean?"

Hardin merged onto the interstate. "I'm going to tell you a story," he said calmly. "You are not to share it with anyone outside of the owners. Neither are they. Please don't interrupt me." He gave Arlo a hard stare, waiting for confirmation.

Arlo nodded, then asked, "Are you sick?"

"Nope."

"Dying?"

"Nope. Just fucking listen and keep your mouth shut."

Arlo seemed surprised but just nodded again. Hardin rarely spoke with so much heat, and when he did, there was a good reason.

Hardin left his stunned friend and determined agent at the inn. Nothing like dumping everything but the kitchen sink in Arlo's lap. The Spaniard was entering into the toughest negotiations he'd ever faced with a warning from Hardin not to disappoint. But that was why Hardin paid Arlo the big bucks. He prayed that the club's owners, known for being staunch family men, would soften their relentless business acumen when they became privy to what was at stake. It could be a win-win or an epic disaster.

Stowe was sitting next to Mac as she worked at her desk when Hardin entered Intrepid. He looked expectantly at him.

"Morning," he said to both, grinning, his gaze bouncing between them, his heart full. His son looked relaxed and happy. Mac just looked fresh and delicious. He ached to kiss her, but it wasn't wise; his relationship with Stowe was tenuous.

"Ready?" Hardin asked him, again overcome with wonder when seeing himself mirrored in the eleven-year-old's eyes.

"Yep."

"You two have a good time," she said, ruffling their son's hair, her eyes and smile lighting on Stowe and then Hardin. "Go easy on Hardin, okay? He's a rookie."

Their son's laughter sounded like music to Hardin, and he slid the sunglasses off the ball cap he wore and over his eyes.

Hardin and Stowe drove to the Wainsoms to pick up Mike and Beckett. Stowe climbed into the back seat to be with his best friend while Hardin exited to help Mike load the equipment and food.

"Hey, Hardin." Cori's husband extended a meaty hand. "Mike. Nice to meet you. Don't you like how our minis leave all the packing to us?" He flashed a smile and nodded to the boys as he said it. Hardin noted Beckett was a diminutive version of his blond father, who looked like he could bench-press a small horse. "They can pack in for the return, maybe with some stinky fish if we're so lucky. Stowe said this is a first time out for you."

"Yeah."

"I brought the extra rod and reel for you. You got your license and a rod stamp?"

"I did." Feeling encouraged by the way everything was going, Hardin had purchased the annual nonresident instead of the five-day.

"Just give it to me when we get there and I'll get you all set up." Mike's eyes lighted on Hardin's boonie. "I see you have a new hat."

"Stowe suggested it." Hardin touched the colorful hat and grinned. "I think he thought I might not wear it."

Mike nodded. "I see your son's wearing the same one."

"I told him I'd get him one. It's what he chose," he said, feeling buoyant. *Your son.* "He needed new boots too. Outgrew the ones he had."

"That's a good thing," Mike said, nodding, regarding

him before putting his sunglasses on. "The spot we're going to is about an hour out."

Hardin closed the gate of the SUV, and the men climbed into their front seats.

Mike whistled. "Nice ride, but the navigation system won't be of any help. I'll take us in, okay? I know the county like the back of my hand. Head south."

Hardin slipped the Range Rover into gear and drove toward Main Street in anticipation of his first father-son outing.

"I expect our boys are going to be plugged in while we drive, which will give us time to start getting acquainted." Mike twisted in his seat and handed them a device with headphones he had pulled from his backpack. "You two goofballs keep it down."

Hardin soaked it all in—how Mike interacted with the boys and how his demeanor, while kind and light, said "respect me." He wore fatherhood well, having parented since Beckett was born. "That'll keep them busy?"

"Yeah, and they'll gripe when I take it away, until their attention is redirected. Then it'll be forgotten."

Hardin kept his eye on the road and nodded. He was eleven years behind in Dad School.

"You'll be fine, Hardin. Stowe's a great kid, and Kenna says you're a good man."

There it was again. Kenna. The name that separated now from then. How to bridge that?

"So, Mike, tell me what you do for a living."

"Damn. Wanted to talk about you and Kenna, but that's fine. We're going to have plenty of time."

Hardin was nothing short of grateful for the time spent fly-fishing. Mike first worked with him, but then Stowe took over, exceptionally patient, much like Mac. After a few lessons, he tried to cast, losing two flies to tree branches. Later, after Stowe attached another fly—tied by Uncle Mike and apparently a work of art—to his line with what he called an improved cinch knot, Hardin found success.

"What else do you like to do besides fish?"

"Summer?"

"Yeah."

"Hang with my friends, hike, swim, bouldering, play basketball and soccer, but I'm not anything close to you."

"What's bouldering?"

"It's a type of climbing but on low rock. We climb without rope, harnesses, and other gear. Well, other than crash pads and sliders so we don't get hurt when we fall. And helmets. Mom makes me wear one."

"Smart, your mom. Got to protect that noggin."

"Wanna try bouldering sometime? If you're going to be around that is…"

"I'd like that. I'll have to get a helmet though."

"Yup. Are you going to be here next week?"

"I am." *I'm not going anywhere, son.*

"Next week then, and just to let you know, you're going to be sore as heck."

"You think so?"

Stowe giggled. "I know so. Mom is in great shape and she could barely move afterward. She got a really long massage."

Hardin dismissed the vision of Mac naked and him

massaging her as soon as it appeared in his head. He cleared his throat. "Thanks for the warning. Should I book a massage before we go?"

Stowe let out a belly laugh. "You just might."

Hardin nodded and cracked a grin, his heart swelling with happiness. Their son sounded so much like Mac at times. It was fantastic.

Standing in the stream under the shimmering sun and impervious to water thanks to his waders and wading boots, he became transfixed with the quiet. Hardin's worries fell away. He was grateful for the hat, sunscreen, and his sunglasses. But he was even more grateful to have this time with his son. To watch him out of the corner of his eye and learn his movements, enjoy his voice and humor and snark. He had a lot of that, typically delivered with a smirk.

All of them took a break from fishing when it was evident the fish weren't biting and the boys claimed they'd die if they didn't eat soon. They found boulders to sit on under the dappled shade and had lunch.

"We'll head up to Slate Lake," Mike said after finishing off his barbecue. "We can escape the heat, fish, and enjoy the views. Hardin, a lake is actually a better place to start. It'll be easier for you to pick up any tugging."

"That's where I started, but you did really good this morning."

Hardin smiled at Stowe. "Thanks, sport."

"Bro, he called you sport!"

Oh shit. Did I mess up?

Stowe rolled his eyes at Beckett. "I can hear, you know."

"No one calls you anything but Stowe or Bro." Some of his masticated sandwich fell out of his mouth.

194

"Honestly, Beck. Where are your manners?" Mike said, sounding disgusted.

Beck wiped at the mess, getting nowhere until Mike handed him a napkin.

"There's always room for another nickname. I kinda like it." Stowe gave Hardin a measured look. "Isn't Bro your nickname?"

"Yep."

"You *are* related!" More food fell out of Beckett's mouth.

"Drop it, Beck. In fact, why don't you start loading the car after you swallow what's in your mouth? Stowe, can you get the rods and boxes?"

"Sure."

Hardin was astounded. Mike had easily halted the line of questioning and separated the boys, protecting Stowe from an onslaught of comments and conjecture.

"Sorry. That wasn't appropriate. Beck was just being Beck. Out of order. Kenna told us this had all just come about."

"Yeah." Hardin's eyes moved to where Stowe gathered the rods and organized the tackle box and then to where Beckett loaded the cooler and picnic supplies. "I didn't know about him, and he didn't know about me. Mac— sorry, Kenna—was trying to protect him, and she had the best of reasons."

"Are you angry with her?"

"No, man. I love the hell out of her. I always have, and now I'm just trying to find a way to make this all good, to be with her and Stowe." Hardin glanced over to where the boys were at the Range Rover, laughing about something. "They always get on so well?"

"Pretty much. Cori and I will sit Beck down and talk to him. Help him understand the sensitive nature of what's going on."

"I appreciate that. Mac and I are trying to navigate this carefully. She's better at it than me."

"From what I've seen today, you do pretty well. Keep giving him the space and he'll come around. He's a great kid, and I'd say that even if I wasn't his uncle."

"Thank you doesn't even seem enough for everything you and Cori and Issa and Doc and so many others have done for Mac and Stowe."

"And just to be clear with you, Hardin, I consider her family, my sister-in-law. We do anything for those we love."

"Yes, we do." Hardin lifted his chin and nodded.

Mike regarded him with a serious look. "She won't move."

"She won't, but I will."

"You're quitting? Jesus Christ, man! How can you quit? You're one of the best to ever play the game!" There were a few minutes of silence, and then Mike spoke again, soberly. "You're serious."

"As serious as a heart attack."

"DAD!"

"BRO!"

"Coming, Beck. The minis call. We act." Mike chuckled. The men stood and Mike held out his hand to Hardin. "I like you, but I love Kenna and Stowe. Don't break their hearts. Do we understand each other?"

"You have my word." Hardin shook his hand and stared back at Mike.

Mike slapped Hardin on the back. "I'm glad we had this talk. Let's go."

He walked companionably with Mike, hopeful he'd earn the big man's trust and respect. He was also pleased as hell. His son had called him *Bro* instead of by his name. It was progress he could live with.

They separated as they fished in the shade of Slate Lake. Stowe and Beckett. Hardin and Mike. As promised, the view was spectacular, reminding Hardin of areas in the Alps. He felt no twinge of emotion when he reflected on that or when he thought of Spain. But when he watched his son, Hardin's heart tightened. His heart and soul were already ensconced in Colorado. He was done, regardless of how Arlo's negotiations went.

"You know, Kenna didn't say much other than you're Stowe's father. She closed up after that. Why do you call her Mac?"

"I've always called her that. It's short for McKenna." Hardin cast his line.

Mike watched Hardin propel the leader and fly a good distance from where they stood in the water. "Nice job. You catch on quickly. She's McKenna?"

"Yep."

"Interesting. We've always known her as Kenna. She's never mentioned the name McKenna."

"She may have legally changed it when she changed her surname."

"It's not Eliot?"

"It wasn't. Look, Mike. I'm not trying to be a prick, but Mac's story is hers. I'm not comfortable discussing it because I didn't ask or get her permission to share."

"She's okay though? Not running from the law?"

"Mac?" He guffawed. "No. She's a woman of great

moral character, the best person I've ever met. She had good reasons."

"But she ran from you and took Stowe?"

Hardin stopped watching his line and turned his head and pushed his sunglasses up, his eyes met Mike's, unflinching. "No. She never ran from me, nor did she *take* our son from me. That's all I can say right now. I'll talk to her and maybe, probably, the four of us can talk about this soon."

"Okay." Mike circled around again. "She said you didn't know about Stowe."

"Nope. I'd been trying to find her for over a decade, but she was smart. Changed her name. Stayed off the grid. But I finally found her."

Mike looked surprised. "You seem proud of her."

"I am. She's smart as a whip. She had her reasons and they were justified."

"And there's more."

"Yes, and you and Cori will have to wait."

"I can't imagine how devastated I'd be if I were in your shoes."

"I felt that way and I'm pissed as"—he glanced at the boys, who seemed far enough away, focusing again on the wonderment that was Stowe—"pissed as all fuck, but not at her. Mac did what she felt she needed to do, and I support her decisions. But at the same time, it kills me that I didn't know my son since before birth. She and I are still making sense of the things that have happened in our past, that impacted us and our son."

"You can't get that back."

Hardin blinked behind his mirrored sunglasses, experiencing an acute sense of sadness. "No, I can't."

Splashing drew his attention to where their boys were fishing. Stowe and Beckett were running through the water toward them.

"Bro! Look what I caught!" A fish dangled from Stowe's shortened line. He beamed a triumphant smile at Hardin.

Before Hardin realized what he was doing, he braced the rod into his hip and ruffled his son's hair. "Well done!"

"I'm gonna release him since we're not having fish tonight. Doc doesn't like fish—go figure." Stowe splashed away as quickly as he'd splashed in.

"We should find another spot. In his excitement, your son disrupted our chances of catching anything else here. Come on." Mike moved toward the shore.

Hardin followed Mike farther from where the boys fished.

"This will give us a better chance. Let's hope for luck. I would have liked to keep Stowe's catch. I promised Cori a fresh fish dinner." Mike waded in with Hardin. They stopped when they were about calf deep. "Stowe's warming up." He patted Hardin on his back.

Hardin was too overcome with emotion to speak, so he just grinned like a fool.

Chapter Twenty Three

S INCE MOVING TO Piñon Ridge, Mac had established a tight group of friends—young females, movers and shakers in their community, known well enough throughout Peaks County that they were sought after for collaboration on projects and outreach. The women regularly met over coffee and for dinners, wine nights, and other activities. Tonight Mac was at the Hazy Rebel with them—Cori, Kai, Emory, and Ronni.

Fortunately, all of them lived in town. Hearty dinners and craft beers had been followed up with whiskey. The plan was to drink and dance all night on the Hazy Rebel's deck. Mac was looking forward to letting loose. It'd been a week, to say the least. Her head and heart were all tangled up.

Kai didn't need to work tomorrow, so the willowy blonde was thoroughly enjoying herself, tossing back the first shot with gusto. Pacing herself, but still having fun, Cori monitored her intake, cutting every sip with water, never sure what parenting duties might be required overnight.

Emory rarely drank. She was usually the designated driver, but tonight they had all walked in and her role would be that of the designated voice of reason should anything look like it was going to go sideways. She downed shots of water.

Mac had opted to begin with water, finishing a few glasses while eating a roast chicken and cranberry salad while enjoying small talk with her girlfriends. She'd switch to whiskey after they moved out to the deck. Owen, a friend and one of the owners, had reserved a choice table for them.

The Hazy Rebel had transformed over the past hour, emptying out when families left, and singles and couples had drifted in, filling the bar or moving to the expansive outdoor area overlooking the Ruston River, which meandered through town. The suspended party lights came on, adding ambience and a sense of intimacy as night crept in.

Rough Riders, a regional country band that performed a combination of covers and their own material, was beginning their first set. Mac and her friends paid the cover, received their wristbands, and pushed the barstools under the high and narrow, raw-edged wood table, preferring to stand.

Kai had ordered the first round of whiskey with a water shot for Emory. They lifted their glasses.

Mac noted the two blondes who were in Intrepid a few days ago as they stood around a small round bar table in the corner. She smiled and nodded to them and received cold stares in return. Her gaze swept over her friends, feeling so much love and appreciation, and gave each of them a huge smile.

"To friendship, through thick and thin. Bottoms up!"

Mac raised her shot glass, knocked against each of the others' raised glasses, and drained it.

Cori signaled to a passing waiter with her empty shot glass. "Another round when you have time, thanks."

Ronni's hazel eyes bounced over the group and landed on Mac. Leaning in toward the middle of the rectangular table, with the other women doing the same so that they could better hear, she spoke above the music. "Bring us up to date on the hunk that you took out on the three-day one-on-one. I helped him at the store. G-O-R-G-E-O-U-S." Her expression took on a merry glint. Teasing, she asked, "Isn't that a break in your protocol, Kenna?"

"I've known him since high school."

Cori wore a shit-eating grin and added. "Rather well, it seems."

Kai glanced at Cori. "He came in for coffee a few days back. I remember him because, well, who wouldn't? Coffee for you, Kenna. Said you needed a pick-me-up and asked if there was something... Oh yes. Something in particular you liked." Her green eyes watched carefully.

Mac pulled at her short denim skirt and squirmed internally, feeling flustered by their interest.

Emory frowned. "Am I the only one who hasn't seen him?"

"Must be. If you'd seen or met him, there's no way you'd forget him. No offense to my handsome, sexy stud of a husband." Cori giggled. Mike was a handsome bear of a man, and she was head over heels about him.

Mac looked at her hands and considered how to begin. This really wasn't an ideal spot to lay it all at their feet.

"Does this gorgeous hunk have a name?"

"Of course he has a name," Mac said, her smile belying the light edge to her voice, her eyes flitting to Emory's. She didn't miss the looks that passed rapidly from friend to friend—surprise, interest, and *you're going to tell us* expressions. "Hardin."

"Hardin, as in Hardin Ambrose? Oh my God! I knew it!" Ronni crowed, loudly slapping the table and drawing attention to their table. "I even said as much when he came in, but he tactfully sidestepped my comments. Damn, girl. How the hell do you know him? Spill it!"

Emory's eyes grew huge. "The soccer player? Jesus, he's... he's like beautiful, Kenna."

"Speaking of which." Ronni sat up, ramrod straight, her eyes suddenly glued to the door that connected the deck to the Hazy Rebel.

Mac's eyes followed Ronni's. Hardin with another man. Another gorgeous one at that. Dark-haired, slim, tall, obviously in shape, similar to Hardin, whom she couldn't tear her eyes away from. *Jesus.*

Hardin did wonders for the light blue button-down he wore, making his aqua eyes pop even more. The sleeves were rolled up, exposing sinewy forearms and his tattoos. Muscular legs extended from the striped shorts hanging casually from his lean hips. Sandals covered his feet. He spotted her immediately. An enormous smile filled his face and confidence emanated from him. Despite the thick crowd, Hardin and his companion ambled easily toward their table as gawkers parted to make room.

"Holy fuck," Emory said, the words whooshing out.

Mac noticed Emory's eyes were locked on the man with Hardin and his, in turn, were all over her. *Uh-oh.*

Hardin slid an arm around Mac's shoulders and pulled her close, leaning down and kissing her, establishing exactly what their relationship was. "Good evening. Sorry to horn in on your girlfriend time."

She was breathless from his kiss, daringly intimate in a public space. It was a kiss of claiming. One that announced to anyone watching, *she's mine*. Fine. Two could play that game. Mac gave him a saucy smirk as her hand snaked around his neck and pulled him close. Her lips hovered over his before kissing him back, her tongue sweeping inside his mouth. Her blood simmered as he returned it.

Hardin broke off the kiss. Heat filled his eyes and the corner of his mouth was quirked up in a sexy grin. In the hush between songs and applause, he said, "I guess showing up is okay. Maybe we should take this somewhere else, Mac?"

She pulled back and grinned at him. In her peripheral, her friends looked astonished. By her behavior or how Hardin had just addressed her?

Arlo cleared his throat. "Good evening, ladies. Maybe we are crashing your party?" He contemplated Hardin. "Maybe not?"

"No. It's fine."

He turned to Mac, who had spoken for the group.

"It's nice to meet the woman who has my friend's heart. I am Arlo."

"Nice to meet you. I'm Kenna."

"Bro's Mac."

"Yes."

Amusement danced in Arlo's eyes before he turned to her friends. He was polite as they introduced themselves. Emory was last. His warm smile grew larger.

Cori slipped away from the table and spoke to a waitress.

"Emory," she said, returning Arlo's smile.

He extended his hand to her, pleasure evident in his thickly lashed hazel eyes. "Dance with me, *mi amor.*"

Openmouthed, Mac observed her friend, one of the toughest women she knew, sway as she stood, then follow Arlo meekly, hand in hand, to the dance floor.

"What are you drinking?" Hardin asked in her ear.

"Whiskey shots. We're waiting on our second round."

"How long are you all staying?"

Things were changing fast. "Not sure."

Owen came over to the table with a tray of shots and more water. "On the house." To Hardin, he said, "I'm Owen. One of the owners. It's a pleasure to have you here."

"Thanks, man. Nice to meet you. I was here last week for lunch. It was very good."

"Thank you."

Nick, Owen's business partner, appeared out of nowhere. "Welcome to our establishment. I'm a huge fan, like Owen. Both of us played in college. Nothing like you though."

Hardin smiled humbly and draped his arm loosely around Mac's shoulders.

More and more people were taking an interest in their table. The statuesque blonde raised her phone, camera lens facing them. Mac grimaced.

Hardin took two shot glasses from their table and gave one to Mac, raising his, fixing her with a deep look, a gentle smile on his face. "To us."

She lifted hers and clinked it against his. "To us," she said and emptied it.

"We're going to slow things down and then take a break," said the lead singer of the Rough Riders.

Hardin tossed his back, then took her hand. "Dance with me, honey."

They hadn't danced since high school, when they were in Stowe, Vermont. That trip, her first time out of Illinois and on a plane, was monumental. Hardin had told her he loved her, and she had told him she felt the same.

Mac stepped onto the dance area, feeling nervous and excited, but that changed as soon as the first chords played. Raw emotion broke in her, and her throat burned as tears gathered in her eyes when the first words of Travis Tritt's "Anymore" were sung.

It was her truth. Mac couldn't deny it any longer; she loved Hardin. She had never stopped. Losing him again would break her. She buried her wet face in his chest, feeling the beat of his heart, his every breath as they barely moved but rocked sensually in the center of the dance floor. Her friends and the people on the deck faded into the background. It was just the two of them.

He danced like he made love. Fluidly and confidently, evoking a passion so intense she was afraid to look up, knowing everything she felt was written all over her flushed face.

Hardin kissed her forehead, lowering his lips to her ear. "You okay?"

She nodded. "I love you, Hardin. So much…" She sniffled. "I love you."

"I love you too, honey," he said, his voice cracking with emotion.

"Closer, Hardin. Please. Hold me closer."

His pelvis nestled in her belly. His hands drifted over

her lower back and pressed Mac even closer, leaving no space between them. His mouth descended, slanting over hers, ready to give and take, his eyes half-open, watching her.

Mac's heart skipped a beat, then went into overdrive as Hardin's sweet breath whispered over her skin, his scent hypnotizing her. Hardin claimed her leisurely, his tongue moving tenderly along the seam of her lips before he devoured them. She kissed him back with equal fervor, losing herself, wanting to crawl into him. Under his skin. Absorb him into her soul. Her fingers curled into his skin through his shirt, then slid down over his tight ass.

Suddenly realizing what she was doing, Mac broke the kiss and looked up at him, stunned by her response in a very public, thankfully crowded, place. "Oh my God."

"Yeah. We're barely holding it together here," he said, his eyes full of heat, fingers playing along the bottom of her short denim skirt. "This skirt. Babe. You know I've always had a thing for your gorgeous legs. I just want to graze on them with my hands and mouth to where they end and another part of you begins."

Mac knew he felt her shuddering, and her core ignited as he pressed her against him. Her nipples were so tight they hurt.

Hardin murmured in her ear. "You need me as much as I need you. What do you say we leave after this raging hard-on you've given me subsides, after we both settle down?"

A blanket of goose bumps raced over her skin. "If you continue to press me up against you like this, we're going to be unsuccessful."

"I don't want to let you go." He sighed and his hands slipped down her backside, fingertips drifting over her ass. "Hm. We have a predicament."

"I'm so very sorry." She grinned up at him wickedly.

The corner of his mouth quirked up in a sexy smile. "I don't think you are."

"Don't look at me like that, Hardin."

"Like what?"

"Like you want to—"

"Hardin Ambrose! It is you!" The statuesque blonde was suddenly at his side, her hand on his shoulder. Her friend, the equally blond and slimmer version, behind her.

Besides interrupting Mac, the woman had ruined their moment and Hardin's impressive arousal. Mac gave her a hard stare.

The Rough Riders finished the song and exited the small stage.

"And to think I thought you worked for *her*," she said, laughing derisively. She ran a long red acrylic nail down Hardin's bicep. "I know who you are! Why don't you stop dancing and we can go party? We'll have so much fun." She was back to flaunting her breasts at Hardin. The shorts she wore barely covered her girl parts. "I'm more your speed."

He didn't seem impressed or upset, Mac observed.

"Uh, look. I'm with my girl. She's my speed. I'm not interested."

She batted her enhanced eyelashes at him. "But you run hard and fast. I've read all about you. I doubt she can satisfy the appetites of a man of your stature."

Mac couldn't help herself and scoffed loudly, not wanting to say or do anything else for fear of escalating things with the bitch.

"Can't believe everything you read and hear, right? There might be another guy here tonight who's open to your offer," he said coolly, lacing his fingers with Mac's and moving toward the table where all her friends and Arlo watched, stupefied. "Come on, honey. Time to say good night."

Chapter Twenty-four

THEY BARELY GOT inside Mac's house before they were clawing at each other's clothes.

Hardin pushed her against the wall as soon as she locked the door, their hot-as-fuck kiss from the dance floor still fresh in his head. "I want you so damned bad."

Of all things, she'd worn a skirt tonight, making it difficult for him to concentrate on much besides getting under it.

She seemed helpless to stop her hips writhing against him. Her fingers raced down the buttons of his shirt. When it was hanging wide open, her hands moved over his sculpted pecs and abs. Hardin hissed when she did it again, lightly teasing his skin with her nails. He ached to relieve the pressure against the fly of his shorts.

As if she read his mind, Mac's hands went to his belt and then to his fly. Biting her bottom lip in concentration, she unfastened both urgently.

He groaned as her slender hand slid inside and encircled him. "Easy, baby."

He unzipped her skirt. She shimmied and it dropped to the planked floor. He hooked his thumbs in the sides of her lace panties and eased them down, nudging them over with his foot to join her skirt. Hardin's heart was hammering, and he swallowed when he glimpsed how she was gloriously ready for him. He wanted to drop to his knees and savor her, but his need was so great he let his shorts slide to the floor, then his boxers, and kicked them to the growing pile of discarded clothing. His shirt came next, and then he hoisted her up, pulling off her tank and bra. Her nipples hardened as he teased them with his tongue and suckled.

"Lock your ankles around me and hold on," he said, pulling her legs, then bracing himself on the wall next to her shoulder with one hand and holding her with his other arm as he pushed deep into her channel, intent on finishing the private dance they had begun on the deck of the Hazy Rebel. "Love me," Hardin whispered before covering Mac's mouth with his, tongue sweeping deep, sliding over hers. He groaned, then pulled back to look deep into her eyes. His soul connected with hers, led sweetly to what they both wanted, what they both needed, taking care of them both.

He swept the damp hair back from her temples. She was feral-looking and glistened as they lounged among the tangled sheets. Like him, her chest still rose heavily from their follow-up ardor in her bed.

Hardin was pretty sure his full heart was evident in the smile he gave her. His thumb pressed gently on her lower swollen lip. "I love you."

Mac's eyes grew shiny. She sat up cross-legged, the sheets bunched in her lap, and reached for him. Her hands cupped his neck and drew him close. "I love you." Her kiss was so tender it brought tears to his eyes.

They beheld each other for a few minutes, grinning like goofs. His stomach growled and she burst out laughing.

"Hungry?" She lifted an eyebrow.

"I am. You've depleted my stores, woman."

"And you depleted mine. Bacon and eggs and hash browns?"

"Sounds incredible. A veritable feast."

"Uh-huh. I need to rinse off first."

As much as Hardin had enjoyed showering with Mac the last time—okay, having sex with her—the tiny stall had been dangerously tight. "You first, then me. I'll help you cook."

She gave him a saucy look before disappearing into the bathroom. "Yes, you will."

The smells emanating from the kitchen made him salivate. Hardin entered, shirtless but wearing his shorts. In contrast, Mac, her thick waves in a large clip, wore only a shirt—his shirt, which barely covered her shapely ass. His mouth watered, wanting more of her.

Mac let Hardin know she knew he was there when she bent over and answered his silent question of whether she wore anything underneath. Nope.

She turned and winked, kissing him when he was next to her, and handed him a knife. "Come be my sous chef, handsome." Half of a red pepper and a small section of fresh broccoli covered the cutting board. "Small pieces please. Tell me about fly-fishing with our son." She pulled a grater and a smaller, thinner board out of the drawer and started on a chunk of cheese. "Havarti okay with you?"

"Perfect." He began cutting the veggies. "He's incredible! The whole day was magical. Fly-fishing was peaceful. Cathartic." He paused and glanced at her, smiling, his eyes glowing. "Stowe caught a fish. He was so excited yet so humble, Mac. I caught one, puny he said, but we got a picture of it."

Hardin put down the knife and trotted out of the kitchen and returned with his phone. "See?" His voice was musical as he showed her the photo. "He started calling me Bro."

Mac broke into a huge smile. The picture wasn't just of Hardin and his first fish, but of him and Stowe with the puny catch. Both of them were beaming.

"Hardin," she said softly, hugging him around the waist with her free arm.

Hardin glanced downward and blinked his eyes rapidly. His voice was scratchy. "Stowe asked if he could be in it. Our first picture together."

"Will you send it to me?"

"I will. He asked for a copy."

I'll get prints and have it framed for each of them. She wrapped the unused block of cheese and returned it to the refrigerator, coming back with an assortment of berries. "These will go nicely with our midnight meal." Mac emptied them into a small colander in the sink to rinse and drain.

Hardin set his phone down and turned, leaning against the counter, crossing one ankle over the other. "Tell me about dinner at Issa and Doc's—that's her husband's name, right? I want to meet them."

"How about tomorrow?"

"It is tomorrow. You mean today?"

"Yes. Today. For coffee. Would you be okay with that?"

"Absolutely. We're both going to need some. Are you working today?"

"It's my day off, but I'll probably go in for a few hours and help. We're slammed."

"I'll help too."

"Thank you for that, babe." Mac cleared her throat. "In a nutshell, I told them you're Stowe's father. That you didn't know about him because I left Illinois when I discovered I was pregnant. And that you've been looking for me for forever and found me and that was all I wanted to say. Then we had dinner."

"Mike probed, but I didn't say much other than to confirm what you'd shared, I think. Everyone wants to know more."

"I'd prefer not to share until Stowe has all the story, in age-appropriate terms of course, and his questions answered. But, realistically, that's not going to happen. Everyone is dying to know. We'll just have to caution everyone to be sensitive. Thoughtful. Patient."

"If Mike is any indication, you're right. I'm one hundred percent on board with you. You lead. I'll follow." He spiked his fingers through his dark waves. "I'm really trying to do my best here, honey."

"I know you are," she said softly. "Open."

He opened his mouth. She slipped a raspberry into it, then followed with a blueberry, brushing the pad of her finger slowly across his lips and giving him an impish smile as she licked it. "To stave off the hunger while things cook." She returned her attention to the cooktop, adding coconut oil to the cast-iron skillet and turning the flame on medium-low.

It was a total turn-on cooking with her, being playfully seduced. Hardin approached her from behind. "Ready for the veggies?"

"Yep."

He added them to the melted oil and then slid his arms around her trim waist, resting his chin lightly on top of her head. "Smells good." His body stirred and he pressed his arousal into the small of her back. "Feels delicious," he said, growling softly.

"We're near an open flame. Behave yourself, sir."

"Kind of matches what's going on inside me, honey."

"Well, as sorry as I am to say it, you need to bank that flame of yours and eat. I can't have you quitting on me later," she said lightly.

Hardin pulled her back from the cooktop and turned her to face him. His hands framed her face and his expression was intense. "I'll never quit on you, Mac. Never."

She kissed him so tenderly it made his breath catch, and then he became lost as it sparked into hungry and hot.

The smell of charring meat and potatoes snapped them out of their kiss.

"Oh no!" She shut off the burners under the bacon and hash browns and inspected them. They had just begun to burn. Mac flipped the bacon and stirred the potatoes. "A little done, but crisis averted. Can you get the plates and forks? Upper-left cabinet. Drawer below it."

Hardin chuckled while he got the plates and forks. "Eggs?"

"Hold on." She ripped off a paper towel and laid it on the top plate, then scraped the sautéed vegetables on top to drain. "Ready."

Hardin emptied the egg mixture into the pan and Mac stirred, adding the cheese and cooked vegetables after the eggs were fluffy. He licked his lips as she divided the vegetable scramble onto the plates, giving one plate clearly more. She did the same with the potatoes and bacon, then pulled two white ramekins from another cabinet and filled them to almost overflowing with the berries.

"Water?" she asked, filling a glass carafe. "We can eat at the island."

"Do you have anything against eating in bed?"

His voice was teasing, easy, but the question caught her off guard. Her body tightened in response. Since she'd left Illinois, eating was done in the kitchen or outside. A strict rule in her home, stemming from growing up and sharing a mobile home of six hundred square feet, of being on top of one another, of always trying to find an area clear of clutter, bugs, and dirt.

"Honey? Are you okay?"

"Y-yes."

"You're not. We can eat at the island. I thought…"

Mac felt awful seeing how confused he was, not sure what he had done to upset her. She inhaled, mentally shaking the memory, and put on a bright smile before leading the way to her room with her plate and fork. He followed with his and the carafe of water.

They set their plates on the nightstand, and after fluffing the pillows, they leaned against the headboard. It was nice. Intimate. The room was dark, lit by the bathroom vanity light.

"Hold on, honey." Hardin had shucked his shorts to join her in bed but padded around her bedroom.

Mesmerized, her eyes followed Hardin's naked form as he moved with lean athletic grace, his corded muscles gliding over each other as he searched for something. "Matches?"

"Yes."

She reached into her drawer and handed them to him. "Here."

"Perfect," he said, lighting the two candles she had lit the other night on her dresser, then turning off the vanity light and climbing into the bed, pulling her over next to him, handing Mac her plate. "It's been twelve years since I picnicked by candlelight, since I made love to you, Mac." Hardin's eyes shone and he pulled the clip from her hair, then he kissed her tenderly. "Let's make this a regular thing."

"Yes," she said, smiling through her tears.

Fingers trailing over her skin woke Mac. She had no idea how long she'd slept having crashed hard, full from their midnight breakfast and sated from making love. "Hey." Her voice was full of sleep. Light from the waning moon streamed in through the window, allowing her to see him more clearly than in the candlelight earlier.

"Hey yourself. Didn't mean to wake you. I'm having a difficult time not touching you. Your shoulders are beautiful, but then every inch of you is."

"Thank you."

"Did you know that you do this puff-snore thing?"

Mac laughed and flipped over from being on her stomach. "I do?"

"Uh-huh. No one's ever told you that?"

"I've never—" She rubbed her eyes then stretched her

218

arms over her head, noting how his eyes raked over her nakedness. "Um, I haven't slept with someone. I was waiting to sleep with someone I loved, and I had this little sidekick."

"Stowe," he said, smiling.

"Yes."

He was on his side, propped up by his elbow, his chin resting on his fisted hand, observing her. "But you've had sex with other guys."

"Yes."

"And you with women."

"Yeah," he said, his eyes dropping to her full breasts, then rising to lock with hers as his fingers traced lazily over the quivering skin of her stomach. "I got involved with a woman a few years back."

"The Spanish superstar."

"Yeah."

"Did you? Did you love her, Hardin?"

"No. It was—" He grimaced and ran a hand roughly over his face, then searched her eyes. "Enlightening. In retrospect, I learned a lot about myself, and my relationship with her clarified my need to find you. You were so fucking difficult to find."

Mac sat up and pulled the sheet up to her chest.

Hardin sat up and faced her, the sheet pooling in his lap. He took a deep breath and exhaled. "I was expected back in Spain this week. When I told you I wanted out, I meant it. Now, after finding you. Discovering I'm a father, well, I'm even more determined."

She reached out and took his hands, playing with his fingers as she talked. "Baby, I don't want to be the reason you quit. I don't want Stowe to be the reason you quit either. You're still at your peak."

His grin was cocky, and a teasing light filled his eyes. "You watch me."

"I've never missed a game," she whispered, her eyes filling and chin trembling.

His swallow was audible, and he pulled her into his arms. Hardin's heart beat rapidly against hers and his voice cracked. "How I wish you'd been there for every game, with our son. It would have been unbelievable."

"Stowe watches too. You've always been his favorite player. He loves to point out you share the name Ambrose. I'm so, so sorry. I never meant to rob you."

"You didn't." Hardin separated from Mac and bracketed her face in his hands, his expression earnest. "You protected him. You protected yourself. And unintentionally, you protected me. You've sacrificed so much."

She watched him fight for composure and it tore at her heart. "What are you feeling?"

"Frustrated. Angrier than I've ever been in my life."

She pulled back. Her eyes met his. "With me?"

"No, not you. Never you. I'm forever grateful. For bringing Stowe into this world. For giving him a wonderful life. For being an incredibly loving and nurturing mother. Protecting him. I love watching you with him, absorbing your relationship with each other. It's beautiful. I hope in time I can have something similar with him, that I can gain his trust and respect."

"You already have those."

"His love."

"It will come. Trust me."

"Stowe's amazing," he said, choking on his tears. "How can I possibly thank you for all you've done?"

"I don't do it for thanks. I do it because I love him more than I've ever loved in my life. He's my world, Hardin."

He wiped at his face. "I understand that. I'm fumbling here, because… because… I love him too. It's hit me like a fuckin' Mack truck." His eyes, wrought and turbulent with emotion, held hers. "I love you so much I can't begin to even put the words together. But what I feel for him, it's beyond what I feel for you. I—"

Mac pulled his hands to her lips and kissed them and smiled at him, tears streaming down her face. "Yes. That's right. You love him fiercely."

"Yeah, it's unreal. Fierce. Right here," he said, hitting his chest with a closed fist. "Raw. I want to be part of your world, honey. Of yours and his, and you and him, mine. I'd do anything for you and him."

"How? You just signed a new contract. That puts you in Europe for a minimum of two more years. Piñon Ridge is his home. Our home. My business. We can't move."

"I'm not asking you to. I would never consider uprooting him from what he knows. Arlo—"

"Your friend that just arrived."

Hardin nodded. "He's more than a friend. Arlo is also my agent."

Mac nodded, pulling her hair back from her face. Things were becoming even more complicated. "Why is he here exactly?" Fear jumped around in her heart.

"The shit's hitting the fan. I didn't show up for training and missed several team meetings. The fines are racking up." He shrugged and leaned in toward her, sounding incredibly calm for what he was sharing. "Rumors are rife in the league because I haven't responded to calls or texts. I've been off the grid. Arlo left me some thirty messages demanding to know where I was. His tone eventually changed to worry that something bad had happened to me. Anyway, I finally called him. Told him to leave me the fuck alone. I needed space. He flew out of his own accord, thinking he could talk me back into returning to Spain, to the club. He's staying in my suite since nothing else is available. Well, maybe tonight he ended up with your friend. They were eye-fucking each other." He snapped his fingers as if he were trying to remember.

"Emory."

"Yeah."

Mac chuckled. "Well, that would be interesting. He seems to be a player."

"He is."

"Em has no tolerance for players. She'll eat him up and spit him out."

"You think so? I want to be around for that."

"Oh yeah, but back to what you were saying."

"Hm. I told Arlo everything. He's gone through the contract and has scheduled a time for us to talk with the owners. It's ironclad. Contracts can only be terminated for three reasons. When they expire. If both parties, that would be me and the owners, mutually agree. Or for just cause. Since I just re-signed, expiration is off the table. We believe the best option is pursuing mutual agreement cloaked in the just cause since I've been absent and at this time refuse to return to my club. That would set up a series of steps to terminate my contract."

"Hardin, what you're talking about is beyond my comprehension. Would you be okay financially?"

"It's all negotiable, but yes, I'm more than fine even if I incur the penalties being levied and have to forfeit the contract salary. I don't live wild and beyond my means, despite what the tabloids report. I want to discuss them, my finances, with you."

"I—"

"You more or less brought them up when Stowe and I went to Intrepid before fly-fishing."

"Yes, but—"

"Hear me out, okay? Let's focus on Stowe and then go from there." He gave her a long look and raised his brows.

Mac pursed her lips, wholly uncomfortable, then nodded. Money was just something she simply didn't discuss with anyone, other than Intrepid's with Cori.

"I'd like to set up a trust for Stowe and any other kids we have."

Any other kids we have.

"Mac?"

"Yes?"

"You seemed to drift off. We can talk later. I know you've got to be tired. I tasked Arlo with getting something drafted through my attorneys. Since he's here, I might as well have him work. All this has been churning in my mind. Taking care of Stowe. And you."

"You're serious."

"Babe, I'm not letting go of you or our son. Our future is us. Hopefully an expanded version of us."

Mac's body shook as she wept.

"Honey?"

"I… I… I don't know what to say."

"Maybe yes? Will you have me, Mac? I love you and I love our son. I can't imagine going forward without you. Will you spend the rest of your life with me?"

Chapter Twenty-Five

LATER THAT MORNING, Hardin and Mac sat in the coveted corner of the Grind's patio under a large umbrella, a spot Kai was known for leaving a RESERVED sign on during peak times for her closest friends. Issa and Doc sat across from them at the round six-top, alternately sipping their coffee, eating fresh-baked scones and breakfast sandwiches, and engaging in light conversation. The morning rush was over and the patio empty except for their table.

Issa and Doc were the parents Mac never had. Hardin was delighted for her and for Stowe, who benefited from being grandparented so lovingly. He had accompanied Issa and Doc to the Grind, hugging Mac and high-fiving Hardin. Stowe sat contentedly at the table after wolfing down an egg-and-sausage burrito, two mini blueberry muffins, and cranberry juice.

Beckett joined them, his eyes bouncing between Hardin and Stowe. "Morning! Mom and Dad are coming as soon as Harper shows up. She's watching the twins this morning." He sat and attacked his breakfast burrito with gusto, chasing it down with swigs of chocolate milk, not saying much until several other boys appeared and asked him and Stowe to play basketball at the nearby park.

"Can I?" Beckett asked his grandparents.

"Don't see why not," Issa said.

Doc added, "Be back by noon, Beck. We'll have your sisters by then."

"Yes, Paw-Paw."

"Can I, Mom?"

Mac smiled, relenting easily. "Go, you silly boy."

"Are you okay if I play, Bro?" Stowe's eyes landed on his father.

Hardin was stunned, never expecting to be asked. "Sure. I'm on board with your mom."

"Cool!" Stowe began to leave and turned back to him. "Noon?"

Mac nodded ever so slightly in Hardin's peripheral.

"That would be great, sport."

Stowe spun and raced out to the sidewalk to join his waiting friends, a huge smile on his face.

Mac squeezed Hardin's hand under the table. His response was an enormous smile.

Doc lifted the carafe Kai had left on the table. His bright blue eyes flitted to Issa. "More coffee, dear?"

Issa nodded at her husband. "Please."

"Kenna?"

"I'm good for now."

"Hardin?"

Hardin pushed his mug a few inches closer to Doc. "Thanks."

226

Cori and Mike came in through the patio, carrying steaming mugs of coffee and plates with burritos and sandwiches. Everyone exchanged greetings as Cori and Mike joined the table.

"Beck just left with the Madrick and James boys. They're playing basketball," Doc informed them. "He'll be at our place by noon."

Cori stretched, then slouched in her seat. "Thanks again for watching the kids."

"No thanks necessary," Issa said.

Doc topped off his coffee and sat back, draping his arm over his wife's shoulders, scrutinizing Mac and Hardin in turn.

Issa sat up straighter, looking expectant, encouraging them with a warm smile. "Well, now that our grandsons have left and we have the patio to ourselves, we'd like to hear your story."

Issa, Doc, Cori, and Mike appeared aghast after listening to Mac and Hardin share the facts. How they had met in high school and their friendship had evolved into love. The destruction of her phone after what ended up being their last night together before he left for college and the explanation of Mac not knowing Hardin's number. Alicia's threat of charging Hardin with statutory rape. His parents' payoff to Alicia for her silence and compliance. The NDA. The restraining orders. The subsequent rescinding of Mac's full ride to NCU. The last-minute change of Hardin's winter-break plans.

Mac also weaved in meeting Carol at the pregnancy clinic, borrowing money from Alicia to fund her escape with the life she carried, not knowing until Hardin told her that the money was bribe money. She also shared for the first time her previous name with Issa and Doc and why she legally changed it to Eliot, surprising Hardin.

He should have known. He'd figured out the significance of Stowe's name—their time in Stowe, Vermont, during high school, when they had first expressed their love for one another. Like Stowe's name, Eliot was of special meaning. T. S. Eliot was one of her favorite poets, one of the numerous poets whose works they had read to one another and discussed at length on dates. Many of his fans and teammates would probably be amused to know what a nerd Hardin actually was under the cloak of his exceptional prowess and skill.

Doc, Cori, and Mike knew about Mac's life since she arrived in Piñon Ridge. Hardin still had some catching up to do.

Cori was the first to speak after Mac and Hardin finished their story. "Wow. Should we continue calling you Kenna?"

"Yes please."

"But Hardin calls you Mac."

"Consider it one of my terms of endearment, Cori." Hardin gently rubbed Mac's shoulder.

A furrow was evident between Mike's brows. "Hardin, you shared your intentions when we went fishing. Kenna, what do you want?"

"I want what Hardin wants. To be together. To raise Stowe and any other children we are blessed with as a family." Her gaze and soft smile touched each of them. "We've got some things to work through, Hardin more than me. He's working on that now."

"How can we support you?" Issa asked, her hazel eyes looking from Mac to Hardin.

"Please keep what we've told you in confidence. We haven't had the opportunity to talk with Stowe. Be patient with us. With Hardin. Especially with Stowe," Mac said, her eyes roving over the people she loved as family.

Hardin made some additional requests. "Give us grace and space. Understand that we may mess up. That the situation may get stressful at times. We don't know how this is going to go, other than we want to be together as a family. Just know we appreciate your support."

Cori's eyes grew huge and full of tears. She wailed. "Oh God. Kenna are you moving?"

"No," Mac said, pulling her into a hug.

"I'm moving," Hardin said in a quiet voice that commanded their attention and had them looking at him. "Here."

"Wow." Cori stared at him. "When?"

"Immediately."

Her expression changed to disbelief. "You're quitting?"

"Retiring."

Issa and Doc were quiet, considering.

"I know you have to get to work, Cori. Mike." Hardin stood and then held Mac's chair as she rose.

"I'll be in later, Cori."

"It's your day off."

"Yeah, but we're swamped. I need to be there. I'll come in for a few hours until things ease up."

"I'm available to help as well." Hardin slid his arm around Mac's shoulders and grinned from her to Cori. "Kind of a win-win."

Mac elbowed him in the ribs playfully.

"Thanks, Hardin. I appreciate it. *We* appreciate it."

Doc, Issa, Mike and Cori got to their feet to leave as well.

"Kenna?"

Mac glanced at Issa. "Yes?"

"With all that's transpired, it seems a good idea to let you know Carol's arriving this afternoon. Of course, it's up to you if you want to keep her arrival a surprise for Stowe."

Mac clapped her hands together and chortled happily. "I think I will. He's going to be so excited! I can't wait to see her! For how long?" She shook her head. "I mean, for how long is she staying?"

"A month. I'm hoping we can talk her into longer. We won't say anything to the children. Doc's going to go retrieve her from Denver after lunch. We thought we'd have a family dinner at our place tomorrow night."

Mac's face was lit up. "I'll bring some of my brownies. And some ice cream. Or maybe the kids could make some?"

"If it's not too much trouble, dear. Making ice cream would keep the kids busy, and it's so good when it's fresh." Issa gazed warmly at Hardin. "We'd love for you to join us."

"I'm looking forward to it! Thanks."

Chapter Twenty Six

THE SOUND OF knocking roused Hardin from his catnap. The small blocks of sleep interlaced among the waking hours were taking their toll on him, but missing out on time with Mac or Stowe wasn't something he was going to do. He glanced at his watch and grimaced, then pulled the pillow over his head and hoped whoever was at the door would go away. It was late afternoon, but he still had plenty of time to shower before Stowe arrived. His son… Hardin smiled to himself.

An impromptu lunch with Stowe and Mac had been a success, followed up with helping Stowe fix the chain on his bike. Hardin could see he had earned a measure of respect from his son. Baby steps.

Stowe had been called away again by friends, to the pool this time, but before he left, he had volunteered to come get Hardin before dinner, under the guise of giving him a personal tour of his stomping ground. Mac had smiled her approval.

Lunch, and being up most of the night with Mac, had left him groggy. It was evident that she was tired too, so they'd parted ways in order to rest up. They planned on another night together after Stowe was settled in at Issa and Doc's. Mac shared Stowe would be even more excited when he saw that Carol—his other grandmother—was there too. He hadn't seen her since she had visited over Christmas and the New Year.

The knocking grew more insistent. Hardin really wanted his last fifteen minutes. If it was Arlo, he was going to chew his ass out. Cognizant of his passion and booming voice during negotiations, Arlo had left to use one of the private offices on the first floor of the inn to call the owners. He was determined to hammer out something in the best interest of his client and friend.

Hardin shuffled out to the spacious, cozy common room that connected both masters, wearing a very wrinkled club tee and practice shorts. He glanced out the floor-to-ceiling glass doors that led out to the balcony and saw that the sun was descending behind the peaks, casting long shadows over ski slopes that were empty in the summer except for occasional hikers traversing them between the forests bordering the runs.

More knocking drew his attention to the suite door that opened to the hall. The thick wood door actually trembled from the force.

"Hardin?"

The pit of his stomach sank, and he stopped in the middle of the living room, shaking his head free of sleep-induced cobwebs. *What the fuck?* He had to be imagining this.

"Hardin?"

What in fuck is he doing here?

"Hardin?"

Goddammit. Both of them. Fucking hell. He inhaled deeply, mentally preparing himself before opening the door.

"Mother. Father." He was too stunned to say anything else but knew his scowl and flexing jaw communicated his displeasure. And that he didn't give a rat's ass.

"Hardin," his father Nathan said, all business, moving past Hardin and into his suite.

His mother trailed her husband, pausing to try to kiss Hardin on his cheek. It was awkward. She missed, her chaste kiss glancing his chin.

Her cool blue eyes assessed him. "Were you in bed?"

Hardin rubbed his face. Closing his eyes as his hand moved over them, praying for patience and civility. He studied her and then his father, who watched him carefully. "I was sleeping."

"It's the middle of the day, Hardin."

"I realize that, Mother. What are you doing here?"

"We—"

Nathan said, "Diane, I'll take it from here."

Dutifully admonished, Diane settled her wisp-thin body on one of the barstools at the counter, facing her husband and son, smoothing out her linen sheath. She fiddled with her pearl necklace as if it were a rosary.

"We've become aware that you haven't shown up for training." Nathan's green eyes bored into Hardin's aqua ones.

Hardin grimaced at his father. "You know I'm an adult, right? You also know that you have no business in my affairs."

"Do not speak to your father like that or in that tone, Hardin."

"Mother, I'm not a child. The two of you showing up

233

here unannounced is"—he raked his fingers through his unruly hair and moved his tense jaw around—"not welcome. I thought I made it clear the last time I saw you that I'd let you know when I want to see you. How did you know where I was anyway?"

Nathan cleared his throat and rocked back on his heels, wearing a smug expression on his face. "I have my sources."

"We do," Diane parroted from her perch, amending her statement after a cool look from Nathan. "Your father does."

"You've been seen cavorting with a local woman. She looks remarkably similar to that girl you took up with in high school."

"Cavorting?" The need to protect Mac and Stowe roared forth. Hardin frowned at his father. "I date women," he said offhandedly, hoping the simple statement and its tone was a diversion, but also very much aware of his father's uncanny ability to read people.

"I understand that you've been seeing only her. It concerns us, especially since you're absent from training." Nathan stared pointedly at Hardin.

"Who I see is none of your goddamned business. Neither is what I do or why I do it. Why don't you and Mother get on your plane and hop back to wherever you flew in from?"

"Insolence doesn't become you, Hardin. We raised you better than that."

It was all he could do to not roll his eyes.

Nathan pulled some papers from the inside of his navy silk blazer. "These are all over social media. Is this woman that same girl from high school?"

Hardin's fury unleashed. "She has a name, Father. But you wouldn't wish to remember it, would you?" He heard his mother's sharp intake of breath but kept going. "And yes, she is the same girl whose mother you paid off. The same girl you slapped with not one but two restraining orders. The same girl you fucked over time and time again! I overheard you bragging to your cronies about having her full ride to NCU rescinded. Did you get off—"

His mother clutched her pearls. "Hardin!"

"We did you a favor," Nathan said angrily.

"Are you fucking kidding me?" he asked, raging. "The hell you did!"

"Do not speak to your father like that!"

Hardin waved at his mother dismissively, then snarled, "Sorry."

"Once a whore, always a whore, Hardin." Diane's face was pinched in fury. "She's a gold digger, beneath your status. You cannot love her!"

"I loved her. I love her still."

"Bro—"

Hardin's head whipped from his parents, locking eyes with the frightened eyes of Stowe, who was standing in the doorway. The door must have been left cracked open. *Fucking Christ.* "Stowe," he whispered.

"Who is that?" Nathan demanded, his face contorted in an ugly mask.

In the moment Hardin glanced at his father and then back, Stowe had disappeared.

Nathan stared at the empty space and frowned. "I thought I heard something."

"You're tired, dear. And all this stress Hardin is putting us through—"

Hardin glared at his mother and ran to the door, throwing it open and looking in both directions. The hall was empty.

How much of the nasty argument had Stowe heard? Jesus Christ. Hardin spun, zeroing in on his parents. "Get the hell out of here!" he shouted, sprinting past them and into the bedroom.

Mac was on speed dial. He held the phone to his ear while he slipped on his socks and tied his gym shoes. The call went to her voice mail.

Breathlessly he said, "Baby, call me."

His parents were still there when Hardin came back out to the common room. "GET. THE. FUCK. OUT." He seethed, pointing to the door. "NOW!" It was all he could do to wait on them to exit.

His parents walked stonily toward the elevator, heads held high as if nothing was amiss. He pocketed the electronic key card and slammed the door behind him, taking the stairs down to the ground floor as fast as he dared.

Stowe was nowhere to be seen. Darkening clouds were gathering over the peaks. The need to find his son intensified.

A driver waited next to a black town car, he presumed for his parents.

Fuck them.

An hour and a half later, Hardin stood on a sidewalk in the center of Piñon Ridge, anxiety eating a hole in him. The clouds over the peaks continued to build, appearing more menacing. He'd had no luck finding Stowe, but then PR was big enough to disappear in, especially for an eleven-year-old who knew every nook and cranny.

Hardin was uncertain why he thought he would be able to find Stowe on his own. In reality, he barely knew this young boy, his son. His hope of dealing with what had transpired had outweighed his common sense. Not hearing back from Mac made it worse. He tried her again. It went to voice mail. "Call me."

Maybe Stowe was with her, telling her about the argument. Is that what an eleven-year-old boy would do? Hardin had no idea, but he wasn't going to wait to find out. He dialed Mac again as he ran in the direction of her house. She picked up.

"Mac."

"You sound out of breath."

"Where have you been?"

"Outside. You miss me? I have multiple calls from you, and it looks like... two voice mails."

He was on her street. "I've been calling you for over an hour."

"I was gardening and putting Stowe's stuff away. There's bad weather coming."

"Is he with you?" Her house was up ahead.

"No... I thought he was with you. Hardin?"

"He isn't. I-I'm at your house." He hung up.

Mac met him at the door. "What the hell is going on?"

"I can't find him." Running and fear made his words choppy. "He took off over an hour and a half ago. I can't find him anywhere."

"What do you mean? Wasn't he with you?"

"He showed up but disappeared almost immediately, upset. It scared me. I wasn't sure what to do. I left you a message right away and then began searching for him in town. Does he have a phone?"

"He does." She called Stowe's phone. It rang from his room. "Shit. I guess he was charging it."

Hardin pursed his lips, trying to make sense of the situation, and exhaled heavily. "I see. When was the last time you saw him?"

"When he left to go meet you. What's going on, Hardin?"

"My parents are here. They were in my suite when Stowe came."

"What?"

"Yeah. Surprise," he said sarcastically. "Why, I don't know. Other than to insert themselves where they aren't welcome. We got into it. I'm not going to lie. It was ugly, babe. I'm not sure how much Stowe heard, but he did hear." His voice cracked with emotion when he recalled the image of Stowe's frightened eyes locking with his. "I saw it in his face, and then he was gone. I looked for him." He wiped at his damp eyes and whispered, "I couldn't find him."

"Welcome to parenting, babe. Worrying is one of its cornerstones." Mac's quick smile didn't mask her concern. She dialed another number. "He'll be home before dinner. You'll see."

Mac's call to Cori, who questioned Beck and Mike, turned up nothing. Neither of them had seen Stowe. Beck checked with his and Stowe's circle of friends. None of them had seen or heard from Stowe either.

The dinner hour came and went. Hardin helped Mac put away the uneaten food and clean up the kitchen. Worry evolved into palpable anxiety as darkness cloaked Piñon Ridge. Lightning bolted across the sky and the wind picked up, shifting one way and then another, indecisive.

Mac's phone rang and she hurriedly answered, not looking at the screen. "Stowe?" she asked excitedly.

Hardin observed her crestfallen face. "Mike. Hi," she said quietly, stilted, then, "Yes."

"Mac…"

Her eyes were full of tears and distress, and her lips trembled when she looked at him.

"Mike volunteers with PCRG. He said to call 911. The sheriff will activate an immediate search." Mac's hand shook as she dialed. When dispatch answered on the other end, she broke into weeping.

Hardin gently took the phone and put it up to his ear, gathering Mac onto his lap, stroking her hair, kissing her forehead. "Hello. Yes. I'm calling about my son. Our son." He took a shuddering breath. "He's missing."

⌒⌒

As soon as Hardin hung up with dispatch, Mike called. "The sheriff has activated a search. We're leaving immediately."

Hardin put the call on speaker so that Mac could be part of the conversation as Mike reviewed the pertinent information he'd been given by the sheriff's office.

"We'll find him, Kenna. Hardin. Stowe's been taught to stay in place if anything should happen. The team knows where to look. We'll be in touch."

Lightning flared and flashed, almost dying into nothingness before again slashing jagged, bright branches across the churning sky. Thunder boomed in the distance, testing Mac's and Hardin's fragile hold on their composure.

Cori, Issa, Doc, and another woman Hardin assumed was Carol, filed in through the front porch.

Kenna stood, her brow furrowed and her eyes glassy.

Hardin rose with her, accepting a hug from Cori after she released Mac.

"Beck's watching a movie with the girls. He connected the dots when Mike got called up. I had to come give you guys hugs, encourage you, as hard as it is, to stay positive. Stowe's a smart kid. Mike, Emory, and the team will find him and bring him safely home." She glanced up at the sky. "This is going to open up any second. I've got to get back and be with the kids. I love you."

"I love you too," Mac said, her chin trembling.

Issa hugged both of them, as did Doc. The woman with graying brown hair and soulful brown eyes was next, wrapping Mac into a massive hug. "Hi, sweetie. I'm sorry this is happening. He's okay."

"I'm so glad you're here, Carol. This is Hardin, Stowe's father."

Carol released Mac and approached Hardin. "May I?" she asked, sliding her arm around in a side hug.

Her touch was soothing. The contrast between his mother's cool touches and Carol's warm comfort couldn't have been more disparate. The support Mac had in this town was what every person should have, and he was grateful it was being extended to him.

"This is a lot, isn't it? Issa and Doc brought me up to speed. I'm happy to meet you, Hardin. I just wish it wasn't under this circumstance. What do you know?"

The sky opened up and hail rained down, bouncing off the house and yard in fury. Hardin shared the details again with the captive audience of Carol, Issa, Doc, and Mac huddled around the small kitchen table. Hardin rubbed Mac's back, who leaned into him. Doc clasped

240

his wife's and Carol's hands, and the women in turn held Mac's and Hardin's.

Doc bowed his head, the dusting of his white hair resembling a halo. "Let's hold our boy in this circle of hope and love. Pray he comes home safe and sound. Soon."

Chapter Twenty Seven

S TOWE CAME TO, chilled to the bone and sopping wet in the dark, shivering in waves, the scree and sharp stones covering the uneven ground biting into his back. He tried to sit up, but the pain in his head made him dizzy and nauseous. Remembering some of the basic first aid his mom and Uncle Mike had drilled into him, he turned his head just before the meager contents from his stomach spewed forth. He wiped at his mouth carefully. Every movement hurt. His left ankle and left arm felt like they were on fire.

His surroundings came into focus. He was at the Zoo, a popular low rocky outcrop on the outskirts of Piñon Ridge where he, Beck, and a lot of other local kids liked to go bouldering. He remembered how he got here.

After tearing out of the Urban, Stowe's fear and confusion about what he had heard between Hardin and the horrible old people morphed into anger. He had turned north. Stomping, then running. When Stowe's initial anger was spent, he had slowed to walking, not having a plan, not paying attention to time, eventually finding himself on the outskirts of Piñon Ridge at one of the closed mines.

The temperature had dropped noticeably, and the wind picked up. Goose bumps covered his bare arms.

Glancing up, he saw the thick, angry clouds swelling above the peaks and moving over PR quickly. Thunder boomed and lightning forked across the sky. There was nowhere to shelter in the open, but the Zoo was close. If he could get to the Perch—the natural indentation under the topmost overhang where he and his friends like to sit out of the sun and take a breather from bouldering—before the storm broke, he'd be safe. Stowe ran toward it.

He had almost reached the Perch when the first fat raindrops splattered on the crag. His hold slipped and his ankle twisted under his weight. Stowe screamed in pain and dropped, hitting the ground hard, unprotected by a helmet or any crash pads. There had been more pain and then nothing.

Now it was twilight. The storm had moved on, and in the diffuse light he could see the sky awash with stars and the moon waning to its full quarter phase. Scorpio was easy to pick out, and he focused on the long string of bright stars, drawn to the one that looked red. Antares, he thought. Or was it Aries? Stowe was having trouble remembering, his mind jumbled and fuzzy. He had chosen astronomy as one of his science modules last year, begging for a telescope after he finished the class, so enthralled was he with the topic. His mom couldn't afford what he wanted but promised to contribute to his telescope fund. He had pooled his birthday money and was still saving what he earned from odd jobs. Mom. She was the best. A tear slid down his temple. Then more. What if they didn't find him? No one knew where he was. *Stupid.* He knew better than to go out of PR by himself. It was one of his mom's foremost rules, and she had a long list of them.

Trying to calm himself, Stowe studied the skies some more, his eyes latching onto something that seemed familiar. Triangle. Season. The Summer Triangle, that's right. His mom had shared some myth about a goddess and a mortal forbidden to see each other. She had looked so sad, he remembered. What were their names? Vega and Altair. Stowe yawned. He was so tired and gave in to the need to sleep.

When Stowe woke again, he was cold. So cold and still drowsy. The stars and moon were brighter now. His head pounded like a jackhammer, and his whole body cramped painfully because of the shivering. Yeah, he'd been so upset hearing the argument. The words. The anger. The things they'd said about his mom. They hated her. How could anyone hate his mom? He should have stayed, but his fear drove him away and now he was in trouble. He prayed his mom and dad would find him. Mom *and* Dad. Stowe smiled and succumbed to sleep again.

"Mike! I found him!" Emory shouted, jogging toward the Zoo.

As mission coordinator, Mike had directed the team to stage their vehicles and other equipment on the old mining road, feeling it was the best place to search from. The surrounding area—replete with crags; boulder formations; and abandoned, boarded-up mines—was a favorite of local kids for bouldering, fishing, tanning, and hooking up. Their rescue group had responded to numerous calls to this place over the years.

The team secured the litter on the ATV they had brought in addition to the emergency response vehicle. They were going to have to carry Stowe out.

Mike ran toward Emory, who was kneeling next to an

unmoving form on the ground. They were speaking quietly. That was a good sign.

He knelt next to her and began assessing his nephew. "Hey, buddy. I'm going to ask you questions, check you out. All right if I touch you?"

"Uncle Mike," Stowe said, smiling through another wave of shivering, then grimacing. "Sure, just be careful. I hurt."

Mike gently pushed the wet dark mop off his nephew's face. "Tell me where."

Mike called Kenna as soon as Stowe was en route to the hospital, letting her and Hardin know their son was on his way to Peaks County for further evaluation. He shared his field assessment that Stowe was concussed, had sustained fractures of both bones in his forearm, and probably had a sprained ankle.

"He's going to be okay. Have Doc drive you. Please. You're too emotional to be behind the wheel. I'll meet you there."

The sun was rising when Mac and Hardin arrived back at her house. Mac was out the minute her head hit the pillow. At the hospital they'd been told they could probably bring Stowe home in a few days.

Their son had indeed fractured both bones in his forearm, but they didn't affect his growth plates or require surgery. Stowe would be in a cast for three to four weeks. In addition, he'd sustained a serious concussion that warranted ongoing monitoring and treatment. None of the bones in his ankle were broken, but Stowe had sprained it and would be following the RICE protocol during his one- to three-week recovery. Their very active son was not going to be happy following the strict resting, icing, compressing, and elevating protocol the doctors had set out. He would be more unhappy when he found out that bouldering was over for the foreseeable future, as was soccer and even riding his bike.

Hardin couldn't shut his thoughts down. He entered Mac's bathroom and stripped, stepping under the cool spray. Maybe a long shower would clear his head. In the span of a week, he had found Mac, realized the love between them was deeper than ever, and learned he had a son and come to love him in a way that was wholly unimaginable before arriving in Piñon Ridge. He would give his life for him. The events of last night had made that crystal clear.

Stowe could have died. Why had the fucking door to the hall been open? But honestly, even if it had been closed, Stowe would have overheard. He had been pissed and loud.

Guilt and responsibility weighed heavy on him. How did Mac do it, parent with such grace? He was raw, scared shitless, all too aware that he was inept in the father department. He would continue to improve, to be what Stowe needed. A knock on the shower door got his attention.

Mac cracked it open, a towel wrapped loosely around her. In a sleepy voice she asked, "Hey handsome, are you going to use up all the water?"

Hardin's blood heated as Mac opened the door farther and her smile turned naughty, her swollen eyes full of emotion. She looked exhausted.

"I know it's a tight space, but can I join you? I'll wash yours if you wash mine." Her eyes dropped to his bobbing erection. "I take it that's a yes?" The towel fell to the floor and she stepped in. "Someone left me in bed all by myself." Her hands slid over the ripped planes of his chest and abs, then traced lower, fisting him and kissing him senseless. Mac rubbed herself against him, panting.

"I thought you were out cold." He hissed through his teeth as she pumped his rigid length.

"Mm. I guess just a catnap. I need you, baby," she said, hoarse and gravelly, weeping. "Right now."

"I need you too." Hardin lifted her, cupping her ass. "Grip tight," he said as he thrust into her, wave after wave of heat consuming him as he plunged repeatedly, the water cascading over them.

She whispered, "I'm never letting go."

He looked deep into her eyes. The fever in them matched the heat coursing through his body. "Me either, honey."

Chapter Twenty Eight

STOWE ARRIVED HOME, subdued and stiff with nagging discomfort from his injuries, a cast on his arm and his ankle wrapped and immobilized. A routine came together easily. Hardin watched over him while Mac worked. Family and friends rotated through to relieve Hardin while Stowe napped, allowing him to work out, run errands, or just do nothing.

Despite being raised by parents who weren't demonstrative, Mac noted nurturing came naturally to Hardin, to the point that she had to talk to him about not catering to Stowe. Caring for him was one thing, but coddling or enabling him... Well, she wasn't going to have that.

Hardin's eyes had twinkled good-naturedly when she had chewed him out one afternoon as they snacked on ice cream Cori and Mike's kids had made the previous night.

"Got it, boss," he said, then flipped some of it off his spoon at her. It had splattered down her face and onto the exposed skin of her chest. Hardin had lapped all of it up and then escorted Mac into the bedroom where he'd taken care of the rest of her while their son napped.

Mac's heart was full to the point of bursting. She had her son home, and he was recovering beautifully. The young man she had pledged to love forever so long ago was back in her life, loving her and their son with a passion that often moved her to tears or took her breath away.

Hardin fed her soul and stepped into fatherhood with masculine grace and wisdom that their son responded to. During their one-on-one time, he had told her more than once how chill Hardin was, how much he liked him. Stowe also couldn't get over how humble he was.

"How is a guy like him so humble? I mean, he's like a big deal."

"Did you ever think that maybe he enjoys being a normal human being?"

"No! That's so cool, Mom."

"Your father puts his pants on like everyone else, one leg at a time. If he forgets that, he risks losing his soul."

Stowe's expression was thoughtful, and she hoped he'd see Hardin as the person he really was, not as the international soccer star.

Mac cheered silently from the sidelines, relishing the progress in their relationship, witnessing the way they began to seek out their own together time without her—private jokes, future plans, and the launch of father-son traditions.

While Arlo hammered out the details of the "just cause" termination with the club owners, Mac's worries turned to Hardin's parents. She found the Ambroses'

quest for control over their son appalling. She broached the subject with Hardin late one evening, after Stowe was sound asleep. They lay in her bed, snuggling, damp in the aftermath of loving one another.

Inasmuch as she had been raised in poverty, Hardin had been raised with money, born with the proverbial silver spoon in his mouth, and yet what they had in common was that they were the offspring of people who didn't view parenting as a priority. The Ambroses hadn't given up and had contacted him through their attorneys, threatening to break the trust, in essence to disown him after he blocked their calls and messages, trying to bring him to heel.

She turned to him and propped herself on her elbow, resting her chin in her hand. "What happens, Hardin? Are you going to be okay?"

"More than okay." His expression was earnest. Quietly, he said, "So will you, Stowe, and any other kids we have."

Mac sat up and reached for Hardin's discarded tee at the end of the bed. She averted her eyes, processing what he had just revealed. It was almost too much, knowing financial worries would be a thing of the past. After scraping by most of her life, more successfully after moving to Colorado and starting Intrepid, it was hard to get her head around and difficult to accept.

Hardin sat up, still naked, the sheets bunched in his lap. He gently took her chin and turned her face to his. "Honey, look at me."

She gazed into aqua eyes that were turbulent with emotion and leaned forward, kissing him softly, wanting to make it all better for him.

"Your kisses. They do so much for me, and right now

they're the balm that takes the hurt away. You help me find my strength. God, I love you."

Mac scooted closer, her folded legs nesting between his sheet-covered ones. She kissed him again, this time with heat, then drew back and pinned his eyes with hers. "I love you too, baby."

"You sure look good in my shirt even though you're swimming in it." That earned him a sexy smirk from her. His thumb brushed over her wet lips; then he smiled softly. "Like I said, I didn't burn through my salary and endorsements. I've invested and it's grown to be substantially more than it was initially. Even if my parents are successful in breaking the trust, it won't have any impact. Got that?"

"I do."

"Good. Boot those worries from your amazing mind, okay? No more worrying about money."

Mac grinned. "Boots. Oh, I like your cleats reference." She kissed him and chuckled. "Booted."

He nodded approvingly and kissed her back. "I played because I love the game. But I also played because it was a road to true independence, no strings attached. While I have my parents to thank for helping me hone the skills I have, years of training and showcases and camps with the best, I'm so fucking tired of the attached strings, the expectations. Look what's going on now, how my parents are trying to control me by holding the trust over my head. Too many have wanted a piece of Hardin Ambrose, one of the MEFL's top footballers. I became a commodity to my club, the league, the world." His voice was filled with anguish. "To my parents." His eyes searched hers and he said huskily, "All you ever wanted was me. All I've ever wanted was you."

As Stowe healed, Hardin quickly discovered their son had a sharp mind and hunger for knowledge. That included Hardin's opinions about a range of topics, including Stowe himself and his parents' history.

Hardin touched base with Mac numerous times the first day while Stowe nodded off, seeking advice on how to navigate the pointed questions and observations their son had made.

She offered very little other than "Keep me in the loop. Call if you really get stuck."

"I am stuck. You're throwing me into the frying pan, honey."

"You're not stuck. You're challenged. The frying pan is a cast-iron skillet, babe. Trust me, practically indestructible. He's your son. And you're his father. Two of the best people I know. I have absolute confidence you'll figure it out."

Hardin had taken a deep breath and let out a jagged sigh, scared shitless. What if Mac had been wrong? But it had turned out she was spot-on. The ensuing days became easier. Especially when he went with his gut.

Conversations ranged far and wide, mostly discovery in nature. Like how Hardin had felt when he found out Stowe was his son and vice versa. Sometimes they tabled a topic until Mac could be there, such as the one about her change of surname.

As he grew more confident, Stowe dug deeper. "Why didn't you and Mom stay together?"

This was the big one. *Shit.* Hardin stood and regarded his son, his leg with the wrapped ankle propped on the ottoman, Homer in his lap. The Lop looked like it was in a stupor as the boy loved on him. "How about I get us some lemonade and granola bars and then we'll talk?"

Stowe looked up, frowning at him. "This is a big one, huh?"

"Yep. It really is."

"Are you comfortable handing this one by yourself, Dad?"

Hardin almost dropped back into his seat, so stunned was he by being called Dad for the first time. Stowe hadn't called him Hardin since coming home from the hospital. It had been Bro. Hardin took a deep breath and searched his son's eyes, startling in their similarity to his, and smiled. "I'm going to do my best. Will that work for you?"

"Yep." Stowe returned his dad's smile, his eyes engaging Hardin's as if he was acknowledging who he was.

"I'll be right back."

Hardin came back in with a pitcher of lemonade, two glasses filled with ice, and granola bars he had picked up earlier from the Grind before Mac went to work. He set the tray on the small table between where he and Stowe were sitting, then filled the glasses and handed one to his son before easing back into his chair.

"What happened between your mom and, well…"

"Why weren't you there when Mom had me?"

"I didn't know. After I left for college, there was a series of unfortunate events." Hardin wanted to touch on some and not others, offer the bird's-eye view of things. "Your mom's cell phone was destroyed, its SIM card taken. She didn't know my number and I didn't know hers." He raised his hand at Stowe's look of disbelief. "I know. Stupid. So fuck—damn—stupid. Uh, let's keep my bad language between us?"

Stowe swallowed his bite of granola bar and rolled his eyes. "I've heard that before, Dad. I'm not a baby."

"No, you're not. But you are your mom's baby no matter how old you are. She's going to chew my ass out. Dammit, chew my butt out if I keep screwing up."

"I won't tell." Stowe giggled and took another sip of his lemonade.

"In the mindless place that teens succumb to, we just plugged our numbers into each other's phone, believing that was fine."

"What about your friends?"

"Nope. Dead ends."

"That's so sad. I bet that's why Mom makes me recite phone numbers from time to time."

"I expect it is."

"Do you know her number now?"

"I do. And I also wrote it down in several places. I'm never going to lose her again."

"Do you know mine?"

"I do. Do you know mine?"

"Yep." Stowe's expression was one of pride. "What else happened? Because more had to happen."

"Everything snowballed." Hardin scrubbed his hand over his face and sighed long and deep. "We weren't able to say goodbye before I left. My parents—"

"They were the old people in your room, right?"

"Yes."

"I heard them," Stowe said angrily.

Hardin turned, leaning forward, his elbows on his thighs and asked quietly, "What did you hear, son?"

"They sounded snotty, like they think they're better than everyone. Are they rich?"

"Very much so." Hardin pressed gently. "What did you hear?"

Stowe set his lemonade down and became engrossed in Homer. He wiped angrily at his eyes, his chin trembling, and gently stroked the Lop's soft mottled fur.

Hardin waited, giving his son time to pull himself together or fly apart.

"They did horrible things. They ruined Mom's life. They ruined your life together. Your mother called Mom a whore!" His crying became jagged and loud. "They hate her!"

Hardin got out of his chair and moved Stowe's leg carefully before sitting next to it on the ottoman. "Hey," he said gruffly.

Stowe put the Lop gently on the floor and stood, balancing carefully, moving into his dad's lap with help. He cried harder, burrowing into Hardin, sweaty with emotion, his heart thundering like mad.

It was surreal, holding and comforting his son, experiencing the fierce need to protect him at all costs. Hardin stroked his back. "Ssh… Ssh…"

"I hate them, Dad," Stowe said into Hardin's neck.

"Are you listening?"

Stowe nodded into his neck and sniffled.

"Hate hollows you, son. It serves no purpose other than to strip your guts out, rob you of your integrity and character. Your soul. You're better than that. So much better."

Stowe sat up and said solemnly, "You sound like Mom."

"I consider that the highest of compliments."

"Can I say I pity them?"

Hardin's mouth moved around as he thought it over. "Um… What you might consider is forgiving them."

"Why?"

"Because it's the best they can do."

"That's really sad. How did you end up so good?"

"Luck, and I had your mom. For a while at least."

"You've got her now."

"I do."

"And me, Dad."

Hardin's heart pounded. He closed his eyes to stanch the threatening tears, but his breath stuttered as he inhaled and his scratchy voice gave away what he felt. "Having you means the world to me, Stowe."

Stowe's arms snaked around his shoulders. "I love you, Dad."

"I love you, son," Hardin said, letting the tears flow.

Stowe pushed away and sat up, wiping his face, grinning at his dad. "You know, Mom says real men cry."

"Smartest woman I know." Hardin grinned back at his son through his tears and ruffled his hair. "I need something besides granola bars. How about I make us some sandwiches?"

"Can we have milkshakes too?"

"Why not?"

Conversation turned to Mac while they ate their turkey-and-provolone sandwiches.

"What are your plans with Mom?"

"She's got her book club tonight. Until eightish she said."

Stowe let out an exasperated sigh. "Dad! No. What, like what do you, you know…"

Hardin frowned at Stowe, not following him.

"You said you have her now."

Ah. Hardin flashed his son a grin. "My intentions."

"Yes."

"Interesting you should ask me that, because there was something I wanted to ask you. Something really important."

From the look on his son's face, Hardin had just confused him. "Are you paying attention, because I want you to give my question very serious consideration before you respond. Stowe?"

"Okay," he said cautiously.

"Will you give me your blessing to ask your mom to marry me?"

Stowe's plate clattered to the floor as he jettisoned from his seat on one foot. His smile was blinding. "Yes! We're getting married! Yes!"

Hardin chuckled and shook his head. "You sure?"

"Dad, I'm so sure! *When?*"

"Hey, sit down before you reinjure yourself, or your mom is going to have my ass." He growled, then corrected himself. "My butt." His brows remained elevated until Stowe sat. "We're going to keep this between us. I need your help, okay? I want to make this special for your mom."

"She's out at her book club tonight, so that's perfect."

258

"I'll fill you in if you promise to nap."

"That's bribery!"

"It sure is," Hardin said, thoroughly enjoying himself. "Deal?"

"Deal."

Hardin ran his idea past Stowe, who made one suggestion. He moved Stowe's nap time back on the condition of helping. As soon as Stowe had his list and was comfortable, Hardin ran the necessary errands.

29 Chapter Twenty Nine

THE DAY HAD been busy and long. Mac was ready to turn in and snuggle up with Hardin as soon as Stowe was asleep. Waiting on their son to fall asleep every night, trying to keep him from knowing she was sleeping with his father, was becoming more of a challenge because she hated Hardin leaving the bed early in the mornings.

She wanted Stowe to hold her in high regard, not see her as a woman who brought men into their home and slept with them like her mother had. Granted she'd never had a man in her house overnight until Hardin arrived in PR. But she wanted to go to bed with him every night and wake with him every morning.

Mac clumped up the steps, allowing the fatigue from the day to overtake her. Book club had been more fun than she remembered. She enjoyed the discussion, although she had to avoid numerous questions about Hardin. Word was all over town after they had danced hot and heavy on the deck of the Hazy Rebel.

Just as she reached for the door, Hardin opened it. He slid her purse from her shoulder and dropped it on the chair next to the door, which he shut behind her and locked, then handed her a glass of wine.

"Good evening, beautiful. A red zin for you." He kissed her warmly, picked up his own glass from the sideboard, and took her hand.

"Good evening to you, handsome." Her eyes bounced around, noting the house was darker than usual. Candlelight flickered on the walls. "Our son?"

The corner of his lips quirked up. "In bed. He was up a lot today."

"Oh." Mac leaned in and cupped his neck, giving him a much hotter kiss than he had greeted her with.

Hardin broke it off and licked his lips. His eyes were dancing. "Honey, I need to know... Are you up for something new?"

Her tiredness evaporated. What the hell was he up to? "Should I shower?"

"Not yet." His breath caressed the shell of her ear, sending delicious shivers racing through her body. "It can wait." The ember in her blood sparked and her legs grew rubbery. "You get to choose tonight. Option A or option B."

Mac knew her eyes had to be as huge as saucers when she looked at him. This was a whole new aspect of him she'd never experienced.

"Do you trust me, honey?" His eyes glowed.

She sighed, relaxing. "Of course."

"And?" he asked expectantly, the playful smile on his face lighting up his amazing eyes.

"Option A."

"Mm. I like option A. Very much. Close your eyes."

"Babe?"

"Close them."

She did. Hardin took the wine from her and set it on the sideboard. She listened to him drink deeply from his glass.

"Hold on. Maybe you need a sip as well." He put the edge of the goblet to her lips and let her drink. When she was done, he licked her lips. "That's very good," he murmured.

Her body was on fire. She wanted him now. Her hands reached for his belt.

"Uh-uh. Keep your eyes closed." She felt him move to behind her. Hardin tied the softest fabric over her eyes, lightly scented with rosemary and mint, which she loved.

"I can't see."

"Then option A is working." He sounded quite pleased with himself. "You have to follow my instructions to the letter." When she didn't answer, he asked, "Mac?"

She licked her lips, unsure what he was up to. "Yes."

Hardin stepped around her. She heard the glasses clink.

"We might want these later," he said before taking Mac's hand and leading her through the house and carefully directing her down the back steps. Once they were outside, he escorted her to where the table should have been, except it wasn't. "Stay."

She moved her head this way and that, trying to sense what was going on around her.

"You can untie the scarf."

Mac reached behind her, surprised to realize she was trembling. Her eyes adjusted as she blinked. The patio was aglow with dozens of votive candles in jelly jars. Numerous arrangements of a fiery mixture of orange roses, billy buttons, goldenrods, sunflowers, and thistle graced white tablecloths covering tables. *Ah, that's where the table got moved to.*

Hardin laced his fingers with hers and dropped to one knee in front of her.

Mac felt as though she was going to faint and swallowed. Was this really happening? She felt and saw how he trembled.

Hardin took a deep, shaky breath. "McKenna Rose Vesley Eliot." He another deep breath, swallowed, and smiled. He spoke slowly and clearly with purpose. "Mac. Twelve years ago, I asked you to not forget about me. About us and our love. I believed our love would carry us through separation and challenges. At that time, I had no idea what we would face, what that might mean. Neither did you," he whispered, dropping his eyes and shaking his head, then gazing at her again. "But we said we would love each other forever. And I do. Love you. Forever. You are my heart. My home." Hardin paused again, stilled his trembling fingers. "I want to spend the rest of forever with you. Our incredible son has given me his blessing. Will you marry me?"

The most joyful tears erupted from her heart, from Mac's soul, and rained down her face, dripping off her chin and onto Hardin's hands clasping hers. All she could manage was to nod and smile like a lovesick fool, because she was head over heels for this man.

"Mom! Answer Dad!" Stowe demanded, stepping forward from the shadows.

She swallowed her tears, and an enormous smile split her face. "Yes! Forever yes!"

Hardin stood and lifted Mac, swinging her around, kissing her unabashedly in front of their son and their family and friends, who appeared from the shadows and circled Stowe. He put her down and extracted something from the front pocket of his jeans—a small emerald-green velvet bag.

He opened the bag and inverted it. "I gave this to you once." The thistle necklace dropped into his hand. "I'm not sure what you might want, honey. In lieu of a ring, I want to give you this again, with the understanding that you will have a ring and soon."

"Something simple?"

"Whatever you want."

Mac turned and lifted her hair, allowing him to clasp the necklace around her neck. She hadn't worn it since she'd left Illinois, but she had kept it because it had been one of the most heartfelt gifts she'd ever received. Obviously Hardin had noticed that it hung over a framed photo of that which was most precious to them—Stowe, her holding him after his birth.

"To the sweetness after the challenges," she said, turning her head to the side and pinning his eyes with hers before planting a long, passionate kiss on him.

"Ew!" Stowe complained while everyone else clapped, cheered, and cried. "That is so gross!"

Hardin pulled their son between Mac and him and grinned. "Sport, remember this moment as an I told you so. Someday you're not going to find kissing gross."

Stowe shook his head adamantly.

Mac's smile was brilliant as her gaze swept over her family and friends, then Stowe and Hardin. "How?" She shook her head. "How?"

Hardin hugged their son into his shoulder. "Stowe was a huge help despite being laid low with his injuries."

"Yeah, Mom. Dad and I divided and conquered, as only Team Ambrose can do. We devised a plan. I made the calls and Dad ran a bunch of errands while you were at your book club."

"You two..." She ruffled Stowe's hair and kissed Hardin again.

Doc cleared his throat. "If everyone would, please, I wish to begin the toasts. Adults, grab a glass of wine or champagne. Kids, help yourselves to the sparkling apple juice." He waited until everyone had a glass of something. "To Kenna, the daughter of our heart. To Mac, the woman of Hardin's heart. And to Hardin, the man who loves this wonderful woman as his equal, who never stopped looking for her. God bless you, son. God bless you both. May you be happy forever."

He raised his glass and drank. The others lifted their glasses and sipped.

Issa stepped forward. "Kenna. You have graced our family with joy, love, and laughter. There isn't a day I don't thank Carol for calling me to help, for allowing us to be there for you, to bring you and Stowe into our family. We love you. We love our Stowe. Hardin, we eagerly look forward to loving you. Congratulations!"

Mac leaned into Hardin and sipped along with everyone else.

"Other than Hardin, I have known you the longest, my dear Kenna. Our meeting was by chance and brief, but oh, how it has unfolded." Carol blinked her full eyes. "Your heart is pure, as is that of the man you are marrying. The two of you are the epitome of true love, and Stowe, you are the embodiment of that. I couldn't be happier for you and I wish you the very, very best." She raised her glass of champagne to Mac and Hardin and the others followed. "To forever."

Wedding planning began as soon as the toasts were over. Kai, Emory, Cori, and Ronni sat Mac down as soon as they had helped Issa and Carol unwrap all the food. Hardin was surrounded by the men, including Arlo, who decided he'd be extending his stay. He had no intention of missing the wedding, and there was a woman whose company he was enjoying.

Stowe had yawned several times during the past half hour. He looked half-asleep on his feet.

Mac motioned to Hardin that the party needed to wind down. She was tired herself despite all the excitement.

"I'll get him to bed, dear," Carol said.

Issa stood and began directing everyone else. "It's been a long, wonderful evening. People are tired and need to get to work tomorrow. Let's help Hardin and Kenna get things put away so they have some alone time."

Within fifteen minutes, the patio was put back together, food was put away, and dishes were either in the dishwasher or washed and drying on the counter. Mac and Hardin said their last goodbyes and locked up the house, looking in on Stowe and making sure Homer was secure in his pen before stumbling into Mac's bedroom.

Hardin pulled Mac close, scenting her hair, then nuzzling her neck and kissing her lingeringly. "Too tired to consummate our engagement?"

"I think so. Sorry. I'm so tired."

"Let me help you get ready for bed, honey." Hardin stripped Mac's clothes slowly, kissing every inch of her as it was exposed.

The drowsiness cleared and her body ignited under the ministrations of his touch, his lips, and his tongue. Hardin

267

brought her pleasure that made her weep. He entered her as it spread from her core, pulsing and unfurling in ribbons, making her entire body thrum.

Sleep was overtaking Mac soon after Hardin pulled out. "What was plan B?"

"The same as plan A. I wasn't taking any chances," he murmured, pulling her to nestle in the crook of his shoulder.

"I love you, babe."

"I love you too, honey." He pushed her damp hair back and kissed her temple. "Now sleep."

Epilogue

One Month Later...

WAITING TO ENTER the large meadow filled with long grass and yellow wildflowers, surrounded by forest, the peaks of the Taurus Range soaring in the distance, Mac reflected on how much her life had changed in six short weeks. It had been a whirlwind since Hardin had shown up in Piñon Ridge. Stowe had his father. She and Hardin had each other, their love stronger and deeper than it had been in high school. They were a family.

Hardin had retired under just cause with the promise of attending the club's biggest match in their home stadium this fall in Spain, where he would be formally recognized and officially retire. She and Stowe would be with him, and they were thrilled to experience just an nth of what Hardin was to his club, teammates, and fans and to spend some time in Spain.

He was pursuing a business venture in nearby Gambol and had purchased not only the house she rented—the only home their son had ever known—but an adorable small bungalow nearby for Carol, who was moving to Piñon Ridge.

With Stowe, she and Hardin had an appointment with a judge in a few days to legally change their son's name, making Eliot his middle name and Ambrose his last and adding Hardin as his father on his birth certificate. Later in the week, she and Hardin were meeting with an architect to begin drafting plans to renovate their home.

Life was good and oh so precious.

She had wanted simple. That's how she and Hardin had begun.

Teenagers. A soccer match. Ice cream. A long meandering conversation that went throughout dinner and most of the evening, recognizing they both pursued being valued for who they were.

Friends. Best friends. Eventually lovers.

She glanced at her engagement ring—a simple band of small diamonds set in platinum. Hardin could have and would have bought her anything, but that was what she chose. Understated. Refined.

Mac felt like a fairy woodland princess in her exquisite dress. Hardin had encouraged her to work with a designer, and the result was a dress that was beyond anything she could have imagined. She had blubbered when she'd worn it for the first time to have it fitted. It was an A-line princess cut, sleeveless and off the shoulders, in ivory. The skirt was a dreamy gossamer combination of layers upon layers of chiffon in different raw-edged lengths; the effect was airy and flowing, and the short train caressed the ground as she walked. The bodice was delicately embroidered in blush, the palest green and purple, and tiny seed pearls.

Mac wore crystal-and-seeded-pearl barefoot sandals,

loving the look while embracing the freedom of not wearing shoes for the ceremony. The thistle necklace Hardin had given her the night Stowe was conceived hung from her neck. Something old. Matching thistle earrings, made of platinum, diamonds, and amethysts, completed her wedding jewelry. Hardin's wedding gift to her. Something new.

A vintage hair vine of crystals and opals and seed pearls decorated her thick, wavy auburn hair, which Cori had artfully woven into a loose knot. Something borrowed, from Issa. She held a bouquet of sweet peas, blush ruffled garden roses, sunflowers, jasmine, fern, and blue thistle. Something blue and lovingly arranged by Carol.

Mac's heart fluttered wildly as the string quartet began to play. The musicians were dressed in black formalwear but barefoot, as were Hardin, Stowe, and the rest of the wedding party.

The sun was descending. The clouds hung at multiple altitudes, enhancing their textures and vibrant kaleidoscope of shifting color, bathing the ceremony in a soft explosion of gold and orange light.

At the arbor, covered in twisting green vines and the same flowers she carried, Mike and Arlo flanked Hardin, who fidgeted nervously. They all wore black tie, as did Stowe at her side since he was giving her away. It was perfect that the love of her life was to give her in marriage to her forever love, his father. Stowe was also charged with the rings.

The minister stood next to Hardin in the center of the arbor and nodded to the bridesmaids when the quartet bridged into another song. It was time to begin. Cori, Kai, Emory, and Ronni all wore the same chiffon V-neck, spaghetti-strap long dress in colors reflecting the greens and blues in her bouquet.

Ronni went first, taking her time, walking the path Mac and Hardin had discovered when they were hunting for the perfect spot to say their vows. After she arrived at the arbor and turned, Kai followed, then Emory.

Cori turned to Mac and clasped her wrist. "I love you, Kenna. So much. I am honored to stand with you. Always."

"I love you too," she said, her throat burning with unshed tears.

Cori turned and headed toward the arbor.

Stowe wiped his eyes and said gruffly, "You're so beautiful, Mom. I love you."

"I love you more, you know." She didn't want to cry.

"Impossible," he said, the grin and the impish expression he flashed her so much like Hardin's. "Just in case you're wondering, I still have the rings."

"I knew you would."

Cori reached the arbor and turned. There were a few beats of silence, and then the quartet played the first chords of "Anymore."

Honorary family and closest friends focused on Mac, expectant and smiling, but they faded to the background as she zoomed in on Hardin, his face shining with joy.

Stowe offered her his elbow. "Are you ready?"

"Yes," she said hoarsely, blinking away her tears, certain her radiant smile matched that of her groom.

Mac glided toward him, the whispering breeze carrying the scent of pine and the warm earthy smell of ripe grasses and flowers. Her eyes never wavered from his.

Hardin stepped forward before she got to the arbor, taking her from Stowe. "God, baby, you're stunning," he said, his voice rough with emotion, wiping the tears from his eyes and capturing her lips.

His kiss was soul-searing, leaving her breathless, and had everyone tittering. They broke apart only after the minister cleared his throat loudly.

"Oops." Mac laughed up at him, brushing both of their tears from her cheeks.

His eyes sparkled. "I love you so much."

"I love you forever," she whispered.

Hardin moved to embrace her again, but the minister interrupted. "Can we begin?"

Mac and Hardin nodded.

"Please face one another and hold hands."

Mac looked into Hardin's eyes, into his soul. They were filled with tears and love. He wiped at them again and smiled. She clasped his hands, intertwining her fingers with his, eager for their future to begin.

MAC'S Chees Pasta Pie

Serves four to six depending on appetite.
Pairs well with fresh fruit or tossed salad.
Reheats well.

Ingredients:

1 pound dry bow-tie or rigatoni pasta, cooked al dente and set aside

6 strips crisp-cooked turkey bacon, drained, cooled, and crumbled (may be done ahead)

1 organic red bell pepper, chopped

1 ½ c. organic broccoli, chopped

½—¾ c. crushed club crackers (can use breadcrumbs or salted crackers but may not have a buttery taste)

6 T. unsalted butter

1/3 c. flour (Mac uses gluten-free)

½ t. kosher salt

½ t. freshly ground pepper

3 c. freshly shredded white cheddar

2 c. milk, can vary amount based on milk type (Mac uses 1 ½ cups of coconut milk)

MAC'S Chees Pasta Pie

Instructions:

1. Preheat oven to 350°.

2. Prepare roux. Melt butter in saucepan over low-medium heat. Whisk in flour, salt, and pepper. Stir until roux thickens and browns (3–4 minutes). Slowly whisk in milk. Stir constantly. Once sauce thickens, reduce heat and stir in 2 c. only of shredded cheese. Stir until melted.

3. Put cooked pasta in greased (buttered) 12-inch cast-iron skillet. Turn on low heat and add cheese sauce. Add in chopped red bell pepper and broccoli. Stir to combine well. Remove from heat.

4. Bake for 20 minutes.

5. Top with bacon pieces, remaining cheese, and crushed crackers.

6. Bake for 10 additional minutes, or until cheese is melted and browning.

7. Serve warm.

A PERSONAL
Note from Sutton

Writing *Hearts Don't Lie* wasn't planned. On the heels of releasing *Afraid to Hope,* Ancient Passages Book 2, in May 2020, I was ready to begin the draft of *Afraid to Love,* Ancient Passages Book 3. The gorgeous cover was designed. The storyboard was filling up, and the lead characters were pestering me day and night, telling me how they wanted to be written and how the story was unfolding.

I had committed to writing a short story as part of a charity focused anthology—*Take Two: A Collection of Second Chance Stories,* commemorating the fifth anniversary of Writers on the River, an author-signing event I was participating in (which ended up being canceled, like untold millions of other events and plans). The proceeds of the anthology go to Thistle Farms, a nonprofit organization located in Nashville, Tennessee, that helps women survivors of violence, sex trafficking, prostitution, and addiction, a mission I am firmly behind.

The short story version of *Hearts Don't Lie* is in *Take Two.* However, it felt unfinished to me. It was incomplete. I needed to finish it.

To date, *Hearts Don't Lie* has been the fastest story I have written. Mac and Hardin's story simply poured out of me. Sometimes writing became so emotional that I had to step away, take a break, wipe my tears. It was a time of uncertainty—COVID-19, quarantines and lockdowns, and other cascading events. My kids were safely home and still in school. Our grocery bill soon rivaled that of our mortgage. Fear infiltrated our lives, and I searched for the calm, the hope, to hold on to the fragility of my faith. I needed to be there for my kids, my husband, and myself.

I wrote for sanity, because writing centers me. I created a fictionalized world based on places I love—rural Illinois, where I grew up, and the mountains of Colorado, which fill my soul.

The result is *Hearts Don't Lie,* Mac and Hardin's story. Their second chance. I believe in ever after. I believe in second, third, fourth, and more chances.

I believe in true love. That is my story.

Sutton Bishop, September 2020

Acknowledgements

Even though writing is solitary work, this author doesn't write in a vacuum. I am grateful to the Goddesses. Your support and our conversations and laughter during video conferences were, as always, a stabilizing force during this chaotic time.

Marjie, thank you for penning "For You," which appears in the beginning of *Hearts Don't Lie*. Taylor, the beautiful cover you created captures Mac and Hardin perfectly as teens. Anne, working with you is a joy. I appreciate you continuing to educate me through the editing process, often with humor.

Jim, thanks so much for talking to me about your experiences volunteering in search and rescue in Colorado and answering my many questions. Please continue to be safe as you risk your life to rescue and recover other people.

To Pam, Enid, and Robbie, thank you for beta reading, for asking questions, for telling me what wasn't working and what else you wanted as a reader. I took every suggestion and critique to heart. A special shout-out to you, Karen, for pushing me when I really needed it, for challenging me to write the best story I had in me. I hope you love the final creation as much as I do.

To my husband Mark and four kiddos—Greyson, Aubry, Josi, and Holden—you are my everything, my ever-after.

WHAT to do now

Hearts Don't Lie is the first book in the Piñon Ridge series—interrelated second-chance romance stories. I hope you enjoyed Mac and Hardin's story.

Please consider leaving a review on Goodreads, Amazon, or BookBub. Thank you.

Do you have friends who'd enjoy *Hearts Don't Lie?* Tell them about it—call, text, post online. Your recommendation is the nicest gift you can give an author.

MORE BY Sutton Bishop

Ancient Passages Series

Afraid to Fall, Book 1 (Ari and Luca's story)

Afraid to Hope, Book 2 (Natasha and Bane's story)

Afraid to Love, Book 3

To find out about new releases and to receive free and exclusive bonus content featuring characters from this series, sign up for Sutton's newsletter at www.authorsuttonbishop.com.

ABOUT the Author

Sutton Bishop enjoys having a foot in both worlds—real and make-believe. She has degrees in forensics and anthropology and a minor in world history. Her writing is inspired by her travels and life experiences. She lives in the Midwest with her husband, their four kids, and a passel of pets.

FIND Sutton online

Website - www.authorsuttonbishop.com/

Facebook - www.facebook.com/sutton.bishop.37

Instagram - www.instagram.com/authorsuttonbishop/

Pinterest - www.pinterest.com/authorsuttonbishop/

Twitter - www.twitter.com/SuttonBishop2
(@suttonbishop2)

"Jungle heat and romantic sizzle combine in the debut novel by Sutton Bishop."

"Bishop writes sex with sizzle and heart—it's more about the passion than hitting all the graphic high points. Bishop is a breath of fresh air in a genre that is losing its passion for romance."

"The chemistry was insane between Luca and Ari. I can't even begin to describe how hot some of the scenes on these pages got (I was surprised I didn't burst into flames a couple times, honestly). The temperature in Guatemala is hot, but damn if these two didn't make it all the hotter."

"Submerging and engaging, pulse-pounding adventure with a slow-building romance. It has many smart, interesting details that make it clear the author has not merely painted a generic background for her novel–she has lived in this environment and wants to give you the experience too."

"Ari and Luca. Oh my goodness, those two characters took my breath away. Bishop gave the reader such vivid details about them, what they'd endured, and what they were experiencing. The most engaging story I've read in a long time. Five stars!!"

"From the first narratives of Mayan mythology to the modern-day story, the reader is swept away like on a wild river ride. Great driven plot, smooth swings and story arcs to keep the reader engaged. It is a 'burning page-turner' that I had a difficult time putting aside to sleep!"

"Sutton nails this story. She writes adventure romance in comparison to other great authors like Karina Halle."

Made in the USA
Columbia, SC
18 March 2021